Amongst

To

Kelly

Lets go on an adventure

M. L. Rayner

M. L. Rayner

Amongst the Mists

?

Question Mark Press

First published in 2021 by Question Mark Press

?

Question Mark Press

Amongst The Mists/ M. L. Rayner. – 1st edition
ISBN: 9798544013679

Cover Design by: Emmy Ellis @ Studioenp
Photography by: PhotoCosma
Promo: Question Mark Press / Elli Toney
QMP Blog Tours By: Zooloo's Book Tours

Prologue

The Brocton Swamp was much more hazardous than young Olivia Bradwell cared to recall. She had trudged through this odorous, algae topped morass many times before. The sensation of mud between her toes somehow provided a strange comfort as she buried her heels into the water's bed. However, tonight was in no way familiar. Olivia had never ventured through the woodlands this late before, and now she could see the reason why. Above a cluster of branches, twilight paraded the sky and left little light to guide her through the bleakness. She was lost. More lost than she dared to admit. Why hadn't she just followed the stream? That question kept knocking about in her mind. Her heart rate quickened with the realisation of the depth of her trouble.

"Stupid idiot," she chastised herself. "Bloody stupid… Idiot."

Sitting on the grassy river bank that evening, Olivia drew aimlessly inside her notebook whatever childlike doodles came to mind. The rain had not been particularly bad over the past few weeks, which allowed the rivers and streams of the area to flow peacefully around the protruding rocks. This was her favourite spot in the whole world. No one would bother her here. It was her place, and it comforted the young girl to think it was her place. Hers alone. The rippling stream brushed past her naked feet, flowing around its bends into the woodland nestled at the edge of the green.

"The voice! The calling voice. That's what it was!" She spoke to the darkness in disbelief, rubbing her tired eyes in an effort to remain focused. After she lost her bearings, she had completely forgotten about that voice.

How could I forget? Olivia thought. Her lips were quivering and beginning to turn blue from the rapidly dropping temperature.

It was the strangest of occurrences. So strange she was doubtful it had even happened. The sun's splendour shone down on the crisp pages of her book as she stretched out for an assortment of crayons. Sighing heavily, she unconsciously listened to the relaxing sounds of the babbling spring and watched the trees as they gently swayed in the near distance. It was then a distant call broke her concentration. Curiosity forced her to raise her blue eyes away from the half-finished sketch.

"Lost!"

Olivia looked around, studying the area where she lay, and tried to determine the origin of the call. Although she listened intently, only the sounds of nature both far and near were evident, and so again she rested and placed her crayon quickly back to paper.

"Lost! Lost!"

There it is again, she thought. Olivia jumped to her feet, causing the crayons to fall and scatter.

"Hellooo?" The girl returned the call as if in song whilst peering along the grassy river bank. "Who's that then?"

The sound of flowing water was the only reply, as she began collecting the now dispersed belongings for the journey home.

"Lost… Lost!"

Olivia's head turned to the side, this time catching the smallest of movements from the corner of her eye.

"Ha!" she yelled playfully, pointing her violet painted finger nail in the direction of the hidden trickster. "I see you, come out. I seen you, I have!"

Her bare feet dashed along the water's edge, sending a cooling spray up each leg. A sharp bend in the bank sent Olivia slightly off balance and brought her to an abrupt halt.

"Oh…" Puzzlement masked the young girl's face. "Where you gone to now?" she called, standing ankle deep on the shore. What Olivia had seen, or what she believed to have seen, had gone, leaving her with only a brewing annoyance the game was not played fairly. She stood waiting, tapping her foot vigorously and impatiently.

"Shout then, you… you mong!"

Olivia waited restlessly before giving up and turning away with a stomp to retrace her steps.

"Lost…" the mischievous voice called from behind, immediately followed by the sound of splashing across the river's surface.

She sprinted farther and farther downstream, committed to catching the caller. But with each bend in the river that was reached, the nasal call was heard farther away.

I'll catch you… You little runt, she thought with a scowl. Her lungs started to weigh heavily with exhaustion. She stopped, hesitant to go on. Olivia waited, watching as the clear glistening water freely tumbled between her legs and into the dimness of woodland beyond. She held no fear of the forest but knew she should not stay. She had prolonged her time here enough.

"I'm not playing now," she yelled. "Gotta go I have."

Olivia waited, and surely enough the reply was delayed in return.

"Lost!" It yelled back through the trees. The vocalisation seemed more distant than before.

"I said, I ain't playing. You deaf or something?" Olivia screamed, trying her best to be heard through the seemingly endless trees.

"Lost…" The caller replied but was perceived with more uncertainty than the last. Olivia tilted her head inquisitively, trying to peer through the thick shrubs.

"You really lost?" she yelled, now beginning to feel a sense of concern. "Or you just fakin'?"

Again she was answered, but the sound echoed even deeper from the dense thicket. The girl cautiously moved forward, following the route of the water. It would be dark soon. She was well aware of that. But as the fading voice cried out from the depth of the woods, Olivia's small body vanished into the endless tunnel of arched trees.

Amongst the Mists

Chapter One – July 1986

At last! His bag was packed. Bran Lampshire sighed heavily, feebly securing the weathered straps before throwing his rucksack carelessly against the corner wall. Laying spread across the unmade covers, he glared up to the dart holes that penetrated his bedroom wall and Michael Jackson calendar. A dart stood firmly embedded in the current date, accompanied by a crudely drawn circle in red Biro.

"The twenty first of July 1986," he groaned. It was an important date for Bran. Possibly the most anticipated day of the year. The summer holidays had officially begun. It was a time to do as little or as much as he wanted. A time where the endless summer days pleasantly all rolled into one. Yet, all of it was gone now. The very idea flushed away with a yank of the chain, sending his desires, his ambitions down the drain.

Why did I agree to this pointless trip? he thought, gazing back towards his beloved Commodore. His friend had discussed the matter for months, arranging every little detail, assuming Bran would willingly accompany him. Bran hated camping, and the call of the wild was certainly no exception, no matter how well planned.

It came as no surprise his parents encouraged him to go. And despite his unwillingness to submit, both mother and father insisted the country air would do him the world of good. He expected the cavalry any minute. The longer he waited, the more he wished the venture had been forgotten.

The faint sound of boyish singing came floating through the window, dashing his hopes to pieces. The squeal of bicycle brakes came to a gradual stop as Bran waited for the inevitable summons.

"Branston!" The loud geeky voice invaded from outdoors. It was Marcus White; he would know that nerdy tone anywhere. They had been pals for as long as he could remember, although now he was beginning to wonder why.

"Branston!" Marcus was obviously irritated as he shouted up towards the crack of the window.

Bran rolled over to his side, muttering under his breath before yelling back.

"What!"

"What? What do you mean, what?" Marcus yelled. "It's time to go."

"Can't, I'm too sick." *Cough, cough.*

12

An awkward pause followed.

"You aren't sick, there's nothing wrong with you. Get down here!"

"You sure it's wise? Looks like rain is on the way. We'll all get soaked."

Marcus tilted his tattered reflective cap upwards, glancing at the clear blue sky, as blue as he'd ever seen.

"It isn't going to rain. There're no pissin' clouds in sight. Get up!"

"It's gonna rain, Marcus."

"No, it isn't, Bran."

"Yes, it is."

"No! It isn't!"

This typically went on for some time. It was a trap Marcus regularly fell for and an exercise Bran thoroughly enjoyed. He resisted the urge to snigger, biting at the corner of his pillow before responding.

"Okay, Okay! Gimme a sec," he bellowed, the bag already slung over one shoulder as he made his way down the stairs.

Marcus waited on the grass, his bike abandoned and leaning against the chalk coloured kerb.

"You know it's classed as rude to shout?" Bran cockily expressed before pulling his bike down from the garage rack.

"No," replied Marcus. "But did you know it's rude to be a complete dick?"

Surprised, Bran smirked. Quick wittedness certainly wasn't a strong point for Marcus, so rather than challenge him further, Bran kindly decided to let him savour the moment.

"OK… so where we going?" Bran asked, sitting beside his friend.

"You really haven't listened to anything, have you?" said Marcus as he pulled strands of brown grass from the dying lawn.

"Nope. Not really." Bran replied with even less enthusiasm than before.

Aggravated, Marcus sighed while dusting the strips of grass from his hands.

"Look! If you don't want to come, don't bother! I ain't forcing you."

Here we go, thought Bran, now sensing what would soon be Marcus's silent treatment. He took a deep breath and gave his friend a playful nudge of the arm.

"Don't be daft. Of course, I'll come," said Bran more convincingly. "Look… I promise you, I won't complain again, alright?"

Marcus's deep frown turned upside down. An appealing smile appeared, and he grunted as he returned Bran's nudge.

"OK then."

"Alright then, pal. So… Tell me. Who else have you invited?"

"Just the new lad, Jack."

"Jack! For fuck sake, Marcus! Why? The guy's a complete special case." Bran's voice heightened, now unknowingly turning the heads of his curious neighbours.

"No, he isn't." Again Marcus nudged. "He's just... just…"

"A fricking psychopath in the making?" Bran interrupted.

"No. Just a little slow is all," said Marcus discreetly.

"Slow ain't the word, Marcus. You said you weren't going to ask him!"

"And you said you weren't going to complain no more."

Bran opened his mouth hesitantly, ready to throw the full range of cursing vocabulary he'd memorised just that year. He stopped himself. A list of inappropriate words hung desperately on the edge of his tongue. He gulped, swallowing the childish remarks back down. He knew full well this was an argument he was not about to win. "Fine! Let's go," he mumbled while they pushed their bikes to the road.

*

Jack Speckle. Or Special Jack, which the kids had unkindly named him, sat patiently at his doorstep. He had waited with anticipation throughout the morning, never truly knowing if his invite was anything more than a spiteful prank. His backpack remained tightly grasped in his hands while his nails scraped unpleasantly across the canvas.

It goes without saying Jack wasn't the brightest kid at school. He had recently moved to town from the northern countryside, his mother only too hopeful he would gain the extra support needed at school. Jack despised his new school, never really understanding why they had to move in the first place.

The sound of boyhood banter approached, instantly breaking his daydream trance. His odd coloured eyes, one blue and one green, widened with excitement. His head turned to somehow gain a view of the restricted garden path. The tightened grip slackened. He let out a sigh of disappointment, slouching back to the door's rotting frame. It wasn't Marcus. Not yet.

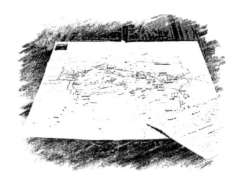

Amongst the Mists

Chapter Two

Jack began to sprint across the uncut lawn, forgetting his rucksack was carelessly placed on the doorstep. A confused gaze washed across his face as he turned to sprint back to his house.

"Oh, for God's sake." Bran impatiently shook his head and pointed in the direction of the running fool. "We ain't even bloody started yet!"

"Shut up, will you!" demanded Marcus. His tone was full of irritation that Bran was not about to take seriously.

"It isn't too late," Bran whispered. "Let's go now, quick before he turns back and –"

But it was too late. Jack had already swung the heavy rucksack over both shoulders, visibly arching his back, and ran back across the well-trodden lawn.

"Hiya, guys!" Jack yelled happily, showing no self-control in his excited projection. A grin was pinned solidly from ear to ear and his sight fixed on the two friends he had begun to think would never show.

"Hey, mate!" said Marcus pleasantly before sternly encouraging Bran to interact.

"Hm? Oh... Hey, Special." Bran was somewhat occupied with the thought of being, well, anywhere but this precise spot.

Jack's smile dropped slightly for the nickname he unwillingly accepted. But now he turned his attention back to Marcus who stood rummaging through his overly large bag. Marcus began to pull the contents quickly from every internal pocket, creating an untidy pile of gear that lay spread across pavement.

"Where is it?" he muttered to himself. "I'm sure it was here." His entire head now became engulfed by the bag as the search went deeper.

"What... What you looking for, Marcus?" Jack softly enquired, taking care not to get in the way.

"His sense of humour," Bran butted in while the chance was right.

A moment later, Marcus pulled out a scrolled parchment. "Ah ha! Here it is!" He waved the object vigorously in the air.

"Here what is?" questioned Bran, shrugging his shoulders and showing not an ounce of interest.

"The map... the map for our trip..."

Bran remained silent, his brow lifted, expecting only to hear something more intriguing in return. Jack remained perfectly silent; hesitant on where to look, his head swiftly turned from left to right.

With the map still held high, Marcus looked at the unimpressed, blank expressions staring back at him.

"Ain't you even excited?"

"Waving a piece of paper around like you're carrying the Olympic torch isn't likely to get our blood pulsing," answered Bran. "Why don't you open that damn thing and tell us where the hell we're headed?"

A short silence followed before the elevated scroll was brought slowly down to the pavement. The map itself was old with shades of brown and green stain that covered the inside surface. The corners were weathered from use: its text in places somewhat blurred. And as the entirety was unrolled, a scent of dust and damp briefly captured the youngsters' sense of smell.

"That stinks!" Jack said loudly, his hand held firmly to his nose.

"It's just old. Where did you find that rubbish?" asked Bran. "It's got to be ancient!"

Marcus spread the corners out, weighing them down carefully to stop the map from scrolling back in place.

"I found it in the old shed out the back behind the book shop. Didn't seem of any importance. But if it was, I still would have taken it regardless. It's exactly what we need."

19

He placed his finger on the map, pointing out their hometown of Bonhil Dale. The town's name had been abbreviated to only its initials. But during a careful study of the faded print, they soon made out the familiar shape of streets they had come to know so fondly. Marcus explained the trip from start to end, not even stopping to take a deep breath.

It was to be a circular route. The envisioned journey would include wild camping, campfires, and plenty of fishing. The route would see them out of town, and with a steady pace they would reach the boundaries of the Sleathton Estate. The journey would take two, maybe three days tops to reach the reserved land. Bran hadn't even considered going so great a distance and frankly hadn't prepared for it.

"That's miles away, Marcus!" Bran called out, disrupting the flow of the presentation. "Why in the name of Greek buggery do you want us to trek so far?"

Marcus paused, his finger still pressed firmly on the print so as not to lose his place.

"It'll be an adventure! Sleathton is the last bit of wilderness we got left. Let's explore it while we can," he said, a gleam sparkling noticeably in his eyes.

Bran placed his palms dramatically to his face, attempting to calm his nerves.

"OK… and just how long exactly is this trip going to take until it sees us back to Bonhil?"

Marcus took a moment to himself, calculating the days required with his fingers, stopping, then

20

recounting them over and over again. Bran stood by, agitated, as he watched his friend's silent count.

"Errr…" Marcus gulped. "Nine days or so."

"Nine days! Are you kidding me?" exclaimed Bran with a high-pitched shriek. He didn't allow Marcus the opportunity to respond. "We can't survive for bloody nine days out there! What we gonna eat for a start?"

Marcus quickly pointed down to a second bag filled with supplies which he himself had accumulated over several months. Unhappy with the whole ordeal, Bran slumped down to the greenery of uncut grass. For the first time he looked to Jack for support.

"Don't suppose you have anything to add to this, do you?"

Kneeling down, Jack looked over the carefully planned journey, as though the whole conversation had never occurred. He paused, rubbing the back of his neck.

"Well…" he said, considering his answer. "Where are we going again?"

"Yup, just as I thought." muttered Bran as he ignored Jack's inquisitive stare.

Chapter Three

Wheels were now in motion. Bran led the way, pedalling as fast as he could through the quiet village streets. His objective was to lose sight of his riding companions. Marcus cruised behind alongside Jack, having no desire to join in Bran's one-man race. Neither of the boys paid any attention to him.

"Come on!" Bran called back.

He pushed on hard, shooting past the town's hall and schoolyard. The narrow road swiftly dropped from beneath him, lifting his bike momentarily from the ground. He knew these roads like the back of his hand, and to prove it he would irresponsibly close his eyes while riding, purely to test his skill. He had done it many times before, although at least a quarter of those attempts resulted in injury.

In the distance, an old abandoned railway tunnel came into view. Bran squeezed, tightening his brakes, stopping in the shade with a grind of rubber. The others arrived shortly after: Jack first, momentarily followed by Marcus. Both faces were red and splotchy, their rucksacks already proving too difficult to carry.

"Heavy, is it?" Bran tauntingly sniggered.

"What do you think? I'm carrying all the damn stuff!" complained Marcus, the words spoken hoarsely with each gasp for air.

Their first stop was much sooner than anticipated. One by one, each bag was emptied onto the tunnel's sleepers and shared equally in accordance to size and weight. Everything was accounted for, leaving nothing amiss before being carefully repacked. And in time Marcus's and Jack's complexion soon faded to a much more natural skin tone.

"Ready?" asked Bran.

"Ready!"

"Me, too!" stated Jack, eager to participate.

The three of them turned back in sequence to the opening light of the tunnel. And watched as the sun blazed down on the sandstone buildings and arranged flower beds of Bonhil Dale, a comforting sight of home each of them had always taken for granted. The bells tolled loudly from the Church of St. Mary's. The daunting echo drifted through the humid summer breeze, reminding Marcus of their strict time schedule.

"We gotta go," he instructed, firmly placing his foot back down on the pedal. In single file they darted over the bumpy planks which would soon lead them to the openness of Quarry Hill. The summer's light soon began to dwindle as they sped on through the underground curve. Jack looked back with a small sense of uncertainty. Bonhil Dale presented itself as nothing more than a speck of light and soon vanished into a tunnel of endless darkness.

"Bye," he whispered softly, making sure his voice would go unheard by the others.

The light dispersed, and just like that the entrance was gone, leaving Jack with only the eerie sounds of bicycle chains rattling off the rock walls as guidance.

*

To Jack's relief, the tunnel's gloominess soon began to end. Sunlight poured in from the exit, illuminating the underground with a sense of paradise.

With the black hole behind them, their pace remained steady, all now aware of how much ground they needed to cover before sunset. Although there were no superstitious accounts of its vibrant yellow fields, the locals referred to Quarry Hill as The Badlands. In reality, it appeared as nothing more than innocent farmland.

When the winter seasons hit Bonhil, the valley would severely flood from the runoff of surrounding hills, pooling into an illusion of a small, still lake. However, it was now summer. The ground lay firm and exceedingly dry. And as the bikes sped through the levelled plains, the breeze blew past and caused the crisp grass to wave and hiss.

In time, the open lands around them began to narrow, ending in a hidden corner where an unstable stile stood crooked between the fences. In turn, each bike and bag were thrown over, landing softly on the overgrown heather. None of the boys had ever ventured past this point before, and even Bran now sensed a little excitement, but he was not about to voice it. An unlevelled path of stones and jagged rocks delayed their way ahead. Cycling was far too risky, and they struggled with pushing their bikes over the cobbled ground. Regardless, none of them minded the walk. The path stayed hidden from the blistering heat, providing them with brief but pleasing shade as they talked back and forth.

"Does this path end soon or what?" Bran yelled as his tyres rebounded awkwardly off the abundant dips.

"Just a little farther," called out Marcus from behind. He, too, was not entirely certain of the confined path's length.

Although Marcus had planned with precision, he was in no way an expert on the land. And now on the first leg of the journey, he started to question his navigational skill. Sure enough he was right. The rocky surface soon began to flatten, smooth, and widen, aiding his confidence as their guide.

"Told you!" yelped Marcus excitedly, making sure he was heard by their cocky leader upfront.

"Yeah, told you!" Jack mimicked, purely in support of Marcus.

The curve of the path finally came to an end, allowing the sun to strike like a hot iron against their pale skin. As they walked, the trees began to lose their towering dominance, and the boys eagerly dashed for the next shadow that spread coolness across the path. Standing side by side, the three figures leaned over their handlebars and gazed out into the view of far-off fields and hills.

"Over there!" Marcus spoke urgently while pointing anxiously towards the old stone road that was visible at the base of the northern hillside. "That's the way."

"You sure?" questioned Bran, now even less optimistic about the distance to be covered before they could set up camp.

"Positive," he replied, brushing aside any doubts before making a head start, his wheels now whizzing down the steep dirt track.

*

The day of pedalling was strenuous. The sun belted down, never once having to break between clouds. And by the time they reached the base of the hill, the day's light had begun to fade. Hungry and tired, all three fell to the ground to rest, allowing the shallow breeze to dry their temples.

Not one of them could believe how rapidly the day had passed.

Camp was set up haphazardly. The chosen spot was surrounded by tilting birch trees that would protect the campfire from any breeze and unexpected weather.

"I'm starving," Bran complained, clenching and rubbing at his stomach, hinting for Marcus to break out the stash of food.

Marcus emptied the hoard which consisted of dry products for the boys to consider.

"What's this shit?" questioned Bran, staring down at the assortment of unlabelled packages.

"Dried food," replied Marcus. "You know? Pasta, noodles, rice…"

Bran's face remained relatively blank but showed a hint of disappointment that slowly turned to despair. A vein on his forehead began to protrude with annoyance.

"Didn't you bring any good stuff?"

"Like what exactly?"

"Like real food, and snacks... chocolate, cakes, crisps, fizzy pops?"

The boys looked down at the piled stash, and the same feature appeared on their faces but for very different reasons.

"And tell me… How the hell was I meant to carry all that? Dried food is traveller's food." Marcus talked like he was explaining to a child. "A little water and you have yourself a plentiful feast. I'm sure we can all go a few days without eating junk for once."

Bran raised the palm of his hand sternly before Marcus had time to continue. "Wait a sec. Did you just say 'plentiful' feast?"

"Yeah…"

"You posh tart."

"Whatever. If you don't want what we have, then starve."

Bran scowled at the patronising tone, shrugging his shoulders before unclipping the water canister that remained firmly fixed to the rear of his bike.

Marcus cooked capably, while, piece by piece, Bran set up the vintage looking tent that was supposed to sleep three.

Jack was given the unwanted task of collecting firewood from around the outskirts of the camp. It was a task set up to fail, though it got him out of Bran's hair, if only for a short time.

"There we go," said Bran, finally standing back to admire his handiwork.

"Nice job!" Marcus complimented.

"Not bad at all, if I do say so myself," said Bran proudly before looking around. "So, where are you two sleeping?"

As the night sky set in, the boys sat comfortably around the crackling flames, eating their first real meal of the day. And despite his previous objection, Bran ate contentedly as he looked back to the shadowy mounds they had just crossed.

Amongst the Mists

Chapter Four

It had been hours, or so it seemed. Olivia was hungry now and yearned for the feel of her mother's comforting kiss on her forehead. She'd followed the cry down the river for some time, never once considering whether she should glance back at the distance behind her. Several trees had long since fallen into the water, turning the channel into an unpredictable trap as she scrambled by.

"I'm coming," she burst out. "Just stay still will you!" *Moron!* The word instantly came to mind without her even considering it.

The clear sound of water travelled through the air and caused her pace to slow. Surrendering to the need to catch her breath, she noticed the light was beginning to fade. So was her patience.

"Lost."

Olivia jumped hysterically. The voice, though only at a whisper, was now so close. She turned frantically, her face filled with apprehension, her fists clenched tight like boulders. *How did you get there so fast?* she wondered. The landscape sloped from the river and into a sunken boggy path.

"Pack that in!" she paused, embarrassed. "You ain't scared me, I –"

Olivia had no time to finish. Short childlike footsteps were heard sloshing through the soggy earth. She heard them so clearly, she could swear they were only yards ahead.

"I got you now, worm!" she whispered with a fiendish smirk, immediately leaving the chilly water and moving toward the middle of the mud path. Drainage was poor in the forest, and, over time, flooding had trickled down the path's centre, allowing an unsightly carpet of grubs to crawl and fester. Being only too careful of where she stepped, Olivia pressed on to claim her prize.

What started as a determined pace for victory began to decrease. Soon, Olivia's feet would vanish into the ground, causing her to slow. Then her legs began to sink.

"Bloody… stupid thing!" The words were distorted by gritted teeth. The unyielding trail had slowed her down so much that it took her quite some time to reach its gloomy end. The thick mud gradually turned into a large, still pond. Olivia had visited this place with her grandfather many times when she was younger. The swamp covered the land for acres, entirely camouflaged by the green leaves swaying gently above her head.

The mud-covered face looked around, but there was nothing familiar. It had been some years since she and her grandfather had walked together through this misty swamp on crisp autumn days. Olivia recalled that much. But as to the reason why they went there, the memory had long since faded. Her grandfather would tell endless tales of such a place. *What was the story?* She couldn't recollect, or she hadn't paid close attention. Either way, she hadn't cared for the old man's evening gibberish. Olivia wished for adventure back then, not lectures.

Being as cautious as she could, she scanned the area for movement and waited for the same cry to resume. But all remained quiet, *too quiet* for that matter. The green layered water was motionless. Not so much as a ripple disturbed its boundary. No breeze blew through the protected swamp, and as she called out with a mighty yell, only the sound of her own uneasy echo came bouncing back.

"Haha… very funny, joker. Come on, give us a clue."

All stayed as still and quiet as in her childhood memories.

"Come out! Joke's over," she called again while peering at the obstructed sky. Daylight had seen its end, and it wasn't until now that the lack of light truly began to creep up on her. From parts of the woodland that she could not see, imaginary eyes pressed onto her. Moving carefully through the murky water, she noticed the darkness take its inevitable form. Soon, only the shapes of the nearest trees were visible.

"Please… where are you? You still there?" She whimpered in each soulless direction, and for the first time she showed a vulnerable streak. Olivia listened intently to the sound of silence, almost pleading for a response. A splash struck the swamp's surface. Its direction was clear, but other than that, all remained invisible. The water rippled with a fading wave that soon brushed up against her thigh. And for the first time, Olivia's heart began to pound into her throat.

"I... I want to go home now. Please… Please leave me alone," she cried, turning to retrace her steps down to the muddy path leading to the stream. Within a moment, much bigger concerns caused Olivia to sob aloud in panic. The path was gone. It was nowhere to be found. She thrashed through the water as if it were a maze, raising her trembling hands to barricade herself from fear. And as she did so, a heckling chuckle echoed through the wall of darkness behind her.

"Lost?"

Chapter Five

It felt strange being so far from home. Without knowing the time, Bran, Marcus, and Jack stayed up until the early hours of the morning. Each of them was only too happy to watch the stars parade in the clear night sky, seemingly shining only for them.

"Who's up for a ghost story then?" Bran asked in a rather boyishly joking manner, breaking the silence of star gazing.

Marcus smiled at the idea, but Jack's thoughts drifted elsewhere, as if he didn't want to listen to anything that would set his nerves on edge.

"Go on then," Marcus sniggered. "We could do with a laugh."

Bran prepared himself, cleared his throat, and edged closer to the dancing flames for effect.

He told a rather predictable tale, one that had altered slightly over the course of time. It was a short story of a married couple. The wife had gone to visit an acquaintance for the evening, leaving her husband to wander about the house alone. As is typical in such stories, a power outage struck the neighbourhood on this of all nights. The man was left in darkness, pestered by a taunting voice that repeated the following words:

I'm a dab hand with a peeler. I'm a dab hand with a knife. I'm a dab hand with a peeler. I think I've got your wife.

The story to Marcus was ridiculous and not at all frightening. Jack on the other hand remained still, his eyes never leaving the same spot on the ground, all the while listening intently.

"You do better then!" Bran challenged Marcus, only too sure that his story would come out on top as the most terrifying.

Marcus chewed on the idea for a short time before retelling the well-known story of The White Lady of Hulme. The story had been relayed time and time again at gatherings, but to Marcus it still caused a shiver up his spine as he spoke the words from his childhood years.

"A gentleman was driving through the country roads as rain hammered down on his bonnet. He came to a sudden stop as his headlights caught the form of a woman in white clothes, standing at a darkened corner of the lane. The woman was quite beautiful but soaked to the bone and lacked an umbrella to shield her from the evening storm. The man sprang from his seat and aided the woman into his car, kindly trading her dripping wet coat for his own. He drove her home, the woman whispering nothing more than an address that was isolated within the fields of Hulme. When he pulled up outside the building, the house displayed in full light from every window. The structure and gardens were an impressive sight to behold. The woman left the car promptly, running up to the doorstep of her home. She turned and gave the man a gleaming white smile as an acknowledgment before she vanished into the house.

"The very next morning, the man slouched into his car. Troubled dreams of the previous night had tormented his mind. He looked behind him, and to his surprise, the lady's white coat still lay damp upon his rear seat. It was then he recalled the woman fleeing from the car, still wearing his long grey coat. So, that morning the man makes a return journey to the stunning country manor, only to find it in disrepair and ruin. The windows are shattered, the door is gone, and weeds grow freely from the weathered brickwork. The man walks cautiously to the open hallway, only to find his coat spread carelessly on an abandoned spiral staircase. He retrieves the coat and sprints back to the car in a fright. As he drives away in a panic, he turns to look back. The woman's white coat is gone."

*

Jack sat huddled, his face buried into the curve of his shaking knees, unwilling to listen further.

"Same old crap. How many times we heard that one?" Bran's expression could be read easily through the dying light. He was clearly not impressed.

"Still gives me the shakes," said Marcus, smirking and again raising his head back to the stars.

"Me, too," Jack whispered, the sound muffled through the gap of his tightly clenched knees.

"What about you, Jack?" asked Marcus.

"Yeah, you got anything for us, Special Jack?" Bran teased, repeatedly poking harshly at the poor boy's ribs.

Jack said nothing, showing no willingness to give in to Bran's playful, yet persistent, bullying.

"Looks like he's not as stupid as you look," Marcus laughed.

"Whatever!" Bran stood and made his way over to the tent without a word, no longer wanting to be considered a fool. Marcus and Jack soon followed, confident the shallow flames would stay confined within the stone circle. The three wrapped up warm within the tent, and although there was little room, tiredness clouded their mind too much to care. Bran's eyes calmly began to close, when Jack began his ghostly tale.

*

Bran sat upright once the story came to a close. "What the hell? I told you he was a psychopath!" forgetting for a second that Jack lay crushed beside him.

It wasn't a common occurrence that Bran would show vulnerability. Hardly ever, really. But when it did occur, the opportunity was much too precious for Marcus to neglect.

"Got to you, did it? Piss your pants, did you?"

Both Jack and Marcus burst into uncontrollable laughter at Bran's expense. His hateful expression stabbed the eyes of his tormentors through the dark before he wrapped the hood of the sleeping bag firmly around his head.

"No!" Bran shrieked before putting his head back to the lumpy ground.

The laughter gradually ran to its end, and as minutes went by, the sound of heavy breathing was heard coming from Marcus and Jack. Bran tried his best to give in to sleep. But the story last told rambled around his restless mind and denied any thoughts of rest.

Amongst the Mists

Chapter Six

That morning they awoke prematurely. The unexpected chill of the early hours had disturbed their sleep and covered the tent in a sheet of glistening moisture. As the tent pegs were pulled, sunlight peeked over the far-off hills. Warmth washed over their faces and revitalised their senses. Another long day of adventure was ahead, and they planned the route like a team, kneeling on the ground with the map laid out in front of them.

The hard mounds around the hill's base made their journey harder than they anticipated. The descending track was far too narrow to allow them to cycle abreast, leaving them no option but to ride single file.

Once the ground levelled, fast flowing water was heard below hidden cliffs. With their hearts now encouraged they rode on, determined to reach the famous flow of Claymore River.

Shortly, white water could be seen from the high banks as they stood along the rocky sides. The river of Claymore was exceedingly well known for its length, stretching over one hundred and fifty miles until feeding into the Northern Sea. They needed to cross at some point, but it was far too risky to swim. There was a guaranteed risk of being dragged farther downstream like a ragdoll, probably to your death. A bridge stood twenty miles yonder. It was boldly indicated on the map.

Hopefully it still stands, thought Marcus, mentally crossing his fingers.

The bridge would lead them to the edge of the Sleathton estate and take them to the last leg of their journey before the real adventure truly began.

"So, we just follow the flow then?" asked Bran casually. The day's objective was turning out to be rather pleasing to him indeed.

"Yup…" replied Marcus. "Though we need to set up camp by nightfall, so the sooner we get to the bridge the better.

"We could make a raft," suggested Jack quickly, though rather wishing he hadn't.

"That's a great idea, you 'tard," replied Bran, not even taking the time to look Jack in the eye. "I'll ride along with Marcus, and you can meet us with the bikes and gear at the bridge. Sound good?"

"Give him a break, Bran. He was only trying to help."

"It was only an… an idea," stuttered Jack.

*

They followed the foaming waters throughout the bright early morning in silence. The sound of the roaring rapids was too dominating to hear each other's playful calls. The descent was so pleasant they could not resist the temptation to race the falling river. As they sped down the path, their handlebars rattled uncontrollably, and their wheels appeared to hover just above the ground. They noticed the waves starting to calm; the river's course slowed to a brisk but steady flow.

It had been an enjoyable morning and a memory that would remain in their minds when they recalled their youth. Wildlife emerged from their hidden homes, causing the boys' eyes to wander from the path ahead. The cheerful call of fluttering birds sang in harmony as they swooped overhead. Wild animals, curious about the commotion, happily sprang out onto the path from patches of tall thick grass. It was another day of warm, clammy weather, but that didn't seem to bother the trio much. With each sudden drop of the river, the fall of water would send a light spray flaring into the air, providing a satisfying sensation as they rode on through the walls of cooling mist.

Crashing his bike to the ground around midday, Bran insisted they rest for lunch. It didn't take much persuasion for Marcus and Jack to join him;

their bellies had been crying out for food for a while now.

They sat next to the soft flow of the river, gradually regaining their strength. Morale was certainly high, and teasing banter harmlessly circled the group. Once they ate their fill, Marcus sneakily took to the edge of the river and cast out a fishing line that he put together himself. His design was flawless, and his technique, although rusty, gave Bran and Jack the impression what he was doing was right. But regardless of countless tries, he couldn't entice even one fish to bite.

"Give it a try later," suggested Bran, now getting rather tired and, in all truth, bored by watching his friend's continual failures.

Marcus reeled in the empty line, disappointed with himself after having made the rod from scratch.

"You'll get one later. Besides, what would you have done with one now?" encouraged Bran while watching his friend stomp across the bank.

"I dunno," said Marcus, shrugging off the conversation and stubbornly collapsing the equipment back in his bag.

For the first time (and last) Jack continued to lead the way. Bran wasn't confident with the idea, and by the look of it, neither was Jack. The boy had no clear sense of direction, and he continued to stray from the path, only to look back for approval.

"Keep your frickin' head straight! What's wrong with you!" shouted Bran, annoyed. "You're all over the place!"

"The water will have you if you fall in, Jack. Just keep heading straight!" yelled out Marcus.

Bran rolled his eyes, never quite understanding Marcus's patient manner towards what Bran considered stupidity and a personality that could never learn.

Soon, the river began to bend, curving around the hilly mounds as though trying to challenge their riding skill. The ride was demanding enough, and they decided to cut through the higher ground. As long as the river was in sight, the day's target could not escape them. Jack eventually drifted to the back and seemed rather pleased by it. He was a follower, certainly not a leader.

The sound of grinding brakes trailed along the dusty ground as Jack came to a stop.

"What is it now?" asked Bran, wanting nothing more than to crack on and leave the bumbling idiot behind him. Marcus trailed back and pulled up alongside Jack, also curious about the sudden reason for delay.

"Look!" Jack whispered harshly beneath his breath.

The other two flashed a concerned glance at one another before panning over to where Jack's interest rested and his shaking finger pointed.

They, too, froze solidly in place. Like a curtain of fog, clouds began to slide apart in the distance. Past the waves of endless fields, giant shadowed mountains reached up to the sky through a foggy ceiling, their peaks fading from view.

"That's it!" Marcus shouted in excitement.

"How the hell do you know?" Bran questioned. "It just looks hazy from here."

"That's gotta be it, Bran," replied Marcus. "The river leads right to it."

There was something Jack couldn't quite put his finger on about what lay ahead. They had come so far from home and the vast landscape was strange and frightening. The grey shaded mountains stood dominantly in their surroundings, intimidating his vulnerable stature as he gazed upon its greatness.

"Come on, Jack," Marcus yelled. Both he and Bran were already some yards ahead.

But Jack did not budge, his eyes unable to prise away from the darkened shadow of far-off rock. He was sure he heard breathing: shallow, earthly breathing that was not his own.

It's just the wind, he thought. As he remained entranced, he began to believe it wasn't he who watched the mountain but the mountain that watched him.

*

Their pedalling quickened dramatically, and within only a few hours the mountain ahead appeared three times larger than when first seen. Its darkened shade had faded and now revealed itself clothed in lively shades of green and brown with trees standing like troops guarding its surface. The Claymore River had lost its relentless pattern of curves and bends, staying almost completely straight. The water's flow again quickened, as though it were enticing them to journey forward more urgently. Marcus looked up. He still couldn't believe they would really arrive at Sleathton as he'd planned. The feeling of excitement motivated him to push his legs harder.

They hurriedly wove their bikes around the pine trees that were haphazardly dotted around them. Soon they would leave open fields behind them and enter a land where they would be surrounded by trees that would block the view of the mountains.

"Stick to the path," shouted Marcus. He tried his best to keep the others in order, though both of them continued to drift off course and further into the jumble of dense woodland. The Claymore River now swerved in and out of the trees like a serpent twisting its way through the undergrowth. Occasionally the sunlight burst through in blinding rays, and although the path beneath the branches was dim and sheltered, beads of sweat fell freely from the boys' brows. The path disappeared under their wheels without warning, though none had come to notice. Their attention was too focused on the challenging ground that lay ahead. Bran overtook the lead so quickly that no one would have imagined how exhaustion caused his limbs to shake.

"Get back here," Marcus warned, now riding faster after his wandering friend. The trees ahead split for a moment, providing the opportunity for him to make up the lost ground. The decision to chase was worth it. And now that the clearing had passed, the view of Bran's thrashing legs quickly left the corner of his eye. His thighs pushed and pushed, harder and harder, until Bran was no longer beside him, and only the sound of his friends' natter was heard from behind. He turned his head back to see, but his attention was drawn elsewhere, past the blur of trees. *What...* he thought, unable to find words. His eyes strained to see what he had nearly missed

"Marcus!" The panicking roar of both Bran and Jack echoed from his pedalled tracks.

Marcus did not have the time to acknowledge. For now, all he saw was blackness.

Chapter Seven

Marcus lay sprawled like a stringless puppet. Alone in a ditch covered in foliage and soil. Bran carelessly jumped from his ride, the bike crashing against a fallen log.

"Marcus?" Bran yelled, slumping down to his friend's side and shaking him vigorously by the shoulders. "Speak! Come on, speak!" He had already accepted that his plea was bound to be ignored. He leaned down, placed his ear to his friend's lips, and waited.

"I... I can't... I can't hear him breathing." His voice sounded helpless and fearful in the current situation. All the while he tried to raise the lifeless body.

He turned back. Jack was still sitting over the red bar of his bicycle, clenching his fists so tightly the tips of his fingers were a ghostly white.

"Go get help, you pratt!" Bran screamed the order and caused Jack to startle and lose his balance. He regained his feet instantly like a duck taking to water while still watching the two pitiful figures on the ground.

"Go... now!"

Jack hesitated a moment longer, not knowing which direction to choose. He started to sprint through the woodland, his legs already pounding

46

from a full day's ride. It occurred to him that if he found help, or if help found him, he might not be able to find his way back.

"Marcus!" Bran screeched again, becoming so frustrated that he actually considered punching his friend in the face. Instead, he looked around.

Water, he thought. His eyes zoomed in on the canteen that had been thrown across the dirt.

He had attended a short classroom session of health and safety only the previous school year. The lesson wasn't at all remarkable, but he recalled a scenario where cold water was used to revive someone who might be in a state of shock. Holding the canteen firmly against his chest, Bran scuffled back to where Marcus lay crumpled on the ground. He emptied the entire contents over Marcus's face causing him to wake in fright, gasping for air.

Marcus looked around as he tried to steady his breathing. He was confused, and his memory was blurry.

"What the hell did you do that for?" croaked Marcus, wrapping his arms around himself to stop the shivers. "I thought I was drowning."

"Lucky for you, you ain't. Although you weren't far off." Bran pointed to the racing river only a metre or two from where they knelt.

"What happened?" Marcus asked, trying his best to recall the events. "I remember," he continued, slurring his words. "I saw something... then... the lights went out." He thought some more before Bran broke the silence.

"Didn't you hear us shouting? We yelled pretty loud. Jack was almost in hysterics."

"No… Well… I heard a noise… But it was faint and sort of distorted. Was that you? Why… what happened?"

Bran stood over him with eyebrows raised, now wondering if Marcus hit his head even harder than it seemed.

"Oh, forget it," Marcus sighed. "We need to get moving and make it to the bridge."

"Make it to the bridge? Make it to the bridge!" Bran repeated with sourness. "You bloody well hit the bridge!"

Marcus hadn't noticed, but the sturdy object which he was currently using as a pillow was drystone, the very edge of that bridge. He twisted around, sending a spasm jolting up his back and causing the bruise developing on his forehead to pound. *Bran was right*, Marcus thought as he looked up from the ditch. From his position on the ground, the dusty red stones appeared to tower above him.

"Well… that came out of nowhere," he said, brushing the dirt from his soil covered knees.

"No. It didn't, Marcus. We saw it as far back as the clearing. Why the hell do you think I fell back?"

Marcus paused, feeling rather foolish but summoning up the words to justify the incident.

"Look, I just didn't see it. OK?"

"You're telling me," said Bran, a hint of amusement now penetrating his words. "You headbutted the frickin' wall!"

"Can we just go?" Marcus questioned in a somewhat embarrassed tone, trying his best to change the subject.

"Fine! But if you're going to act like a complete retard for the rest of the way, we're gonna have to find you a helmet."

Marcus attempted to raise himself but soon realised he could not. He bellowed in agony, the pain in his back too intense for him to move, let alone stand.

"You OK? I'm done playing nurse with you for the moment."

Marcus ignored the remark, far more concerned about the pain in his back. He was trying to rub out the constant ache when he noticed there was someone absent.

"Where's Jack?" he asked with a frown.

"Ah, shit!"

"Where is he, Bran?"

"I swear, if I haven't gotta look after one special case, I've gotta look after two."

Bran ran over to his bike, jerking it up from the dirt.

"I sent him for help. The moron's probably gone looking for it up a tree!"

"Go find him," said Marcus, his face still scowling from the tormenting pain that stabbed his lower sides.

"I will. Just… Just don't move. Last thing I need is for you to go wandering off, too."

"Does it look like I'm going anywhere?" Marcus spat out through clenched teeth. "Go... now!"

"There'll be no need for that."

A deep, humble voice boomed past a line of trees. Their heads turned to see a figure almost camouflaged against the backdrop of the forest. A man walked swiftly towards them, stopping just short of the tip of Marcus's toes.

"It right that you boys got into a spot of bother?" the man asked, his sunburned face partially protected by a very full and untamed gingery grey beard.

None of them spoke. They were too focused on trying to determine who this man was and how he appeared seemingly out of nowhere. Jack appeared a few steps behind, looking relieved to see Marcus awake and talking.

"Young Jack here tells me one of you've had an accident," the man said. "Quite shook up was this young fellow when he bumped into me. Even implied you may be... well, you know, on the other side."

Bran and Marcus looked at each other with uncertainty, both hoping the other would speak first.

"However, I can see that's not the case, thank goodness," the man continued, never once indicating he had physically exerted himself.

"The name is Degg, Gregory Degg, if you so wish to be formal about it. I run the lodging house about half a mile north. Good job your friend

50

bumped into me when he did, I was just about to head on home.

Bran broke in, tired of dancing around Marcus's lack of ability to speak.

"And what exactly are you doing out here, Mr... Degg, was it?"

"Yes, it's Degg, but plain old Gregory will suffice just as well. And to answer your question, chopping firewood. Please don't judge. Have you any idea of how costly it can be to keep a lodging house heated?" he said while rubbing his thumb and finger together. "Well, I can tell you, it's not cheap. Dried wood is very expensive these days, especially during the winter months. It burns a hole right through my trouser pocket, if you'll pardon the pun. So, throughout the year I wander into the forest and source what I can, ready for the autumn."

"No judging here," said Marcus, becoming more at ease with the talkative gentleman.

"Hang on a second," Bran interrupted, still not altogether convinced of the man's defence. "If you're chopping wood, where's your axe then?"

Gregory gave a resounding laugh from the belly up.

"My boy," said Gregory, still laughing, "if I was to come marching towards you through the woodland with an axe in my hand, I assure you, you'd have thought my intentions to aid this young man not at all honourable."

"I guess so," replied Bran, although his response would go unheard under the man's infectious laughter.

"Now, my friends, if you think it at all proper for me to call you that, tell me exactly what occurred here."

For the next few minutes, Gregory Degg remained absolutely silent, listening to Bran and Marcus as they bickered over the smallest of details. Jack, as usual, said nothing, never keen on involving himself in any kind of social dispute, no matter how big or small. When the telling of events had ended, Gregory stood quietly, handling his beard as though deep in thought.

"I see," he said, his concentration never straying past the stand of trees. "And tell me, young man, what exactly do you believe you saw?"

Marcus scouted from one pair of eyes to the next. "I… I…"

"Yes, young man?"

"I… don't remember."

"Yeah, because you didn't see shit!" Bran teased. "You just don't wanna 'fess up to the fact that you made a complete tool of yourself. Too hyped up on rice and noodles, that's his problem."

Marcus said nothing in return, but proudly presented Bran with a swift two finger salute.

"Now, now, boys," Gregory protested, raising both hands in order to calm the mood. "The way I see it you have a couple of options. One. You rest up here for the evening. It is what you originally planned after all. And in doing so, see how this young man's injury fares. Option two." He raised a second finger in the air. "You gather what you can and call the journey short. Or –"

"No way!" Marcus yelled out, determined for the trip to go ahead as scheduled. "I've planned this trip for months!"

"Shut the hell up, Marcus, and let the man finish." Bran whispered loudly enough for all to hear, including the old man himself.

Gregory looked around him. Again, all waited for him to continue.

"Or…" he began where he left off, "you can come down the road with me. I have a spare room vacant at the lodging house. It may do your friend's injury here a bit of good to sleep in the warmth of a real bed rather than on the cold, hard earth."

He cleared the dryness of his throat before continuing. "Of course, it is a matter for yourselves to discuss. I shall retrace my steps and retrieve my axe and timber, returning to you presently."

And just like that, Gregory Degg stepped back into the dimming woodland from which he came. His crunching steps faded quickly, until they could be heard no more.

The three boys spoke quietly at first, unsure whether their words would travel any distance.

"What you think?" asked Marcus.

"I'm in," replied Bran willingly. "Anything beats sleeping in that shitty tent of yours."

"I dunno, he seems nice enough. It's just…"

"Just what?" Bran asked.

"Well… Dodgy, isn't it?" Marcus questioned. "Think about it. Stranger in the woods entices three boys back to his rural lodge."

"I think you have this obsession to think the worst of any situation," said Bran. "And plus, a stranger in the woods enticing three boys back to his rural lodge sounds a lot like one of your straight to VHS movies. This guy could be complete gold dust."

"I'm not sure," Marcus said, attempting to force his stiffening body to a sitting position.

Jack stepped forward, picking up his bike and wiping the mud from his worn leather seat.

"I think…. I think we should check it out." He paused, waiting for a following. "If we don't like it, we… we don't have to stay. He was very helpful when I called for help, after all. We need to remember that."

Bran smirked, overly pleased that another opinion was closely in line with his own.

"That's the spirit, Jacko!" Bran cheered. "And I believe that's two against one. Don't worry, Marcus. If he turns out to be a complete perv, Jack here will take one for the team. Won't you, Jack?"

"Absolutely!"

Amongst the Mists

Chapter Eight

livia woke, lying motionless and floating in the shallows. Her weight barely touched the water's murky bed. Fluid filled her ears. She could hear only the sound of the ripples as the water gently washed against the side of her face. She remained still. A thick mist had descended, covering her body. She watched its peaceful gliding flow, her body weightless, her mind (at this moment) calm while the thoughts of flying through endless clouds piqued her imagination. Was she awake or asleep? She herself didn't know, didn't care. But as the mist broke, the physical sense of flying shattered, and memories came flooding back of how she came to be there.

Olivia sat upright with a fright. She coughed and spluttered, heaving up the grime which had somehow worked its way into her fragile lungs. It was so very cold. Freezing, in fact. For a time, all she could do was grasp her arms for warmth. She stood up slowly. The only sound was the lapping of the water. She looked around and quickly searched her memory. There was just one problem; this was not the place she remembered. She had been brought here and left to soak in the unforgiving mud.

Where is this? she thought as she looked in every direction, removing the clumps of hair that stuck to her face. But where is the ribbon her mother had put in her hair? It was gone.

The night was still at its darkest, but she could tell not all was the same. The trees, although still towering like giants above her, stood much more dense than she recalled. And in between, scattered boulders appeared, faintly materialising through the brume. Never had she stumbled upon such a place before, the idea of what secrets it held troubled her even more.

Olivia began to walk carefully through the marsh, her submerging feet squelching with every step. When she finally reached the closest stone, she rested. Her head lay flat on its damp, slippery surface to catch her breath. It occurred to her that despite her desperate desire for help, she still remained mute. She worried that if she cried aloud for help, the response in return could bring her harm. So for now, she remained silent, stepping cautiously from rock to rock.

I'm getting out of here, just keep moving.

The words repeated around her head again and again, feeding her determination to make it past the forest's edge unharmed.

Just follow the rocks.

Amongst the Mists

Chapter Nine

Once the four had passed the stone bridge, the trek to the lodge was not demanding. Gregory guided the boys up a steep dirt path and then to a wider road, out of sight of the river. A wall of green trees lined either side of the road, seeming to go on forever, which in turn provided the bluest break in the sky.

"Is this Sleathton?" called Marcus, leaning over his bike to ease the pain from the crash.

Gregory looked back as he walked, his axe weighing heavily upon his shoulder as he spoke.

"The border, yes. Won't be long now, boys. Just farther on up this road," he said, showing little interest in discussion.

"Hey! My hat!" Marcus shouted, rubbing his hair. "I've lost it."

"Bloody thing went flying into the river as you crashed." Bran was not at all sorry to see the end of it. It was a dreadful hat, its material reflecting every colour of the rainbow.

"That was my favourite hat, too!" There was no way Marcus could conceal his disappointment.

"It was your only hat, you plank."

They all walked on, the flattened road a luxury to travel. Gregory stepped out from the shadows, and for the first time the boys were able to look at him in the evening light. The old man trudged onwards, his upper back arched uncomfortably forward (or so it seemed), providing the impression that bearing weight on his shoulders was part of his daily duties.

It didn't take long until the relative ease of the hike ended. Their bags felt heavier; their legs began to tire. Yet the road kept stretching farther and farther, without any bend or dip in sight.

"How much longer?" Bran was impatient and rather tired of the same, seemingly endless view.

"Not far." Gregory answered without turning to look back.

Jack walked at the rear, as he usually did. He listened, trying to catch sounds of the wilderness. Neither a whiff of a breeze nor a bird's trill could be discerned. The only sounds were the ticking of loose bike chains accompanied by the thud of each man's step. Soon, scattered buildings loomed through the shrubbery, though they were not at all welcoming. The owners of these homes had apparently long since departed, leaving the wooden shacks to rot and slowly collapse. At first, it was only Jack who took the time to observe the dilapidated structures. The other two were far too fatigued to notice. Jack said nothing about the matter, this was the wilderness after all, and he would soon come to terms with the neglected look of forgotten homes. A weathered sign leaned out from the overgrown ferns, its lettering partially covered by a thin layer of muck.

W lcom to T ym .

"What the frig does that say?"

Gregory turned when he heard the question, not knowing who had asked.

"Thyme... It reads, Thyme." There was not a hint of pride in his elderly voice. "It was a thriving little community once. No doubt you've noticed the houses set back from the road?"

Bran and Marcus immediately shook their heads. They finally took note of the structures that were barely standing upright behind the wall of conifers.

"Why would they leave?" asked Bran, mostly to himself.

"People just do. You live somewhere then you leave. That's just life." Gregory shrugged off any suspicion the boys may have insinuated.

"What! Everyone? That ain't normal," stated Bran. "This place is completely deserted!"

The old man suddenly halted and turned to face the shadows that followed him. His expression was somewhat grieved, and his head hung low. Swinging his axe to the side, he rested the handle against his thigh. "And I suppose you know the meaning of the word normal?" He wiped his brow with his unravelled sleeve.

"Well... It's a little odd, don't you think? People don't just abandon an entire village." Bran's words slowed while speaking, as though he were somewhat hesitant to question the old man who bore an axe.

A short pause followed, none of them entirely sure of who would speak first.

"Nothing odd about it." Gregory broke the silence. "Plus, you're wrong. The village isn't entirely abandoned." He swung the axe effortlessly back over his shoulder and began to make his way.

"How many live here then?" Bran shouted outright.

"Just me." Gregory answered loudly and began to belt out a tuneless whistle.

The boys glanced from one to the other with indecisiveness, concerned about making the decision to either follow their newly found acquaintance or simply make haste and vanish into the bush.

"OK then… this guy is clearly a nut job!" said Bran, not caring about his choice of words or how loudly he said them. "You!" He pointed his finger in Marcus's face. "You never said anything about this place."

The map was jerked from the side compartment of his rucksack. After tracing their route, Marcus followed a dotted line to where they supposedly stood.

"There's no Thyme on here?" he asked in confusion before he threw the map to Bran for further examination. In turn, it was passed to Jack. Gregory continued walking down the road with no desire to convince or enlighten his followers. The evening was drawing late, and the setting sun had already begun to turn the distance to an unappealing bloodthirsty orange. Despite the boys' mistrust, a comfy bed was far too inviting to chance offending their host.

"It's only for tonight," Marcus urged. "Please. Might not be so bad when we get there."

Bran said nothing more. He only shook his head at the thought.

"Hey, Mr Degg! Hang on." Bran shouted. He and Jack quickened their steps to catch up to the patiently waiting axeman, leaving Marcus to waddle slowly behind with his suffering.

Chapter Ten

To the boys' surprise, the lodge house was far beyond the unsightly image they each anticipated. A wood chip path guided the four from the roadside, curving through the dominant overgrowth until reaching the rustic lodge. It was an old limestone building with a newly installed timber extension on the rear. An old water wheel hung loosely affixed to the side wall, its aging frame showing black decay and neglect, giving Marcus the impression that rivers once flowed freely through Thyme. But now the wheel remained dormant as it had for many, many years. The gorge below that once served its purpose was now only a gathering of dried rocks across its cracked, dusty bed.

The boys rested their bikes against the trunk of an old oak tree, while they still looked uneasily over the house. All of them waited for any reason, any excuse, to give them the cue to leave.

They followed the old man further up the loose path, watching the windows and door of his home as they approached. The house itself was set much farther back into the woodland in comparison to any neighbouring building, and fallen walls could be glimpsed through the swaying branches of the trees surrounding the lodge.

"Not so bad… is it?" Marcus sounded less than confident in his judgment.

"No, it's… it's fine." Apparently, Jack, too, was unsure about the place he had chosen to rest.

"At first light we leave, right?" Bran had ignored the question at hand and asked one of his own. The others nodded in agreement and urged him to step over the threshold

"Right. Let's get it over with," he said.

*

"Please, boys, this way," Gregory directed from the front. He guided the boys through the cramped lodge house, its hallways at times so narrow that one couldn't shake away the unnerving sense of claustrophobia. Making their way up the wooden staircase, the steps called out (as if pained) as they creaked and cracked, accompanied by a rattle from the unsteady handrail. Bran was sure the floor would give way before they could reach the upper level, causing them all to fall to their certain doom. Framed pictures were hung carelessly across the damp walls, all resting at unpleasant, crooked angles.

The pictures represented a variety of forest scenery, each image different in colour and mood. *Odd,* Bran thought as he considered the choice of theme. *You would think he'd get tired of the sight of trees.*

A door swung open for them at the end of the hallway, revealing a room whose interior was at once suspicious and gloomy.

"Hold fire," Gregory muttered, his body disappearing into the blackness. "I'll let in some light."

Within seconds, the light from the evening sunset spilled into the room. The boys jumbled inside, each rushing through the doorway to bag themselves a bed. The room was small, but it didn't matter. There were beds, two to be exact, but anything was better than sleeping on the hard forest ground. Bran bagged the single bed, pushing against Marcus and Jack in panic to reach it first. The double bed that sat by the window, two boys would have to share. They didn't care for the situation but were willing to make the best of it. *The sleep would be worth it,* thought Marcus.

"I'm sorry I can't offer you a larger room, boys," the old man said. "I don't get too many visitors these days, so I prepare only a few rooms at a time, just in case."

The boys gave a smile of polite appreciation in return, though each of them eagerly waited for Gregory to take his leave.

"My living quarters are located at the rear of the house should you want anything. I find it much more to my liking so I won't be seen puttering where any guests are staying. Food, should you want any, will be when the chime hits seven. Again, you will find this provided in my living quarters, which again, is located at –"

"The rear of the house?" Bran interrupted. "Yeah, we got it."

Marcus gave a swift kick into Bran's naked shin, embarrassed by his friend's impolite manner. Old Gregory caught sight of the painful stub and waited for their childishness to cease before continuing.

"Hmmm… yes, quite. Well, as I said, when the chime hits seven. For now, rest yourselves, get some sleep. Oh… and where are my manners? I almost forgot. Welcome to Thyme."

Chapter Eleven

T he door expressed its displeasure with being opened by creaking loudly before the latch clicked firmly into place. The boys were exhausted from the recent trek and took no longer than a minute to find comfort on their soft feather pillows. None of them spoke; only rest occupied their tired minds. Jack fell back. His head dropped into the fluffed-up pillow, causing both sides to balloon beside his ears. He watched as the light of the setting sun struck the pane of glass above him. The agitation of the bed caused a display of dust specks to liven and dance frantically in the air. Closing his eyes, Jack thought only of his body's aches and pains. This trip was proving to be more challenging than he ever imagined. But to him, it was OK. Because now he had friends, real friends. And that, deep down, was all he truly wanted.

*

The sound of puttering below disturbed their peace. There was nothing at all sinister about the sound, and since they had no concerns, they all sat up sluggishly from their curled positions. The dim room was now dark, giving them the sense that the hour was late and everything around them was peacefully at rest. Marcus pressed down hard at his watch, activating the backlight which pierced his eyes in the process. "Get up!" He yelled at the others as he sat upright, for the moment forgetting about his current wounds.

"Uh… Why?" Bran moaned, unwilling to lift his head away from the comforting warmth.

"Get up, both of you! It's eight thirty." Marcus had allowed himself to get into a rather emotional tizz.

It took only a second before the boys vacated the room and were scurrying back through the narrow hall. The building was dark, too dark to be conducive to their wanderings. Six palms felt along the surface of the walls at either side, scanning for a light switch.

"Found it!" Jack called with accomplishment.

A short pause followed as they waited for light to brighten the hallway.

"Flick the bloody switch then, you idiot!" Bran remarked, still half dazed and tired of making his way through the shadows.

Click, click, click, click.

"I am!" stated Jack as the noises appeared again. *Click, click, click.* "It doesn't work."

"Great," said Bran.

Feeling their way through the lower level of the house, and stumbling more than once, Bran was first to notice a faint glow peeking underneath a door at the end of the hall. He followed it and led Marcus and Jack without explaining what enticed him. He grasped the handle and twisted it slowly. The door opened to a dimly lit room. A kitchen.

Several candle sticks stood on a solid wooden table, the candlelight flickering in response to their entrance. A partially consumed glass of red wine was in the centre, and to the side was the opened bottle. Although they hadn't decided to stay, the smell of dinner cooking on the stove made the choice easy. The outer door swung open, and in walked a dark figure, masked by a backdrop of darkness. The light of the candles revealed the old man.

"So, here you are then. I did wonder whether you'd make your way down here at all. I waited some time, you know, but couldn't take the chill in my old bones any longer. So I decided to nip outdoors to fetch some firewood. Come, come, don't just stand there. Please take a seat, rest yourselves. I imagine you're rather hungry?"

Each of the boys slumped to a seat, thinking only of their bellies and the possibilities of food. Whatever bubbled away on top of the hob smelt delicious. So much so, that as the food was ladled from a very large pot, it caused Bran's mouth to water and Jack to drool embarrassingly.

Gregory placed the three steaming bowls down on the table alongside an ice-cold jug of cloudy lemonade.

"Ah, nothing quite like a homemade rabbit stew, is there? Tuck in boys, there's plenty more if single servings don't suffice."

Bran didn't need telling twice. He sat shovelling down the meat and fluffy potatoes that were swimming in thickened gravy. As for Marcus and Jack, they ate steadily, not wanting to cause discomfort to their grumbling stomachs. Eating contentedly, they paid no attention to the dim room lit by candle flame. Gregory squatted by the fire grate, his old knees cracking as they slowly bent. The fire soon caught, causing the room to glow and their hearts to warm.

"So," the old man began. "I trust you managed to find sleep? I thought it sounded too quiet overhead."

The boys nodded, each of them far too involved with their meal to respond politely.

Gregory continued to talk, and talk he did. He spoke of the seasons, the winters, springs, and summers. He griped about the upkeep of the house, the sadness of being alone, each amongst other facts that held the interest of not one of the boys. Still, Bran, Marcus, and Jack nodded along all the same. Marcus's mind wandered, noticing items within the room that grabbed his curiosity.

In the far corner of the kitchen stood a large pamphlet stand, very much like any ordinary stand you'd find situated at tourist spots. There was, however, one distinct difference compared to others he had seen. The inner tray to every slot was empty, holding only a thin sheet of dust.

The sign above, painted in large gold font, ironically read. *Things to do in Thyme.*

A depressing sight, thought Marcus. His eyes scanned the upper walls. There were many pictures, but none were of the old man or even any people. All of the pictures looked to be original works depicting nature.

"You like my work?" asked Gregory. He, too, was looking at the paintings above him.

Marcus gulped down a mouthful of stew before beginning to speak. "Your work… all of them?"

"Yes. Call it a hobby if you will, but it seems to pass the time. I apologise if the house seems flooded with these old paintings. I don't consider myself an expert by any means. I just very much like to paint and struggle these days with where to store them." He sat back, taking an inelegant swig of wine. The dark fluid stained the tip of his moustache as the glass was lowered from his lips.

"What's that?" asked Marcus, pointing towards a large framed picture that hung just above the fire beam.

"Hmm… oh, that," Gregory spoke, adjusting himself to where the picture hung at a slant. To be truthful, he was rather disappointed that the conversation had strayed from his own handiwork.

"Tis just an old map, is all."

"May I see it?" asked Marcus politely.

"As you wish."

The damaged frame was removed from the arch and placed flat on the table. The picture in question was old and faded, but Marcus had begun to develop a keen interest in maps. With an eye for detail, he noticed a particular location instantly.

"Look," Marcus pointed. "Bonhil Dale."

Bran quit chewing a chunk of rabbit.

"And… why exactly do we need to look at that?" he slurred. "We've lived there our entire lives. Hardly exciting, is it?"

Jack and Gregory gathered around the table. "See here?" Gregory pointed while taking control of the map. "This is where I found you. And this," he pointed again, "this be where you rest now." He pressed his index finger against the glass. The shadow hovered over what appeared to be nothing but printed wilderness. The village of Thyme did not appear on his map either, very much like their own.

But... Why? thought Marcus, now reading between scattered markings. Gregory had been right enough in the matter. The village of Thyme sat just below the border's edge of Sleathton. It would take only a few hours to reach its boundaries.

"Why is Thyme missing from the map?" asked Marcus, looking up to the elderly figure standing to his side.

"Well... it's just not on this map."

"It's not on our map, either," replied Marcus, pulling the scroll from his jacket pocket.

Gregory studied the scrolled map with interest.

"Ah, you see, your map is in fact many years older than my own. The village of Thyme was constructed in the early fifties for leisure tourism. And, well...once the trading stopped and the home owners left, Thyme in effect ceased to exist. Even for the map makers, so it seems. You'll have a pretty hard job finding a map that displays the word Thyme."

"So… why'd they leave?" Bran questioned with a bowl and spoon still in hand. "Or, should I say, why is there only you left?"

Gregory Degg slumped back down beside the fire. The warm glow of the flames brightened the side of his sun beaten face.

"I..." He thought for a second more. "I suppose that is a fair question. I've come so accustomed to the village looking a complete shadow of its former self; I forget how it must appear to outsiders wandering through. Quite the ghost town, wouldn't you agree?"

"You can say that again!" Bran was now leaning back, his stomach was full, and the button on his trousers was ready to burst.

Gregory made himself comfortable in the wooden chair, his back towards the flames. He filled his wine to the brim as he thought of the words to say.

"Very well," he grumbled. "I've spent many a season alone in this house. Many seasons boys, waiting, listening, watching, but above all, wishing."

Confused, the boys stared deep into the man's sad eyes.

"I'm sorry," the old man said, massaging his temple. "Do forgive me. I forget myself at times. If you wish to know, allow me to start at the very beginning."

Amongst the Mists

Chapter Twelve

One by one another boulder was reached. *Would this trail ever end?* Olivia thought. Her confidence was beginning to wear thin, and her sobs betrayed her frustration.

She persistently moved on, sometimes sprinting to the next rock. Her heart throbbed in her ears. The fog thickened, occasionally portraying the stones as shadowed figures. Several times she was convinced that human shapes floated in front of her. She stood her ground, only to discover that when the fog thinned a little the rough, uneven surface of solid rock would appear.

She wished for daylight. My God, did she wish for daylight. She wished for the sun to rise, for white clouds to drift above, and for the vibrant green of the hills and trees she loved so dearly to be her friends once again. It was a trying wish, one she knew would not be granted immediately, or even soon for that matter.

Again, she took to a straight line until the dark shape of a stone peeked through the murky air. She rested on it. Her mind was tired and now numb to any sensation of cold. Olivia had been walking for hours, yet she felt like she'd made no progress. She had no impression that her desperate escape was close to its end. She sobbed a little, losing the small sense of bravery that before pushed her so strongly forward. Resting on the rock, she thought of earlier that day. Why did she follow the calls? Those pestering calls now tormented her mind.

"You're an idiot," she whispered. "That's why!"

Olivia had heard the stories, heard the tales. Over time, she had decided they were nothing more than fables, simply stories to stop her from wandering far from home. After all, there had been no sightings in years.

Was it true, any of it? she asked herself, though her mind was already made up. Her belly cried in hunger, but she dismissed the idea instantly. How could she think of food at a time like this? She needed to move and move now. If she didn't, Olivia knew she soon would not move at all.

Again, she pushed herself firmly away from the rockface. An efforted grunt escaped her when both feet began to sink into the gruelling muck below. A steady wheeze rattled about in her chest. The fog was becoming so thick she could choke on it. She waved her hands about as if she were moving a weighted curtain of mist. Her steps were loud and her breathing heavy as she strained both eyes to see through the murk. Something lightly tapped at her shin. No, not just one tap, but several. They felt like nothing more than floating twigs. She knelt down, waving the mist away with the flick of her wrist. Olivia's gaze froze as the surface revealed crayons floating in the shallow water; the crayons that had fallen from her pockets. She looked around her surroundings in panic. Tears flowed unabated as she tried to understand what was happening. Olivia had travelled full circle. The rock trail had led her back to the very place she had awoken. She looked down at her submerged ankles, blubbering as she did. The thought occurred to her; whatever dragged her here had no desire to let her leave.

Chapter Thirteen

The kitchen door had been closed and locked, effectively silencing the sounds of the night. The candlelight settled to the calmness of the room and illuminated the old man's face as he prepared himself to speak.

"I had travelled to Thyme from the south during the summer of 1952. The word that year was passed from ear to ear of a new settlement to be constructed. Its location, to be scattered within the open wildness of Sleathton's forests. Its goal, although to encourage settlers, was to bring tourism to the wild and out of the over populated cities.

"For a time, the houses seemed to fly up. It seemed at each waking dawn a new family would be seen arriving into the village from far away. I had moved here not alone, but with my wife and granddaughter, eager if only to make a fresh start. For months it was a happy place. Our Lodge… this Lodge, was always busy, always full. It was a joyous time. Our business thrived, and we plodded gaily through life."

A noise broke the old man's flow. Jack had fallen asleep where he sat, his arms outstretched and resting on the table with his head lying peacefully in between.

"He almost looks normal with his eyes closed," said Bran who spoke with his own face disgustingly smothered in gravy.

The company fell silent; both Gregory and Marcus stared in reproach at the boy who hadn't stopped gorging.

"What? I never know which bloody eye of his to look at, that's all," continued Bran.

"Hmmm," mumbled Gregory while watching the young man slumber. "Maybe he has a point. Perhaps it is far past the hour to speak of such matters."

Bran shrugged off the idea of listening further. He was never much for stories, his own impatience exceeded whatever the narrator had to say. Marcus on the other hand was eager, he always had been, no matter what the tale.

"No, please carry on, Gregory," Marcus pleaded, his willingness to listen far greater than that of his companions.

The old man sat back once more. "Hmmm... Very well. Now, where was I..." he pondered and scratched his beard before having another gulp of wine.

"Ah, our business thrived and we got through life happily. I remember now.

"Well, who were we to know? Who were any of us to know? During our first winter, the purest horror would strike the village of Thyme.

"A boy. A young child only five years of age should go missing. His mother claimed she saw him playing innocently amongst the trees on that early morn. Within the blink of an eye he was gone. She protested frantically. Of course, the village folk worried, but they thought nothing sinister of such an incident. The child could have simply wandered off. Young boys do such things, don't you know?

"That morning the men of the village gathered, determined to find the missing child and return him home to his hysterical mother. We searched long and hard into the night, returning without having any luck. But we were still quite hopeful. The next day we wrapped up and set out again. I remember the frost that morning as we began to walk the trail, the grass standing on edge like sharpened blades of ice. Despite the cold, it had only been one night, so the logic of survival was still favourable. Well, we checked every hole, every hollow tree, the rivers, and the lakes. We searched the boundaries like a hound to a fox. Still, we returned home with bowed heads and empty hands. The child could not be found."

"Don't tell me," said Bran, "he was at home all along."

Gregory turned and threw the needed logs into the withering flames.

"No… Quite the opposite. We never found him. He was gone."

Marcus sat at the edge of his seat. He took in every word, not wanting to miss the smallest detail.

"Then what happened? Did you just give up?"

"On the contrary," the old man continued. "We spent many weeks searching, eventually coming to terms with the fact this would no longer be a rescue search. It would be one of recovery. A grown man can last much longer in the woods. But children, they have neither the knowledge nor the instinct of survival, especially a boy of only five years.

"Times were indeed sad. However, over the course of the following weeks, people began to settle back into their normal lives. They were beginning to accept the conclusion that what they had feared had indeed come to pass. The search parties became less frequent when the men were convinced there was no chance of finding the boy.

"I remember it well. In due course, the men gathered to put the choice to a fair vote. They asked if the searches should be stopped so normal life might continue. We all agreed, me included. The searches would end that day.

"We made our way back through the forests. Each of us had a sickened feeling in our gut. The thought of explaining our decision to the child's mother was too emotional to bear. We followed the trail home in silence. No one, not even I, spoke a word.

"To our surprise, a clatter of voices pierced through the distance, travelling up from the lower lands of Thyme. We ran as fast as our legs would allow, many falling en route. I seemed to lead the way while the others followed to the hillcrest overlooking the huddled village. The women ran amok below. Each of them were shrieking loudly and pulling on their children like they were rag dolls. By the time we reached home, many had secured themselves behind locked doors. I remember… A woman. Yes, a woman lay tormented on the cobbled roadside. Tears flowed from her eyes; her rose coloured cheeks frostbitten from the cold of the day. She was sobbing into her apron as I uneasily looked around the area. Regardless of words not being exchanged, somehow a part of me already knew… Another child had vanished."

*

A brief break was taken from the telling of Mr Degg's story. The boys' jug was soon filled, and a fresh bottle for Gregory was pulled from the rack and uncorked. The old man returned to his seat, his face showing no emotion as he listened to the faint howl whistling down the chimney.

"My, it's getting late," said Gregory, glancing back to the wall clock. "Would you boys care to retire?"

Jack still lay soundly asleep, only the deep breathing reminding others of his presence. Bran didn't care to listen to any more. Although the story had become intriguing, he could very well sacrifice hearing the ending in return for sleep. Marcus sat forward. Bran knew too well his friend would want to hear the tale until its end.

"Please, carry on," begged Marcus. "You've gotta finish it now."

The old man took a deep heavy breath and sighed. "If you insist." His tone was more troubled as the story went on.

*

"By the time we heard the second child had gone missing, another boy at the age of eight, the day had already begun to lose its light. The group of men who had ventured out earlier that day were exhausted. But somehow they returned to the forest, urging themselves on, this time to find the child and bring him home."

"But you couldn't find him, could you?" Marcus interrupted.

"No…" He paused, bowing his balding head. "No, young man, we could not." Gregory's heart was heavy in his chest.

The old man stood, his knees again cracking under the pressure of his weight. Making his way over to a corner unit, he shuffled about in the drawers.

"You boys like Chopin?"

"Is it a kind of cake?" asked Bran.

Marcus rolled his eyes, embarrassed.

"It's a composer, you idiot."

"A what?"

"A composer. You know, Beethoven, Mozart?"

"I know what a composer is!" said Bran, attempting to divert judgmental eyes away from his obvious humiliation. He took a moment longer as they waited for his response.

"Got any of those Shakespeare tunes?"

Chapter Fourteen

The needle gently rested on the spinning vinyl, sending a comforting crackle around the room. The flames appeared to sway in time with the tranquil sound. The old man returned to his seat as the music began to play. The piece was written for only a piano, the tempo slow and sad.

Bran scowled. *Why didn't they just say piano music? Fuckers!*

He thought the sound was depressing. It was also somewhat spooky. Not at all in a good way. Yet, this time he stayed quiet. Marcus said nothing, paying no attention to Bran or the eerie sound of Chopin. Instead, his sight remained fixed on the old man.

Gregory sat, his eyes closed, slowly bobbing his head with the rhythm. His face strained, holding back an emotion he had learned to bear. He exhaled, almost forgetting about the visitors sitting at his table. His head ceased keeping time, and his hand that had been conducting the music rested on his knee. Again he began to speak.

*

"The searches went on. Yet, not so much as a hair did we find in our efforts. We just couldn't understand it. No witnesses, no trace. It was as though they vanished into thin air, like they never truly existed at all. Local authorities were again informed. And again they disappeared as quickly as the missing children. Times were different back then. The police in these parts had very little authority. Their job was to keep the town as quiet as possible. Each week became harder than the last for the locals. Come Christmas the remaining search party decided to rest. We had missed the company of our own families greatly over the months and wished to spend time resting by the side of our own fires. The peace did not last even the day. As I sat on that Christmas morning, my granddaughter playing happily upon my knee, a heavy bang struck at the door. My wife, she…. she wailed at the man at our doorstep and ran frantically to me. Our neighbours' daughter had been taken."

"Taken?" Marcus was now very intrigued by the old man's words.

Music continued to spill out from the speakers, somehow fitting the story being told.

"Yes, taken. You see, this time someone watched the child leave. The family's eldest son

83

told the household what he had witnessed. He had watched his younger sister take interest in a view beyond the window pane just before she sprinted out into the frosty wilderness. He followed her, never letting her know of his presence. The child, he said, was speaking aloud. To what, he could not see, could not hear. But when his patience had been tried enough, he allowed himself to be seen and demanded her immediate return.

"His demands, however, fell on deaf ears. She did not acknowledge his adolescent proclamations of authority, nor did she stray from the path. The boy ran after her and watched as she slid behind the thick leaves.

"He came to a blind turn, but alas, his sister was not there. He did not feel at all alone as he stood watch. He called out for his sister, knowing by now he would be left with no alternative other than to retrace his steps to inform his father. He turned. A twig snapped loudly beneath his foot, sending a shiver up his spine. 'Help!' a distant voice echoed through the quietness of the woodland. The frightened young man looked around him. He knew very well that this particular cry came from no child.

"Well, now it was apparent. Someone was stealing Thyme's children. Three children in three months, soon to lead to its fourth. The men no longer carried walking sticks and lanterns. Instead, they lugged pitchforks and guns, now determined to end the life of another. And who could blame them? I, for one, could not.

"December spread into January and then into February. We had found nothing and deemed ourselves failures to the village. I returned home late and kissed my wife upon her lips, my granddaughter upon her cheek. I fell into the deepest sleep, only to be woken late that evening by the sound of frantic screams. I ran to the commotion, half asleep, half awake, finding my wife lying on our grandchild's rug. The bed covers had been torn from their place in the search. The cupboards and hiding places about the house had been opened and investigated. My heart broke that day. As I lay slumbering in my armchair, peacefully dreaming, my granddaughter stepped away from my protection. I was guilty of failing her.

"Shortly after that, the settlers began to abandon the village, too afraid the same tragedy was bound to befall their loved ones. The houses were left unlocked, the doors wide open, and their walls over time began to fall, like the very memory of Thyme."

The two boys exchanged a worried look, unsure whether to believe this actually happened.

"And your granddaughter?" asked Marcus.

"What of her?" he asked unhappily.

"Well… Did you ever find her?"

"No. No, I did not. And to be truthful, I have spent too many a year searching."

"Then why don't you just leave like the others?"

"Because…" He thought a moment. "Just because one is gone, does not imply they are dead. I stay in the hope of that thought. It is a feeling I believe in very strongly. Unfortunately, my wife could not bring herself to believe the same. It was inevitable for us to part after that."

A silence circled the room, soon followed by dimness caused by a dying candle.

"I stay here, son, in hope of her return. Regardless of living or spirit, I will be here… waiting."

Amongst the Mists

Chapter Fifteen

"Come now, it's time you all retired." The old man spoke softly, guzzling the last of what remained in his glass. The vinyl record had already been turned over. The next piano piece struck an uncanny resemblance to what had already played. The boys left the table as they were told, waking Jack from his corpse-like sleep. He jumped up, terrorised by the realisation of where he was. But his fright was short-lived. He gazed about the dimness of the room; a dazed expression plastered nervously on his face. Half awake, yet half asleep, he recalled how he had come to be there. By morning, he would barely remember being woken at all. The old man insisted they take the last burning candle, but it supplied little more than a few minutes of flickering light.

Jack finally rose from the hard wooden chair and wearily walked to the hallway. Removing the candle from the table also removed most of the soft light from the kitchen, leaving the old man with nothing more than the glowing embers on the grate as he continued to sit and nod his head to the music.

With the door firmly closed behind them, the boys made their way to the upper quarters of the house. Although they were at ease with the narrow hallways, it did feel like the walls were closing in around them. The candle lit the way well enough. When they reached the upper level, Marcus raised the flame to illuminate the artwork.

"All trees," he stated.

"And?" replied Bran impatiently. His steps were intentionally heavy.

"You'd think he'd get tired of painting them."

"Well... You don't get tired of talking shit."

"Whatever," uttered Marcus under his breath, not willing to take the childish bait. The day had been long enough already.

Marcus continued to pan over the crudely hung artwork, in some strange way admiring the old man's persistence that spanned decades. The weak glare of the flame hovered over a large summer portrait. The leaves were bright, the flowers vibrant. And to compliment the pleasantness of the artistic mood, a round beaming sun marked the sky with streaks of yellow and white dashes. Another painting followed, although strikingly similar. It was without a doubt an impression of autumn. Its vivid colours of orange, yellow, and brown were prominently featured, reminding Marcus of his favourite season of all. In fact, he would go as far as to say that if the image included a pumpkin or two, he'd probably have wanted it for himself.

They continued down the hall, the seasons forever changing at his sides. Summer, Autumn, Winter, and Spring, many of which had been duplicated time after time but remained fixed to the wall all the same. An owl shrieked from the outside world, the sound piercing the rooftop and loudly echoing its way through the halls of the house. The sound was followed shortly by a rodent's death scream.

"Jesus Christ!" yelled Bran. "I almost had an accident."

They broke out in nervous laughter, grasping their mouths tightly so as not to cause Gregory concern from below.

"What do you think it was?" whispered Jack, secretly uncomfortable with the idea of it ever happening again.

"It'll just be a stinking rat that got what's coming to it," said Bran, feeling no empathy for the creature's abrupt end.

Jack couldn't help but feel some sadness for the helpless rodent. He loved most things, especially animals. The fact of the matter was, if he were to think such an incident regularly occurred, a choking lump would swell in his mouth and tears would form in his eyes.

With the bedroom door now in view, Bran and Jack pushed past Marcus, eager to reach the comforts of their beds. It was what they expected when they agreed to stay here, after all. Regardless, Marcus seemed to be in no rush. He stepped back into the hallway, immediately catching sight of a painting that was hanging differently from the rest.

After studying the patterns made by the brush strokes, he determined the painting was in fact a night portrait of Thyme. At first, he could see nothing but the black and grey paint smudged across the canvas. He thought there was something else, though, something he had missed; something he hadn't quite understood. There was more to this particular picture than just an evening with trees, and Marcus, as curious and devoted as he was, wanted to know the whole story.

"Get in here, and shut that sodding door!" Bran was ever so ready to put his head down to sleep.

But Marcus did not listen; his concentration was consumed with the final piece of art. The candle light scattered across it. Up, down, left, right. He almost gave up on the idea, until suddenly, there it was. He saw it.

As plain as day you might say. How he could not have caught sight of it previously was beyond him. It was so clear. His eyes were fixed. And now he hoped, wished, that if he observed its strangeness for long enough, what he saw would retreat and hide in the stygian patterns where they originated.

"Bran!" Marcus whispered harshly. "Bran!"

"What do you want?" An irritated and muffled voice called from beneath the thickness of warm covers.

"Come take a look at this."

"What?"

"This picture."

Bran tossed about in the bed, his head reappearing from beneath the quilt.

"What? Why?"

"Just come take a look will you… Please!" Marcus begged with a hint of desperation in his voice. He needed a little help to find some peace of mind after his recent discovery.

Bran swung his feet to the floor and stomped across the loosened boards, if only to impart his irritation.

"The old man best have painted a picture of your mum's tits. Otherwise, I don't give a toss!"

It was typical for time to run out as it did, and regardless of how Marcus felt, the flame of the candle slowly flickered and faded into darkness, followed by a brief stench of smoke.

Swallowed in the lightless hallway, both friends stood close, guided only by the cast of the moonlight as it lit that section of the hall.

"So… what is it?"

Marcus looked away from the outline of his friend to the wall, which was now in darkness. Discouraged, he pointed to where he guessed the middle of the painting should be. "You see it?"

But Bran could not even see the movements of Marcus's hand.

"See what? It's pitch black out here."

"The picture!" shrilled Marcus, earnestly urging Bran to witness what he had seen.

"Calm down, it's only a painting."

"There's just something about it."

"What?"

"I dunno, something odd."

Enough was enough. Bran was tired and determined to rest. He walked back to the bedroom, pushing Marcus along the hall.

. "Sleep on it," he said. "You never know, it may come back to you."

It was the perfect persuasion. It helped him to get Marcus to finally wind his neck in and also let him get the rest he so desperately wanted. Finally, they settled. They weren't surprised to find Jack collapsed on the bed. He had already escaped into the land of dreams. Outside the wind blew wildly, but from where Marcus lay the stars twinkled brightly, shining through the thin material of the poorly hung curtains.

"Bran?"

"Hmm?"

"What do you make of old Gregory?"

"What you mean?"

"Well… you reckon the story's true?"

"I don't know, mate. You know what old folk are like. My grandfather makes up crap half the time. It's got to the point no one even listens anymore." Silence filled the room before he continued. "What I'm saying is, yeah, it's terrible kids went missing. But, did anyone think they may have just run away. Adults tell what suits them all the time. Makes them feel a little bit better on the inside. If it helps, let them do it. That's what I've come to understand anyway."

Both said nothing more and turned to face the cold surface of the wall. Marcus closed his eyes and was deep in thought, but in only a few minutes his concerns escaped him and his body relaxed as he welcomed sleep.

Amongst the Mists

Chapter Sixteen

ll was quiet now. The same as it had been for all those countless lonely years. The music had faded gradually as the record reached its end. The needle had been guided into a constant loop of crackles and scratches. Reminiscing took a lot out of the old man. It had been some time since he dared let his mind go back to those days when Thyme stood proudly. So long in fact, he found it all the harder to believe such terrible events actually happened.

How long had it been since he last had guests? Real guests. And not a desirable illusion of his own selfish wants. The old man brooded over the question he knew could not be answered. It had been so long he'd started to feel like some form of a wandering spirit himself. He had been left alone in a village that all others had long since forgotten, neglected and left to rot amongst the long-abandoned past which clung effortlessly to his tormented soul. Always being alone during the night never fazed him. The darkness had become a friend, and there was nothing to fear from it. Although from time to time he recalled many memories that filled his spine with ice, the darkness was never one of them.

The old man exhaled heavily, tilting the back of his head against the wooden frame of his chair. His breathing soon indicated a very clear sign of emotion before he relented and broke into sullen sobs. If any truth could be said of the darkness, this was it. It was the perfect camouflage, a mask for the needy, allowing the opportunity for any proud soul to unleash their guarded emotions and express their neglected burdens without the cruel wrath of watchful eyes and judgment. The old man wept, crying aloud into the silent night. He crossed his arms around him, holding his torso tightly to control and calm his nerves. As his sobbing subsided, so did his need for air. His chest loosened, and his shoulders relaxed and dropped to his sides once again.

I should have told them he thought, wiping the snot from his nostrils and trying his best to prevent the fallen runs from hitting his shirt. *I should have told them everything.*

It goes without saying the story told that evening was not in any honest way complete. He pondered on the idea, the memories, the fear.

What would they have thought of me if I was to tell them the entirety? To tell them… what I witnessed when searching for those children? I know what they would think. Nothing! That's right. Nothing! They would not have reason to think. Their legs would be far too busy. They would flee. Yes, without doubt. They would flee. And I would be left to worry about the consequences.

Moonlight peered in through a dirt smeared window. The glass pane was held upright with the help of a single slotted plank. Gregory faced the sheet of pale light and watched the shadows gradually shift in the clouds. The old man was tired. The desire for rest was relentless and lingered deep in his bones. Yet his brain remained flooded with concern as he continued to consider his predicament.

What... What if they didn't run? What if they thought me only a fool? That I was nothing but an old man who had lost his marbles. An old man who had nothing better to do with his remaining years than to entice children to his broken home and feed them stories. Those stories would instil fear in the mind of any grown man or woman, let alone a child.

"Ah, enough with your infernal insecurity." Gregory stood up and reset his train of thought. He swung open the rear door and stood taking in the late-night air. Like the house, the garden showed no resemblance to the glory of its former years. The forest, once skirting the border of the land, had now completely reclaimed the gardens. He listened in peace to the softness of the breeze.

And yet, no matter how quiet these once familiar forests seemed to be, hidden shadows lay in wait for him everywhere he turned.

He was well aware he shouldn't have drunk his fill. He knew that. The need to ease his mind was far too tempting to resist. The drink indeed helped, far more than anything else. It was the dreams he could not escape. The dreams bound him to his past. Memories shackled him and forced him to watch and relive the same old events as though it were only yesterday. He would awaken howling in fright most nights: the sweat pouring from his forehead, the bedsheet cold and wet from perspiration. There was no escape, nor was there any lasting relief. The dreams were now a part of him, a reminder that he failed the village and his granddaughter. These he could never put right.

During the same holiday period every year, Gregory would sit and stare at the table after having just collected the several metres of rope he had used to hoist a kayak in the community shed. He sat, and he drank. His eyes never strayed from the bundle of weathered rope. One particular holiday was all too much. It was an anniversary, but not at all one worth celebrating. He would continue to stare while he drank, fall asleep, and dream. He would startle awake and remember. Then he would stare all the more.

It was on one of these most festive holiday evenings that his particular ritual had broken him spiritually. He bolted into the forest, the rope clenched firmly in his hand, and found the perfect usable tree. The desperation for it all to end was far too powerful for him to take note of his trek there. He easily threw the rope around a reachable limb. The noose rubbed firmly against his neck as the branch bent from his weight.

Is it really this easy? he thought as he kicked the rock from beneath him. The burn tore around his neck, sending a fire running sharply down his throat. He felt the strong pull, wishing to touch the soft earth just one more time. He thought the devil himself was dragging him down to the new home he believed he deserved. Bloodshot eyes of the swinging man watched as the trees danced, throwing peace at his torture. It was time. Breath was not important. Vision blurred. The only sound was the swinging rope. Eyes closed. A dark shape crept from the shadows of the trees.

He fell to the ground with an unpleasant thud, choking and gagging on the fine night air. His decision to stand was made far too quickly and sent the agitated man toppling into the mud. By the time he regained himself, the shadow was gone. He sat, not caring about the cold or his regrets. Frustrated, he removed the noose from his neck. The rope had snapped from the weight of an old and desperate man. "God damn you!" he yelled aggressively at the rope. "God damn you…" The outcry caused his voice to croak and break. He had an overwhelming desire for death, but he could not seem to accomplish even that task. His inability to succeed caused the tears to flow. His heart was completely broken.

Something shifted behind him. A branch snapped. Creeping feet shuffled. Turning quickly, he listened. His eyes opened wider, his jaw dropped, and he spoke only one word.

"Grandchild?"

Amongst the Mists

Chapter Seventeen

Jack awoke from a disturbing dream; the type of dream that would now be lost forever. The cool night air surrounded him, causing his senses to heighten. He looked around, noticing a ghoulish moonlight descending on his friends who looked like mounds as they stayed securely hidden beneath their quilts.

Jack wondered if he should wake them. But what would he say? Would it be worth Bran's abuse which would surely follow? No, not on just the whim of a bad dream he could no longer remember.

It would be absurd to wake them.

And with that thought, Jack moved his clammy palm from the blanket that stretched up and over his friend.

Unease flourished within him. For what exact reason, he was not sure. He felt unsafe and vulnerable, as if at any moment his soul would be snatched and fed to the empty darkness. Desperation coursed through his body, somehow feeding the urge to leave the warm mattress and reach out to open the small, sash window. Jack pulled firmly, but the swollen frame held shut. It would not budge no matter how much brute strength he applied. Jack was in no way what anyone would describe as a physical child. A well-appointed opinion would suggest the boy was nothing more than short and weedy. Yet still he continued to pull. The pane would not give, and his mind would not calm. He rested his head on the glass. The window's cool surface pressed satisfyingly against his forehead, causing him to calm and close his eyes. His breath formed a thin fog that spread across the glass. He sat watching it form and unconsciously etched his name on the clouded glass while his mind wandered away from the repulsive imagination that pulled him from sleep.

Jack woz hear.

Blowing over the childlike writing he cleared his canvas, providing an all new page on which to write. He paused, then lifted his finger again.

JAck mRs HomE.

Reminiscing about home soothed his mind. He longed for the comforting space of his bedroom, the presence of his doting mother, and all the security he felt at home. It wouldn't be long until he was back in Bonhil Dale. He just needed to push on and leave his worrisome dreams where they truly belonged.

Bran tossed in bed, chattering with a dreamlike mumble: words that not even Jack could interpret. Jack's palm swiped the glass, removing his clouded words with one swipe. It was as this streak was made and the hand brought to a finish, he noticed a dark shadow standing beside the thickness of the outer trees.

Jack rubbed roughly at his eyes, not with disbelief but to reassure himself of what he saw. He looked again. Yes, the solid outline of a person remained. Jack smiled rather hesitantly, purely to determine if a pleasantry would be returned. It was not. Nothing was given. Its shape remained as solid as before, and even through the haze *it* appeared to be more like a statue than anything living.

It reminded Jack of a cartoon called *The Snowman*. Everyone had seen it. Everyone had loved it. Every child anyway. The concept came flooding back of how a pasty-faced ginger kid, during a winter's snow, created a snowman one day that by night would magically come to life. The rest of the story wasn't important. The point was, it terrified Jack. The very idea of an innocently made snow sculpture prowling the grounds of his home as he lay in bed sent hairs to stand on end. Many people have fears; some of spiders, some of clowns. Yet nothing scared Jack more than running past a snowman. Its large coal eyes would follow his every step. The idea, he understood, was nothing more than a child's vivid imagination creating something from his wildest dreams. But as he looked down to the dark stillness, he thought:

What if it was just as easy to create something from a nightmare?

The shadow moved to reflect the nervous stare from above. Again, Jack held his glare. The very suggestion that what he witnessed was real caused him no end of doubts. He turned to the snoring figures next to him. Neither was stirring in their peaceful sleep. He surveyed the room, knowing full well nothing lurked inside the house.

No... nothing, he thought but checked again anyway. He returned his attention to the land beyond the window and again focused on the trees. The shadow had gone. Just like that. It suddenly just ceased to exist, disappearing back into the night from which it came. "Wake up!" he whimpered under his breath, accompanied by a rather heavy self-inflicted slap to the face, trying to shake away his delusions. Again, he peered from the window. And just as before, the blurred shadow was there, standing as though *it* had never departed. *It* waved at Jack, showing no pause in its gesture. Stunned, Jack threw himself back from the windowsill, smashing flat against a stocky wardrobe, his sight still fixated below. The wave stopped, *its* hand twisting abnormally as though to beckon him nearer.

An unnatural sensation surged through Jack, lifting the fear, the worry, and hesitancy lingering within him. He no longer cared about anything, and like sand falling through fingers, his feelings dissolved. A childish smirk was illuminated by the moonlight.

As though tangled in a dream sequence, he found himself outside, walking barefoot on the sharp wood chip path with no memory of how he came to be there.

His feet took him ever closer to the forest. The night was as black as ebony, but he could not perceive the darkness. Even as he strayed into the dry, grey grass, his inner consciousness told him his predicament was nothing more than a pleasant stroll on a delightful summer's day. He knew where he was headed. A voice called him there. A voice he didn't know but felt a mystic urge to trust. While his surroundings were as deathly as a country churchyard, the sky above burst alive with bright city lights. The branches parted like a theatre's curtain. Beyond it was the sight of nothingness. A black hole. Just a few more steps and he would be part of it, disappearing into the unknown, vanishing without a trace.

Chapter Eighteen

Come morning, the sky drew crisp and clear. The rising sun cast an amber tint over the limestone, awakening the boys with its brilliance. They sat upright, still tired even after their night of undisturbed sleep.

"Time is it?" questioned Marcus, his wide yawn throwing off his speech.

"Early," replied Bran as he tucked his head back under the covers to avoid the blinding rays.

"Have you ever seen the sun that colour? I haven't."

"Exactly! It's too bloody early."

Marcus had already noticed Jack was not in the room and quickly concluded he had gone to the lower quarters for breakfast.

"Come on, we best get up," said Marcus while he pulled up his clothes from the floor.

"Where you reckon Jack got to, then?"

Bran sat upright, his eyes clouded with sleep, his hair messily on point.

"He's probably already gone down for his bowl of Special J?"

"Very good."

"I thought so."

The house appeared deserted as they wandered through closed off rooms. There wasn't the slightest trace of Jack. In the kitchen, the glasses from the previous night still stood tall on the table, a moisture ring circling each base. The grate was over filled with ashes. The boys sensed no one had been in the room that morning. The rear door remained ajar, calmly swinging and allowing sunlight to seep through. Beyond, a jungle of nettles surrounded the paths. Marcus and Bran ventured outside, the sun's warmth so much more inviting than the chill of the house. They would wait for someone to return, and here was as good a place as any.

So, they waited. The morning passed without a sign of their friend's return. And what concerned them even more was the old man himself could not be found wandering his grounds. Still, they waited, passing the time with idle chat which soon turned sour in debate.

During the course of the afternoon, they decided to venture away from the house. The path led them back to the road. As expected, the road was quiet, and no one passed by. The longer they waited, the more Marcus felt overcome with worry.

"Where the hell has he got to?" he moaned, trying his best to hide his frustration. "And where the hell is the old man? In a few hours it'll be dark."

Bran was off the road, trying to climb on a tree branch. His lack of success was rewarded with a nasty fall. He wobbled drunkenly to his feet, shaking off thousands of fir needles that had embedded themselves in his clothes.

"I don't get what you're worried about," said Bran, diverting attention from his fall. "The crazy old loon's probably just disappeared off to chop wood again. And knowing Jack, he's so frickin' gullible, he's probably agreed to help!"

Marcus didn't respond. There was something more to it. He had a sense for this type of thing. Not a case of visions or gift-like messages, it was purely a gut instinct. And his gut told him something unfortunate had befallen his friend.

"Look!" Bran's temper was beginning to shorten. "You're panicking over nothin'. What's the odds of both of them disappearing?"

Marcus shrugged and still watched the roadside for movement.

"Exactly! I'm telling you, Jack will be fine. He's probably helping the old man right now."

Marcus sighed deeply, in some slight way thankful for the sentiment that helped calm his mind.

"You're probably right," said Marcus. "We do need to get moving though. You really think he's OK?"

As Bran turned and started walking towards the house he called back "Absolutely! I've told you, he'll be fine, unless…"

"Unless what?"

"Unless… that Gregory is some kind sex pest."

"Oh, great! Thanks for that!"

"What? It happens, you know. Kids like us get taken away and touched up in the woods all the time."

"Jack is not being touched up! You're such an idiot!"

*

The afternoon dragged by slowly, much more slowly than they'd liked. There was little to do but sit and wait. They ate, helping themselves to the store of food they found on the kitchen shelves. They somehow knew their host wouldn't mind the self-service. Marcus perched himself at the side of an armchair and scanned a collection of books unevenly piled in stacks of ten or twenty. He enjoyed the odd read, however these books piqued no interest in him. For starters, they were hardback and lacked their dust jackets. Some had bindings as frayed as a discarded paperback. He tossed the first few aside, barely taking the time to read the title. They were covered with years of dust, and when opened they smelled damp and musty. Each title was more disappointing than the last, and he huffed his disinterest at the content.

The Origin of Species, by Charles Darwin. Trees Worth Knowing, by Julia Ellen Rogers. The Life of Bees, Familiar with Flowers, Rocks of Time, Art of Growth, crap, crap, crap, crap, crap! he thought as he slouched back into a well used chair and allowed the towered books to lean. He tried to save them, reaching out to keep them in balance. The top book began to slip. And like a game of Jenga, they all toppled, fanning their pages across the floor.

"Oh, whatever!" he groaned, dismissing the jumbled heap before falling unhappily to his knees.

Marcus gathered the chaos and began restacking one book at a time. A small leather-bound volume weighed heavy in his hand. It was in pristine condition. On the cover was a faint groove of imprinted characters. He wiped the surface carefully with the hem of his shirt. Taking his time, Marcus held the book towards the light, guiding the tips of his fingers across the leather before reading the title silently. *Amongst the Mists.*

Chapter Nineteen

For some unknown reason, probably brought on by the crushing boredom, Bran took it upon himself to explore the house. He was hoping to find a note, anything really, to indicate the whereabouts of Jack and, of course, the old man himself. The afternoon soon turned to evening, and slowly the feeling of concern began to evolve and fester.

Bran fell down on the unmade bed. He had an unquestionable predicament swimming around his brain concerning the need to stay another night in Thyme. An extra night wasn't so bad. After all, he could think of worse places to bide his time. But what if they hadn't returned by morning? Or night? Would he and Marcus continue with this tiresome game and wait even longer? If it was a game, Bran didn't like it, not in the slightest. Keeping himself calm was one option. Encouraging Marcus to see reason was quite another. Marcus was an emotional chap. It was a personality flaw that had been with him throughout their school years, and Bran felt sure it would not dwindle away with age.

Impatience itched within him. My God, what he could be doing with his precious time right now. And sitting in a dank old Lodge in the middle of a village that apparently no longer existed certainly wasn't on his to-do list. He heard the intermittent thuds as items collapsed somewhere downstairs. He listened as Marcus's muffled voice complained from the room below.

"Oh, whatever!"

Bran relaxed, knowing his friend was safe and sound.

The chime of the landing clock had struck the hour. And if correct, the bells vibrantly sang out six o'clock.

Six already? Bran turned to his side. The rays of the remaining daylight leaked through the window, slowly sinking down the walls and onto where he lay. He closed his eyes and tried to shut out the annoying glare.

Maybe it's time we left to find help. He wondered. *Maybe... staying here really wasn't such a good idea after all.*

Bran lay deathly still. He had convinced Marcus that nothing bad would happen to Jack.

He would be fine. That's what he told him. It was a statement based on false hope.

What if something really did happen to Jack? To the both of them? What if now it was too late? The questions frazzled his brain like a high-speed merry-go-round, never slowing to give him answers.

A sickening foreboding clenched his stomach. He had had such sensations before, most often when he felt he could have done more, much more. Bran often portrayed it as guilt.

What have I got to be guilty of? I ain't done nothing!

The realization of his own selfishness presented itself as clear as the streaks on the window. He sat up, feeling utterly ashamed of his choices. How could he have just sat here? And not only him, but he had convinced another to do the same.

Placing his hand to his face remorsefully, he turned to the window to determine the remaining hours of light. He paused, then started to smile. His guilt faded, leaving no trace that it was ever there.

The door swung open and rebounded off the torn floral wallpaper, striking the intruder as he entered. It was Marcus. Excitement shone deep in his eyes, indicating a conversation would shortly follow.

"Check this out," said Marcus. In his hands he carried a black leather book. Although not overly large, it fell on the bed with an unexpected *thump*.

"Hey, you listening?" said Marcus.

"Uh, what?"

"I said, check this out."

Bran's head leant to his side, hardly expecting to be impressed with whatever Marcus had sourced from this dingy old house. He shrugged, not giving the item the time of day before looking away.

"You could act a little more interested."

"It's a pissin' book, Marcus!" His tone was patronising and clearly indicated now was not the best time.

"Take a look at it then!" What little patience Marcus had left was being tested by his friend's arrogant attitude.

Bran lifted it to his lap and fanned out the worn-out pages.

"Amongst the Mists... Sounds like utter shit! I've never heard of it." He tossed the book back like he was discarding junk.

Marcus snagged it and flipped through chapters in an attempt to gain Bran's interest.

"No, me neither, but look. It's a book on local myths. One subject is related to Sleathton. How mental is that? I haven't read it all, only the first few pages. But it's pretty damn interesting. Might have something to do with Jack disappearing," he said jokingly. "What you reckon? Want me to read some of –"

Bran jumped up from the bed, arms flailing and determined to speak.

"Shut the hell up about the goddamned book!"

Marcus paused, then slammed the book closed, making no effort to discuss his findings further. Bran paced the room. His temper flushing his face to a bright rose red.

"What the hell are we doing here?" said Bran who stopped and motioned his hands to elicit a quick reply.

"What you mean? You know why. We're waiting for Jack."

"Why? He isn't coming back."

"What?"

"You heard me."

The room was silent. Apprehension electrified the air as Marcus waited for an explanation. Bran had noticed it. Sure, it took him a little time, but he had found it all the same. All Marcus needed was a little push. A gentle nudge in the right direction, and he would see it, too. A sideward glance, a nod if you will, was made in Marcus's direction. It took more than once for Marcus to take a hint. He stared on blankly.

"Errr…"

"Look at the window, you turd!" said Bran in despair.

The orange sunset was blinding his eyes, and he held up his hand to block it. And as he did so, the light caught the window just right. Perfectly in fact. *How did I not see this before?* thought Marcus. There, camouflaged on the grimy pane of glass was the perfect scribble, its letters readable to all.

JAck mRs HomE.

"So… what are you saying? He's just ran home?" Marcus examined the handwriting only inches away from the tip of his nose.

It was a very strange development. It was difficult to believe something as simple as a three-word smudge could turn their suspicions around so easily, even if it was spelt piss-poorly. Still, the writing indicated a possible explanation as to why their buddy had legged it. And after further inspection, it was without a doubt, no question, Jack who wrote the words.

"Selfish git," shouted Bran. "That bloody little sod. Just wait till I get my hands on him."

Marcus could now fit all the pieces together. It was so blatantly obvious.

"Reckon Gregory took him back then?"

"Of course he has. That goes without saying. We'd have been waiting here like a pair of mugs until the old man returned to break the news."

Marcus considered their options, wondering if Bran wanted to continue their trip at all. *Why didn't Jack just tell us?* The question poked at his mind like a sharp splinter in flesh. "So, now what?" He was ready to lip sync Bran cancelling their adventure.

"Well," Bran paced slowly before continuing, "I say we get packed and make a break for it. It will be dark within the hour. The sooner we leave the sooner we can make camp."

"You want to carry on? With the trip I mean?" asked Marcus, truly surprised his journey would not be cut short for the sake of one selfish act.

"Of course!" Bran barked his reply and pointed his finger to justify his point. "If that special little sod thinks he can put everything on hold with the snap of his fingers, well, we'll show him. And as for the old man? Let's be gone before he returns. I don't think I can take another night of rambling garbage."

"Yeah, let's do it!" uttered Marcus, his rucksack at the ready as he began to button his coat.

"And do it we will," said Bran. "Just the two of us. The way it always should have been."

114

The little black book was tucked safely away into the sleeve of his pack. The intention was simply to borrow it, though it was never clear how it could be returned. They left the grotty room, closing the door with a heavy-handed slam. Bran scurried for the staircase, the width of his bag scraping the wall panels at either side. He was eager to leave the house. There was something about Thyme that didn't sit right with him. The emptiness for one. Regardless, they would see the back of it now, with never a need to return.

The forest painting of blackened night still hung slanted upon the wall, catching Marcus by surprise as he stopped to study its depth. He had forgotten all about the grim looking impression of night, and he carefully scanned over the canvas, searching for whatever it was that caused his hair to rise and his pulse to race.

"You coming or what?" a voice urged from the bottom step. The sound of an unbolted door latch followed, as the opening remained patiently held for Marcus's leave.

"Yeah, I'll be right down."

Chapter Twenty

How could it have come to this? Olivia's mind begged the question. It had been nothing more than a normal day. A relaxing day where she was a part of the rivers and the elegantly swaying trees. She had done it many times before. *What made today so different?*

She sat crouched in a rock faced corner. Her only familiarity was the group of crayons floating on the surface of the filth around her. She had almost given up. The idea to stay hidden seemed far more sensible than running astray.

"Someone will look for me. Yes, and when they do, they will find me here, in this spot."

The thought was appealing enough, but she had great doubts it would ever really happen. She had great doubts about many things. Like how she was alive for one. She was so cold and had been for too long. Olivia wasn't stupid, she knew very well cold could kill. It was lethal, something the human body could withstand for only a given time, depending on circumstances. That was a fact. So why could she no longer feel its biting wrath? She felt cold for sure, frozen to the bone. Her matted hair had begun to stiffen like icicles. The feeling persisted but would never send her into a deep sleep so she could escape this taunting madness.

She placed her fingers on her wrist. A strong pulse beat just below her skin, indicating her reality.

Oh. Not dead yet, she thought sarcastically, huddling further back into the arch of dampened stone. Olivia closed her eyes and listened to the vacant sound of dewdrops falling freely from the trees to the swamp below. *Mustn't fall asleep. Mustn't fall asleep.* The words repeated, playing around in her head like a broken record left to run its course.

*

She awoke from a dream. The dream was not special but provided her with a deep inner warmth of home. Olivia reviewed her surroundings, peeking out from her den of nature. Although disgruntled, she felt as though sleep had protected her for hours. Yet the skies and land around her were still in darkness. *Where the hell is the sun?* It was not the first time she had wondered about the absence of sunlight, nor would it be the last. It seemed like days since she had felt the sun against her skin, and she wondered if it would ever happen again. Would the sun ever make itself known? Perhaps. Perhaps there was some reasonable explanation behind it? An eclipse maybe, or some miraculous freak of nature. She dismissed those possibilities. Whatever was going on here didn't feel like it affected the rest of the world. This was for her, and her alone.

The dribble repeated and broke the silence. *Drip, Drip, Drip, Drip. Drip, Drip.* It was so irritating! As easily agitated as she found herself now, Olivia could muster patience when she chose. And right about now, her patience was beginning to run thin. She cupped her hands over her ears, blocking out the noise and replacing it with the muffled sound of the sea. She started to sing. Not aloud, but in her head. Not just any song, either, but the words of an old poem her mother would recite on winter's nights.

> *Winter's sights show bleaching white,*
> *A breathless voice so quiet*
> *Carries gloom, yet feels delight,*
> *Its time was short though overstayed.*
> *Hearts forged in ice can feel not warmth*
> *Although they travel far and wide.*
> *Their howling songs through hollow nights*
> *Dissolve the earth by scorching light.*

What! She thought with a subconscious jerk, her heart pounding like a bass drum. *What is that!* Olivia loosened the pressure from around her ears. She listened then pinched herself. Oh yes, she was awake. And she knew exactly what she'd heard. It was a voice, not of just one person but two. The sound permeated the vastness and drilled through her ears and into her consciousness, forcing her to rise to her feet.

"HELP!" screamed Olivia. Her fragile tone trembled in reaction to the pure distress. She had never heard herself screech in such a way; so fearful, so desperate. If help was not at hand, she sensed only death awaited her. An energy surged within her she didn't know she had. She heard the distant voices more clearly, charging in from every direction.

"Help me! Please, I'm here!"

Olivia didn't stop. Wouldn't stop. No matter how much her toes would sting and her legs would bruise. She would not fail. She would find help, or help would find her.

They're getting closer.

The very thought excited her beyond belief, sending adrenaline gushing through her veins as she kicked off from the ground like a feverish mule. The sound of footsteps on dry land serenaded her as she circled a mound raised up from the swamp.

"Where are you?" she muttered to herself. There was no time left to wonder. A sound drew closer, faster. If she were too slow, this rare opportunity would be missed. The unmistakable sound of bicycle chains clinked through the woodlands, but she could not guess the speed. Instinct encouraged her legs to sprint. If she were to stay put, her unknown rescuers would pedal right on by her. Oh, how she would rejoice when finally rescued! And in a short time, the tale of how she had come to be lost would become nothing more than an amusing memory. Maybe even to Olivia, once acceptable time had passed.

She tried to picture what her heroes would look like when they emerged from the unknown. Tall, dark, dashing. A collective of her VHS heartthrobs. But she wasn't fussy, she'd accept help from anybody who was willing.

There it was. She caught a glimpse of movement through the trees. She shuddered and gave out a croak-like whimper. The realization that they were people… real people… was enough to break her. She could hear them riding closer and closer. All she needed to do was wait.

"Over here!" she screamed. Excitement took over the young girl as her arms flung briskly about the air. A beaming smile. A happy thought. It would last only a minute. The sound told her the pedals were rotating faster, drawing in the ground between them. Her waving became hesitant, and the smile stripped clean from her face. Something wasn't right. She watched the figures hover through the dimness. They were there all right, this was no dream. Olivia would soon wish it were. As the moon cast its light from the heavens, the horror came before her. They held no features. There was nothing. No faces, no personality. The moving shapes resembled nothing more than blurred shadows alone. Their voices relayed only a distorted gurgle. The sound of racing bikes stopped. Faceless shapes scouted the land, grunting back and forth as though in meaningful conversation. Olivia hid, terrified by the inhuman sounds, and clasped her jaw to control her panicked breaths.

Within a split second, the voices dispersed. Olivia reappeared from her hiding spot, raising her head through the thicket. No sign of the shadows existed. They had withdrawn without a hint of movement or direction.

"What the hell was that?" she asked in the peace of night, believing all hope was truly lost. Whatever they were, they were not here to help. Neither did she know if they were aware of her existence. They moved weightlessly. That much she knew. *Ghosts?* The idea was shrugged off instantly. She didn't believe in ghosts. Never had, never will. It was a stupid suggestion, and she kicked herself for implying it. One thing was for sure. The shadowed beings had gone, leaving Olivia to wander alone.

Chapter Twenty-One

The boys dared not wander back onto the road. The possibility of coincidently bumping into their new friend Gregory was not worth their time or effort. Instead, they ventured over the rear of the property and headed for the hills which would lead them deeper into Sleathton. Marcus had checked the map with precision. Twice in fact. He tried to hurry the journey along, though Bran followed slowly behind. There was no path, and the steep incline was far too difficult to ride. Never had Bran expected the forest to be so dense. It felt as though every obstruction befell him. When he had almost reached the hilltop, he swore blind that every branch, bush, and ditch had it in for him.

It was a warm evening, an evening not at all suitable for this kind of trek. Yet, once they reached the summit, the crest of the hillside curved downward to a smooth open slope. A cool breeze blew through their hair on the easier descent. They didn't have long. They both knew that. It was their only agreement when leaving the house. *Get out of Thyme and make camp.* That was the plan. They hadn't shaken on it but agreed on the matter like men.

Camp was set as the dusk deepened. A small patch of grass, surrounded by a wall of brown stone took their fancy. By the time all was done, both were tired, weak, and confused by the day's unusual events. And even with all the bottled-up frustration, neither one of them wished to speak of it. Both knew that unfiltered words would cause irreversible regrets.

The campfire crackled from the collapsing deadwood, the disturbance sending up magical sparks that danced in the smoke. They ate their fill considering there was an extra portion to split. It was some kind of a breakfast in a tin that they had swiped from the old man's home. Surely it would go unnoticed. His larder was mounted with food, though mainly tins. The labels had been stripped from each container, providing a potluck experience of jelled cuisine. Bran hadn't been fond of the meal, and the knowledge it was stolen hadn't made it taste much better. Still, he didn't complain but looked over at Marcus who sat with an empty tin in his lap and his nose pressed between the pages of a book. Bran huffed loudly, a knack he found most beneficial when expressing his undying boredom. A grunt was also used, but Marcus's eyes looked no further than the lines on the page.

"Why did you take that thing, anyway?" Bran had no real desire to ask the question, but it broke his target's concentration.

Win! he thought as Marcus lifted his head, fanning the pages in his hands.

"I don't know. Just thought it was interesting, that's all."

A blank stare flew back past the spitting flames. Bran's features were an array of shadows and orange light.

"What?"

"Interesting?" Bran questioned.

"Well, yeah. Listen, you didn't see half the shit piled up in that room. This book kind of jumped out at me. So, as I just said. Yeah, it's interesting."

"Girls are interesting, Marcus. The day when you can finally stop looking through those magazines your dad keeps under the mattress and put study to good use? Now those things are interesting."

Marcus closed the book, setting it down to his side.

"They're art magazines, I told you!"

"Then why do all the pages stick together?"

"Shut it!" snapped Marcus, rising to his feet and turning to walk away.

"Hey, I'm not judging. If I could stash a collection of Ben Dover magazines under my pillow, you wouldn't see me leave my room for a week. You'd think I'd been lifting weights." Bran laughed loudly and stood up. "Hey! What's the matter? Where you off to?"

"Going for a piss. Reckon you can cope on your own for one minute?"

Bran slumped back down on his folded coat. A silent chuckle tensed his chest and forced his shoulders to bounce. Things were starting to ease back into place. And although picking at Marcus's dad's 'art collection' probably wasn't the best topic to start with, it got the banter flowing.

Irritated, Marcus trudged on through the outer camp, searching for a spot where he would no longer fall victim to Bran's continual taunts.

*

His stream gradually died. The sense of relief was almost too satisfying to describe as he slowly returned along the darkened path, fastening his trousers as he walked. He used the flames to guide him. The fire now only a glimmering flicker in the distance.

"Marcus." A hushed voice called as he walked, its whisper bouncing through the woodland in all directions.

"Give me a second!" yelled Marcus. He was so close to the site he could smell the unmistakable scent of burning wood.

"You don't need to tell me your every move," suggested Bran, his faint outline seen resting beside the blaze.

"What? You just called me!"

"I never called you."

"You did,"

"No, I never."

Marcus stopped dead in his tracks. He had the uncomfortable sense he was being watched. He became so concerned that it placed his already anxious mind further on edge, and he rapidly scanned the darkness.

Is someone watching me? He saw no one. *Was anyone calling?* He could no longer tell. The sounds of the sleeping woodland influenced the

125

night. The quietness seemed by no means peaceful. Still, he concentrated on the trees although the view was constricted by a thin layer of mist.

"What's taking you?" yelled Bran, never once budging from his comfort.

Marcus turned his suspicion to the nearest clump of saplings. His nerves felt shot. The very idea of someone lurking within the deep, dark wood brought back memories of those gothic childish stories.

Hansel and Gretel. Billy Goats Gruff. The Pied Piper. The stories no longer scared him, of course. But they were the stories that would beg every child to check twice beneath their bed. These were the tales to make one want to leave a trail of breadcrumbs. Marcus had come to accept these facts, the stories being only scary tales, but out here there was the familiar sense of repressed fear creeping up on him.

Get a grip. He chided himself while pacing across the ground. The soft turf cushioned his steps along the camp's boundary. He sat down with a thud, opening his book to the folded page. He needed something, anything, to steer his thoughts away from those grim fables. And reading, well, reading was by far his best option of escape. He had found his place in *Chapter 2.* His index finger dragged over the thin stained paper to guide his vision. He'd almost lost himself, too, almost, before Bran abruptly doused the flames, sending the black letters into a sudden state of nonexistence.

"Sorry, were you reading?"

"You know damn well I was!"

"I swear I didn't."

"Then you swear fuckin' badly!"

The hiss of smouldering stones gently faded. A cloud of steam evaporated where they sat, catching so thickly in the back of their throats that they wanted to gag.

"Oh, come on," said Bran with a shrug. "It was only a joke."

Marcus pushed down on the grass, eager for a verbal altercation. Instead, he packed the book away as best he could. He held his tongue, knowing full well once that battle began, they would be sparring until sunrise.

"Don't ignore me. I said it was only a joke," repeated Bran. His expression now hardened with an angry stare.

"Who were you talking to out there, anyway?" asked Bran, his determination to speak not about to let up. Marcus stopped, he set his bag down, and he turned while he considered an answer.

"I… I wasn't talking to anyone."

Bran raised his eyebrow in disbelief.

Lying prick!

He wasn't as stupid as Marcus thought. Far from it. And if he didn't get answers right now, he would never let Marcus forget it.

"Don't give me that. I heard you," he said, waving his finger in the direction of the path.

Marcus hesitated. "I thought I heard something but I didn't. OK?"

"You thought you did?"

"Yeah, I thought I heard you call me."

"No, no it wasn't me."

The first slight breeze drifted its way through the camp, lifting the steam and causing the tent door to flap.

"Exactly. It wasn't you. So, forget it!"

Regardless of this open-mindedness, reality or not, it wasn't what Bran needed to hear right now. They were miles from anywhere. The last thing he wanted to chew on was the idea of a woodland wanderer. He stood quietly, sticking to the spongy grass of the camp. And once he gained his night vision, he shifted around to look beyond the fallen trees.

"What are you doing now?" Marcus snapped. He watched as Bran hobbled about the ground like James Bond's retarded cousin.

"Am I the only one concerned with what you heard?"

"Or didn't hear."

"That's not the point."

Marcus made his way over to Bran, reluctantly joining in the amateur stakeout, trying to help put the boy's mind at rest. They waited. Still there was nothing. Yet Bran would not budge. He was willing. No, willing was too feeble a word. He was determined to find something, anything, that would prove Marcus's theory correct. So again, they sat and they waited until the hour had grown late.

*

"Let's just go to bed," begged Marcus, his joints beginning to ache from kneeling. "There's nothing out here."

"No!" replied Bran. His mind was firmly set.

"What are you expecting to find? I'm the one who heard something, not you. There's nothing out there, I'm telling you."

The night was starless, making it difficult to know how late it really was.

"If you think I'm getting in that tent when for all we know Gregory is hunting us down, you can think again."

Marcus, bellowed out with laughter. It was so loud that a colony of birds flew out of the treetops in fright. Never had he thought his friend so pathetic before. It was a ridiculous notion. And it was an impression he would never live down.

"Is that what you think?" asked Marcus. "You really are a nutcase."

"I'm just saying we don't know the guy, is all."

"You're right."

"Really?"

"No!" Again Marcus cried out with laughter. It wasn't like Bran to get into such a tizz, especially over something as simple as unheard voices. However, he was not one to be made fun of, either. Marcus would push him only so far. He knew Bran's limits. And right then, he was currently hitting the line.

"Stop laughing!" exclaimed Bran, swiping his leg viciously and removing Marcus's feet from the ground. The impact as he landed flat on his back reminded Marcus of the almost-forgotten pain of the recent past.

Marcus gasped, the wind from his lungs knocked clean out of him. The instantly regrettable action brought Bran to tower above him. Marcus was an asthmatic, had been all his life. And without the aid of his puffer, Bran knew the consequence. He sprung over to the tent, pulling out the innards of Marcus's rucksack until a light blue container was found. Marcus wheezed, snatched the inhaler, and hatefully grabbed Bran's shirt. He could have punched him. He wanted to. The action would have been well justified should anyone come to ask. Instead, he pushed with all his might, sending Bran to the ground and causing several buttons to fly loose from his red checked shirt.

A small price to pay, thought Marcus as he desperately wheezed for relief.

Bran had seen his error, he was human after all. And he felt the remorse that came with being fallible.

"Sorry, pal," said Bran. He meant the words. A hand was offered to Marcus, who still lay curled on the ground, his inhaler grasped tightly in both hands as though it was the dearest of treasures.

"Forget it," replied Marcus breathlessly.

Bran pulled his friend to his feet. The wheeze of his lungs was now beginning to sound more like high-pitched whistles.

A loud piercing scream enveloped the woodland. For a second or two, they both assumed it was a prank pulled by the other. It was a dreadful sound. A miserable sound. A sound so haunting it caused Bran to bolt. Marcus didn't realise it until he turned to speak, but Bran had dived headfirst into the tent, burying himself beneath the sleeping bags. His only thought was of his impending and immediate death.

Moments later, Marcus tugged at the cover.

"Come on, Bran, get up."

"Are you kidding me? Can't you hear that!"

"Yes, but –"

"But nothing. There's something out there I'm telling you. And… it'll have us."

"Yes, but –"

"Quiet," hissed Bran, bringing his shaking finger to his lips. "Keep your voice down, will you!"

Marcus sighed, still listening to the painful screams in the night behind him.

"Bran," he whispered. "It's only a fox."

The movement ceased under Bran's layers as he considered the concept. "A what?"

"A fox… Just a fox."

"It sounds like the frickin' devil!" replied Bran. His head reappeared from under his sleeping bag.

It wasn't in any way an unusual sound. For anyone who lived in the country, the painful scream of a fox's howl would be considered nothing but natural. It was surprising Bran had never heard it. But it explained the reason behind his actions.

"What the hell did you think it was?" asked Marcus, biting his top lip in a poor attempt to hide a grin.

"I dunno…" Bran was thinking of all the possibilities to justify such a cowardly response. "Could have been old Gregory?"

"If that's the case, he'd have to have a pair of belting pipes on him."

Bran laughed a heartly belly laugh, causing his sides to tense and head to ache. No longer did Marcus feel the need to keep his smile hidden or locked away. He accompanied Bran in humiliating laughter, and they spoke far into the night. The sound of the woodland screams became less threatening until eventually they were barely acknowledged at all.

Amongst the Mists

Chapter Twenty-Two

The next morning, they slept late. So late that the morning had well and truly passed. They ate breakfast quietly, both starting to feel the effects of sleeping in a dingy old tent.

They broke camp and rode farther south and deeper into the hills of Sleathton. Dark grey clouds thickly matted the skies above, foreshadowing the summer storms to come. They kept their pace, riding faster and harder through an area where the growth of trees formed cave-like tunnels.

Marcus thought of Jack. He'd be home by now, back in the comfort of his own room and alongside his fussy mother. And on that note, the old man would have returned to the deserted settlement of Thyme, discovering his last guests had departed. Marcus couldn't help but feel a little sympathy for the old man, too. It mustn't have been pleasant living how he had for all those years. Not a soul to speak to or friendships to share. Gregory Degg endured the loneliness of his life. And that, Marcus thought, was the saddest thing of all.

"Wait!" Bran instructed. Yanking up on his brakes which almost caused Marcus to crash into his rear tyre.

"Did you hear that?"

They listened. But Marcus heard nothing unusual, only the call of a bird or the shake of colliding branches swaying innocently around them.

"No, what?"

"Shhh!" Bran lifted a stiff finger to the air, halting Marcus from any further interruption. Still, they heard nothing. And then, the silence was lost.

"What you hear then?"

"I dunno," Bran shrugged. "Sounded kind of like a girl."

"A girl? Are you mental? What would a girl be doing out here? What did she say?"

"Jesus! Twenty bloody questions! I never said it was a girl. I said it sounded like a girl."

"OK, so what did this girl sound like then?"

"Hell should I know. It was just high pitched and, well… girly… You know, a girly kind of sound."

"Right…" Marcus questioned, his front wheel beginning to turn as he pedalled off in front.

It was a difficult day, the hardest either had faced. The sky grew dark with clouds, confusing the mind with a sense of misplaced time. Still, not an ounce of drizzle fell from the heavens. The air felt mildly humid, giving the premonition of coming showers. It was only a matter of time.

They followed the most sensible trail on the landscape. It was much smoother now, and after an afternoon's ride, it was most welcoming to see the grey-topped mountains peek over the woodland ceiling. There was no intention for adventurous climbing. Not on this trip anyway, and neither had the desire to consider it. A break in the shadows presented for a very brief time, revealing the vast bodies of two grey mountains and the rock pathway between them. As they got closer, the path appeared to be a tighter squeeze than Marcus had hoped. The two of them would make it through. That was unquestionable enough. However, it was far too optimistic to try lugging their bicycles.

Marcus assessed the narrow walkway. The upper walls collided together, and the ground claimed the unpleasantness of jagged rock pointing up like spears. He slumped down on a mossy mound and allowed himself time to think.

"The bikes won't fit, Bran," he said, trying to concentrate on the rolled-out map. This was the route he had chosen and if he turned back now, his plans would fail.

"OK," said Bran, "then we just ride around them?" The idea to him seemed perfectly logical.

But as usual, nothing ever was simple with Marcus.

"No good," replied Marcus, holding up the map and fully concentrating on the print. "You can't tell from here, but these mountains run a rather strange circumference around Sleathton. We need to get to the middle. Here." He gave a tap on its centre.

"So, we can't find another way?"

"No. Not without losing a day… two at a push."

Bran was exhausted and, to be perfectly honest, had become exceedingly fed up with the whole ordeal. Still, he wasn't about to prolong this god forsaken trip any more than intended. Not even if it killed him.

"Leave the bikes," remarked Bran, bluntly. It was a simple solution, though a proposal Marcus had not foreseen.

"Leave them?"

"Why not! We can get them on the way back, can't we?"

"It's a suggestion."

"Look, mate," dictated Bran, "the way I see it, it's the best option we got. You wanna reach the centre of this stupid estate, don't you?

Marcus nodded.

"Alright then, let's just do it. I'm certainly not prepared to sacrifice another twenty-four hours biking around a hillside, all for the sake of seeing more boring trees. My feet have enough blisters!"

He was right, of course. The plan wouldn't work. For one, they didn't have enough food.

Although Marcus had no desire to retrace his steps, it appeared he had very little choice in the matter. He glanced over the crinkled map repeatedly, planning a route that would return them to the opening of the mountain path.

Alright, I got it.

"Let's get the gear together and make our way through," said Marcus, with a new determination in his voice.

The passage was exactly what they had expected. Narrow walls with sharp stone edges grabbed at their clothing in an apparent attempt to impede their progress. Deer scat lay matted across the ground, and the mountains rose like enormous tower blocks.

Now this is an adventure! thought Marcus, his heart singing soundly in his chest. Bran, on the other hand, was not so inspired. He was tired, always hungry, and had already covered his favourite trainers and jeans in scattered stag shit.

Bloody fantastic this! he thought, wondering how in God's name Marcus found enjoyment in such inconvenience.

The passage began to widen, and one behind the other they stepped onto exposed, dry ground. A spectacular sight was before them. Even Bran, a boy with very little appreciation for nature, stood mute. He wouldn't admit it, but the view took his breath away.

"Wow, it's stunning," said Marcus as he looked across the outlands. It was exactly how he imagined it. Wildflowers exploded, sprouting up from lacing tree roots. The plants and trees flourished, sending the amazing smells of nature into the open air. Nothing was left to the imagination. It was perfect.

Yes, they had finally made it. And now the hard work was done. They would set up camp near the closest lake and spend what little time remained of their adventure not worrying about anything other than having fun.

"I know that look," said Bran patting Marcus on the back. "There is fun. And there's your idea of fun."

Marcus smiled guiltily.

Amongst the Mists

Chapter Twenty-Three

Thunder crashed in the dryness of the afternoon sky. The clap was so powerful it caused the ground to tremble. Bran had never heard anything quite like it. Not in his lifetime, and he didn't savour the experience. With each beating thud, the bass of nature struck him. The feeling of an invisible barrier pushed firmly on their chests, demanding they stop. They didn't wait for the clashes to end. They ventured on, soon becoming accustomed to the peals from the sky.

The day drew on, the clouds remaining thick like bundled wet cotton. The colours grew darker with every upward glance, saturating the sky in hues of taupe and slate grey.

Marcus led them through the closest wood, following unreliable trails in the mossy earth that bordered the hill's base. Bran noticed instantly the woodland was different here. It was a darker forest. The forlorn trees clustered together here as if in fear, their branches entwined in search of anything to give them strength. Nettles were prolific among the hearty grasses. And despite their sombre impressions, the boys strode forward.

Nature walled up all around them. Hand-like twigs grasped skin and clothes, desperate to prevent their passing.

Camp would be in sight soon enough, thought Marcus. They just had to keep moving.

But still it made no odds. The more progress made, the more they grunted and groaned. And the forest floor became more hazardous. More intimidating.

That's it, I've had it, thought Bran. He had been thinking about giving up for some time now, making mental notes to quit this untenable quest. He looked down at the scrapes and cuts which patterned his flesh. He felt the urge to scratch at the itch crawling under his skin. He was truly at his wits' end.

This trail will never stop.

With exhaustion beginning to take its toll, his conscious mind persuaded him to rest on a toppled tree trunk.

"What's the matter with you?" asked Marcus. He was secretly happy taking a break himself.

Bran lay sprawled over the rotting wood. His eyes firmly shut, his breathing deep and unsteady.

"Oh, just leave me be!" he mumbled. "Just let me die in peace."

Marcus sniggered. It was this predictable style of overacting he had gotten so used to over the years.

"I'm not kidding!" continued Bran. "I'm done!"

"We're almost there!"

"You've been playing that card for ages." Bran complained vehemently, lifting his head just a little while he spoke. "You'll have me walking to my death!"

Marcus turned away and surveyed the land around them. *It had to be nearby.*

Observing beyond the wild growth, a single step submerged his foot. It wasn't until he felt water sloshing around his ankle that he pulled back. He again leaned forward and pushed aside the tall grass that was hiding an algae covered pool. Marcus forced himself deeper through the friction of the surrounding weeds. It took no more than a moment. Then with one wave of his hand, the misty tomb of Mother Earth evaporated. Beyond emerged the vision of a glistening, motionless lake. In perfect stillness, the surface was a polished mirror capturing the storm ridden sky.

I've found it.

*

They walked casually along the pebbled shore, the crunching of stone loud beneath their feet.

It was such a relief to escape the confined space of the forest. And for a time, satisfaction overcame them.

The more they walked, the lighter Bran's spirit became. He caught sight of an object almost too odd to be out here in such a forgotten land. But there it was... an old wooden boat was firmly stuck to the mucky bank, the bow line tied down to a large rock. Its rope was withered with age, almost to the point of disintegrating. The child buried just below the surface of each boy emerged joyfully as they scrambled aboard and sat against the creaking frame.

"Reckon she still floats?" asked Marcus.

"Only one way to find out." An excited eagerness filtered through Bran. "You still got that fishing line?"

The camping gear was carelessly thrown on the shore's edge. They still had plenty of time to get comfortable later. Even Marcus agreed it could wait. He had been waiting for a chance to test his skills the entire trip. Now was his chance. He quickly assembled the rod while Bran pulled at the knotted rope, its tension lessening before releasing with one nimble snap.

"Give her a push!" Bran yelled, drawing on energy he thought was lost.

They heaved forward, pushing alongside the boat's edges that had been long held secure by a shallow grave of muck. They tried again, determined to see her float.

"It's not gonna budge," said a discouraged Marcus.

"Oh, it'll budge. She just needs a little encouragement, that's all."

They lined themselves up, clenching over the fragile wooden beams, their feet twisting and grinding into the soft bedded shore, awaiting the final call.

"Push!" The word was shouted almost in sync. They pushed and heaved together, doubtful they could resurrect the little boat even with their combined strength.

Finally, the underside slid from its place. The sound of wet earthy suction releasing its hold was so satisfying!

They pushed the old row boat down the bank, and the stern hit the water first. The entry formed ripples that danced across the lake's mirrored surface.

They high fived, immediately feeling rather childish in doing so. Unbalanced, the boat rocked as the boys kicked their legs over the side to climb aboard. Surprisingly, the structure seemed solid. Not a leak sprang through its unstained planks as the oars were placed in the locks. Bran paddled outwards, having no sense which direction they faced. The lake was smooth, and rowing came easy to him. He soon quit paddling and let the boat wander in the middle of a motionless world.

*

"Here comes another," chuckled Marcus. His excitement caused him to pull on the line too forcefully. The moment seemed to have exceeded itself. Sure enough, the fading pattern of green and brown shimmered as it was freed from the shadowy depths.

"Careful! You'll pull its brains out yanking it like that!" instructed Bran.

This would be his third catch, and a generous one at that. The trout swished its slime coated tail in panic as its body was pulled carelessly from the water. It flipped violently before feeling the blunt point of an oar's end. And quickly, it exited life without further struggle.

"That's enough now, yeah?" persuaded Bran, a force of guilt washing over him as he watched the fish twitch its last.

Marcus, although overly enthused by a fair day's catch, agreed to Bran's terms with a nod. It wouldn't be right to kill more. He was no killer for sport after all. And to prove it, the trout he caught would be served as tonight's dinner. He collapsed the line and offered to help row to shore. The small boat was turned clumsily; Marcus had never rowed a day in his life.

Bran happened to feel it first. Small gem-like drops fell on the centre of his forehead. There was no time to prepare. As the short-lived sprinkling grew to a torrential downpour, the thunder crashed loudly overhead. Neither dared to look up.

The rain pelted down, rebounding around them and giving the illusion the lake's surface was as solid as hardened ground. Marcus continued to row, but his motion was too irregular for any meaningful progress. Bran hadn't noticed. He was far too involved shouting commands from the front in an attempt to guide them to the shore. A dim spark of lightning caught the corner of their eyes, then struck the water. And the thunder rolled across the lake.

"How much farther?" Marcus was breathless as he wiped the rivulets of rain running into his eyes. "We're like drowning rats out here!"

"Don't stop!" yelled Bran. "Just keep rowing." His words were partially muted by the multitude of thunder claps. To be entirely truthful, Bran wasn't too sure himself. The distance hazed in and out, making it difficult to distinguish land from water.

Still, he told Marcus nothing. He knew Marcus would panic, and it was an extra problem he wasn't prepared to deal with right now.

The whole idea of seeking refuge had become rather pointless. Soaked clothes hung heavily on their bodies, the excess water dripping from their shirt hems. They should have been on the shore by now. Shouldn't they at least have seen it?

We must be rowing in circles, thought Bran.

"Just let me take over for a while," Bran shouted, spitting out rain water that had seeped past his lips.

The boat rocked left and right while Bran again readied himself to row.

Boom!

Thunder and lightning struck simultaneously. The rumble faded in the distance as the fury again began to build. And just as the sky quieted and only heavy rain was in their thoughts, a swishing sound, followed by a loud distinct plop, filtered through the rain. The boys remained still as statues to prevent the boat from tipping. Curiosity pushed them to peer over the side to investigate, and they tried to squint past the thick, grey haze. The rain dulled their senses. The splashing continued like a panicked soul insisting on recognition. Just as they considered speaking, a voice assaulted their hearing and echoed around the lake. Each heart skipped a beat when they heard it.

"Drowning!"

Amongst the Mists

Chapter Twenty-Four

In the hall were the lingering smells of spices. Olivia hastily kicked off her wellingtons, abandoning them to topple on the door mat. The same aromas permeated the house every year at this time when her mother made some of her favourite treats.

Peeping around the kitchen door, she caught sight of her mother, wearing her usual apron, as she poured the spiced batter into her favourite cake tins.

Mmm, spiced pumpkin cakes, Olivia thought as her eyes widened and mouth began to water. *I'll just sneak one,* she promised herself. After all, pumpkin cakes were a rarity, a valid excuse to create something so delicious out of what would usually be classed as squirrel food. She had carved the pumpkins herself this year, making sure to scrape out all of the pumpkin's innards in hopes of extra cakes. And now that irresistible smell infiltrated each nostril, Olivia couldn't resist.

She crawled on hands and knees; the table over her concealed her presence. Her mother danced on the other side of the table. She hummed an infectious tune that Olivia didn't recognize. She only knew her mother's soft voice provided her with a sense of deeply hidden joy and peace.

Olivia smiled and waited for precisely the right moment, excitement causing her breath to quicken. She raised her hand to the table's edge, slowly feeling along the surface.

Easy, easy, the word repeated in her head as her fingers dragged softly across the festive tablecloth.

Almost, almost... got ya!

Her hand was lowered down gently, clutching at the delicate paper casing that held the cake.

Mine, it's all mine! A victorious smirk accompanied her greedy thought. She smacked her lips together, taking in its warm, tangy smell before opening her mouth.

"And what time do you call this?"

The voice came playfully from above her, along with a heavy-handed knock to the solid oak table.

Olivia giggled as her head protruded from the hanging cloth. She looked up, her mother down. They exchanged glowing smiles while her mother wiped her flour coated fingers roughly against the pocket of her polka-dot apron. She loved her mother dearly and hoped to inherit her elegance and beauty one day, but most of all, she hoped to be given her voice. Olivia had been gone only a couple of hours, but when she looked into her mother's eyes, it felt like they had been apart for an eternity.

"And where, might I ask, have you been?" Her mother grabbed her mischievous daughter and tickled her under the arms.

"Out," Olivia managed to say between the bursts of laughing fits, while her warm pumpkin cake rolled across the floor.

"Out?" her mother teased. "Out where?"

"Just out, out," laughed Olivia, escaping her mother's hands and dashing for the doorway. She peeked hesitantly past the frame.

"Well, we've been waiting on you," her mother replied as she returned to her baking. "Go sit with your grandfather. Dinner will be ready shortly."

Oh, not that old goat, she thought, reaching down to grab her cake as she made her way to the lounge. She crept in silently. Her grandfather sat sunken in his armchair, as he always did, endlessly mumbling as he slept. The impression was undeniable; his dreams were far more appealing than his reality.

Olivia snuck past him, comfortably sitting herself down on the floor beside the sofa. It was warm and cosy here, thanks to the radiator that gave out a hearty warmth as she leaned peacefully against the padded seat.

Her grandfather groaned again, his mouth fully open while his crooked neck rested awkwardly upon his bony shoulder.

Daft old goat. She smiled while raising her brow. She got comfortable while looking down at her long-awaited snack. Gently, she peeled back the crisp wrapper that crackled as it came loose from the cake's sticky sides.

At last! She thought as the wrapping lay on the floor.

"Where have you been?"

Olivia jumped, the cake springing from her grasp but was luckily caught in mid air.

"Jesus!" she spoke angrily under her breath, knowing all too well the daft old codger couldn't hear an elephant fart if he was listening for it.

"Afternoon, Grandfather."

"Uh, what?"

"I said 'Afternoon!'"

Olivia's grandfather leaned forward in his chair, his dentures almost slipping from his mouth as drool stringed unpleasantly down to his shirt.

"Where have you been?" he asked again.

"Out."

"Out? Out where?"

"What is it with everyone? Just out!" *Ya deaf old bat.*

Olivia tried not to smile but remain focused on the old timer staring back at her. He reached out for his walking stick that was always at his side. Olivia didn't quite understand why he owned it. He never used it, not once. Other than to hold in his chair, that is.

150

"You've been wandering about those woods again, haven't you?

Yup. "Of course not, Grandfather."

"Hmmm. I'm no fool, girl. It will do you justice not to mistake me as one." He pointed his stick to the window. "Don't think I don't see you from this here window, every day skipping off our land like a foolish child."

"Well, I am a child."

"Wah?"

"Nothing."

Olivia was in no mood. It was the same discussion day in, day out. Night, after night, after night. *Stay clear of the swamp, Stay clear of the swamp, Stay clear of the swamp.* God, she wished he would change the blooming record. If the local swamp was so bloody dangerous, why on earth had he moved so bloody close to it in the first place! What was she expected to do with her youth? Sit alongside him and listen to his grumblings about the weather, tales of stamp collecting, and daily complaints of his many aches and pains? She thought not.

"And here's another thing," the old man said, prodding with his stick and breaking Olivia's idle day dream. "Stay away from that swamp!"

"Yes, Grandfather."

"I could tell you stories that would cause your hair to fall right from your scalp, girl."

"Yes, Grandfather."

"Not sure if I ever mentioned it before?"

"Yes, you did, Grandfather."

151

*

In a short time, the old man's ranting subsided and a deep snore filled the room. Olivia was glad of it, overly glad in fact.

Finally, peace at last. Olivia sighed as she buried her shoulders in the cushions. She picked up her cake and waited for something else to disturb her. She brought the cake to her nose one more time, then took a bite. She savoured the taste as it danced on her tongue. It was glorious! No, it was sensational! She ate contentedly, watching the snack become smaller by the second. She could never tire of the sweet, spicy cake that stuck like glue between her teeth.

Wait. She thought, her mouth stuffed with the last remaining bites. *Something doesn't taste right.*

She kept chewing, but the sweet, fiery taste she remembered had somehow become a gross and bitter paste that caused her to gag. Even though she was reluctant, she spat it out all the same. Olivia knelt down, gazing at the semi-masticated blob. Familiar fear grasped at her heart.

Mud?

She straightened the balled-up wrapping, only to find the pink flowered paper smothered in dark coloured muck. She quickly tossed it away. "What's wrong, child?" an old voice called.

Olivia knew the voice. She turned to reply, but instead screamed in terror.

Her Grandfather lay dead in his chair, visually decaying as she stared at the dreadful image. His frail skin sank back into his bony face, slowly discolouring to a sickening colour of yellowy green. She pushed herself back to gain more space between them, and both hands submerged in a dark, murky ooze. The nearly forgotten cold had reattached itself fiercely to each leg. And as she backed away, the corpse of her grandfather twitched, his bones cracking as he stood. His deathly eyes watched her every move.

The sound of her mother's humming, once so soothing, slowly whirled into an unrecognizable screech as Olivia ran to escape the house.

"Lost... Lost!" her grandfather shrieked. The familiar voice brought tears to her eyes but did not give her the courage to look back.

A cackle she knew droned behind her, its taunting tone bringing back a dreamlike memory she almost forgot existed.

"Lost!" The voice called again as she turned to confront the source.

A shadowed mass hovered and howled. Its reflective eyes, as white as stars, pierced her soul.

Olivia awoke in fear, remembering the dark place she lay, the sounds that brought her there, and the feeling she was far from safe.

Amongst the Mists

Chapter Twenty-Five

Water began to fill the bottom of the boat. Breathing hard, Bran pulled the oars, taking them slowly forward. The weather around them had worsened, and now they could see only a few yards ahead. The sound of the heavy rain blurred into an unusual whirring noise. But they knew they were nearer their goal. The sound of panicked splashing grew louder with each stroke of the oars.

"You see anything?" sputtered Bran while he tried to catch his breath and relieve the burning sensation that clawed up both his arms.

Marcus didn't reply. He anxiously leaned over the bow, trying to catch even a glimpse of who was out there.

"Drowning!" the voice gurgled.

"Starboard!" yelled Marcus, frantically pointing to the right.

Bran manoeuvred the boat and, in spite of being almost completely spent, continued to fulfil his duty as oarsman. The evening sky faded around them, although they were too preoccupied to notice. They ignored the downpour they had once tried to escape as they searched through the water.

"Drowning!" The voice echoed again and disappeared into the air. Although nearer, its source appeared not to be in their direction of travel.

"Portside!" Marcus cried, again waving his arms aggressively.

"Just say left or right!" Bran cried out in frustration. His patience and energy were beginning to run on only fumes.

They had just travelled from that very direction.

How is that possible? thought Bran, lifting the oars again from the surface. Could it have been they were taken by current? Dragged at the mercy of the lake regardless of their efforts? Or, was it as simple as losing their bearings? It had been known to happen to many, so why not them?

"Drowning!" the voice yelped. It was now so perfectly clear they could not understand its visual absence.

"Wait!" demanded Marcus. Bran raised the oars and allowed the boat to drift.

Marcus had seen something. He thought he had. Unless his mind was prone to trickery. He peered into the cloud ahead and waited. The splashing had ceased, the yelling grew silent. And now all that could be recognised was the sound of rain drumming against the structure of the boat.

Come on... Come on, Marcus thought, his eyes never straying from the same suspicious spot. For a time, nothing happened.

"What is it?" asked Bran, for some reason using a rather hushed tone.

He stared on through the murky space. And with good instinct. A shadowed arm lifted from the surface and slapped back down to the lake.

The voice yelled out again, followed by their reassurance that help was on the way.

Bran witnessed it, too. A figure, desperate and panicked, thrashed in the water. If they had been a moment later, the figure would probably be dead.

It was an unpleasant thought, but the sight in front of them raised their hopes to new heights. Bran rowed on like never before. Adrenaline coursed through his veins, urging him to forget his exhaustion.

The boat drew nearer. The figure's shadow was hopelessly crawling through the white water.

"Hold on, buddy! We're almost there," shouted Marcus, trying his best to offer hope to the poor, unfortunate soul.

The shadow stopped and stared. Its thrashing eased. Its kicking went limp. And as it looked toward the slowly approaching vessel, its form swiftly disappeared, sinking below the misty surface.

Marcus plunged his hand through the surface of the lake, reaching into the empty cold. Bran rose from his seat and scrambled across the boat, nearly sending Marcus plummeting to the lake's bottom.

"Come on… Grab on!" Marcus cried out at his own rippled reflection.

Bran snatched an oar and submerged it to its limit. He cautiously shifted it around in motions resembling the stirring of a cauldron.

"Anything?" asked Marcus.

"No… nothing," replied Bran with a shake of his head.

He continued to stir the oar around in the water. The thought of his possible observation of a death by drowning was horrifying.

Suddenly, the oar froze in place. Bran could no longer force it to budge.

"You got them?" Marcus asked with fearful shock.

His eyes seemed to pop from his skull as they peered into the abyss. He gave a swift nod, steadied his breathing, and began to pull.

He gave it his all, every ounce of strength that remained in his petrified body. Air bubbles broke the surface, shortly followed by a sluggish but desperate hand reaching for help. Marcus gripped it tightly as wet skin on wet skin tried to slip apart. He and Bran heaved as one, pulling on the body that felt like it was weighted with a ball and chain. Dark black hair lay flat on the person's face, hiding any semblance of consciousness.

"One more, and heave!" screeched Bran.

The two fell backwards violently, leaving the lifeless body to lay limp in the bottom of the boat.

They glared down, terrified at the thought of death having already claimed this person's life. It was a boy without doubt, that was clear enough. But how did he come to be here? And all alone?

"Check his pulse," said Marcus, hoping that Bran would display the needed bravery.

"You check the bloody pulse!"

"One of us has to!"

Both remained where they were and the rocking of the boat soon stilled.

"God's sake," exhaled Marcus as he reached a hand out to the lifeless body. He laid only a finger on the neck when the boy startled and cornered himself in the helm of the boat. He trembled in pure terror, shaking uncontrollably.

"It's alright," encouraged Marcus, holding his hands up with his palms out as a subtle sign of peace. Bran was quite different. He was scared, quivering on the spot with an oar tightly held in both hands. If needed, he was ready to swing, sending the boy back to the depths from which he came.

A reassuring hand wrapped around Bran's shaking fist, as Marcus desperately tried to calm him. Shock consumed their utterly fatigued bodies as they stared into the brightest eyes they'd ever seen. One blue eye, the other a vibrant green.

A quivering lip turned wearily into a strangely confused smile. And with that, the rescued boy sat upright.

A stillness fell across the lake, the eerie atmosphere causing goosebumps to stand sharply on end. And despite all he had witnessed, Bran still held the oar desperately waiting for any excuse to use it.

"Jack?" whispered Bran.

"Hiya guys."

Chapter Twenty-Six

T he boat jolted, the force throwing the boys violently forward without a chance of bracing for impact. The rocks along the shore crept invisibly beneath them, piercing the underbelly of the weakened bow. Beginning as a trickle, the water soon flowed faster as the puncture was freed from the offending rock.

Bran lay awkwardly on his side after the fall sent his head bouncing off a stationary seat plank. He looked around in a stunned daze wondering who had struck him. Muffled voices drifted in and out as he tried to focus on a blurry silhouette standing over him. A hand reached down and indicated he should grab hold. He followed the scrawny arm up to a smiling face and familiar eyes.

A distorted voice finally became clear enough for him to recognise. "Take my hand."

Bran took it weakly just before his sight faded away. The figure picked him up, and within seconds Bran realised he lay flat on the cold, pebbled shore. He was surprised to see Marcus already there reaching out to help. The world was spinning, and he could do nothing to stop it. All the voices and sounds merged into one. The trees, no longer rooted in solid ground, floated and swirled around him. Clouds and figures glided in the air. He remembered nothing after that.

*

By the time he woke, darkness was beginning to fall. He sat up too quickly, and dizziness clouded his mind once more.

"You OK, mate?" Marcus shouted, rushing over from prepping the evening's meal. Camp had already been set for the night. The tent was assembled, pots and pans lay jumbled, and a blazing fire gently warmed him where he sat.

"What happened?" Bran asked, rubbing at the back of his head. "I had the most obscure dream."

Bran continued to speak, but was soon distracted by footsteps approaching the flames, causing him to stumble over his words.

"You!" Bran shouted. He scowled and weakly rose to his feet. "How the hell did you even get here?"

Jack said nothing but stood stiffly with his arms filled with firewood, his unblinking eyes staring directly into Bran's. He smiled.

"Answer me, Jack!" Bran demanded. "How did you get here?"

An uncomfortable pause filled the camp. Jack's eyes never strayed from his.

"I followed," replied Jack, softy, before turning away to feed the flames.

"Don't turn away from me!" yelled Bran.

But it was too late. Jack had already walked away, past the camp and into the trees. And again, there were just the two of them.

A hand firmly gripped his shoulder, as he allowed his body to gradually relax.

"Calm down," whispered Marcus. "You won't get anywhere asking such things. Believe me, I've already tried."

Bran chose not to reply. He was still dizzy, and the back of his head thumped in time with his heartbeat. He sat by the fire, its spreading heat unable to quell the chill of his shaking bones.

"How long was I out for?"

"Not Long. I debated on looking for help, though I couldn't be sure I'd find you again. Plus, you were breathing, even vocalised the odd mumble from time to time, as if you were asleep."

A bowl was gently passed to him, steam rising from the rim. "Eat up, mate. You'll feel better."

Bran looked down, *Not more broccoli and cheese pasta.*

"What happened to the fish?"

"What do you think? They went down with the ship, of course."

Bran looked down at the steaming but disgusting bowl of slop.

"Don't get picky on me, eat up," said Marcus. "This is just as good."

"I seriously doubt that."

*

The night rapidly intensified in around them. And for the first time since they began, Bran ate without a word. His mind was far too busy contemplating everything that had happened. Yet, no matter how many times he tried, the pieces wouldn't fit together. His memories and thoughts remained scrambled like a long-forgotten dream.

The surrounding trees swayed in a gust of wind that blew through the camp. Bran raised his face from his palms. As he did, Jack returned into the firelight. Like before his arms were filled with deadwood. He came and sat crossed legged by the fire, the wood still held tightly in the ridge of his arms.

Bran gave a look that could only be interpreted as hateful. It made no difference. Jack just looked back at him, but only at him. The flames reflected something wonderful in his wide, unblinking pupils.

"You got some answers to give, Jack!" chided Bran, putting his bowl down and pointing a trembling finger. "I'll ask you again, how'd you find us?"

"I followed," replied Jack, his face unchanged as he dropped the wood and rested back against a tree.

"Bullshit!" cursed Bran before looking at Marcus, whose mouth was full. Completely baffled, he stared at Bran in return.

"I know a liar when I see one," continued Bran. "What the hell is your game! Making us worry like that."

Jack said nothing in return but gave a slow, uncaring shrug, severely impacting Bran's temper.

The camp filled with silence, and for a time only the sounds of insects were heard in the summer's night air. They ate in awkward silence, none of them knowing what to say to one another. The plates were cleared, except for Jack's whose food remained untouched. He did nothing but stare at Bran.

"What? You got something you wanna say to me?"

Jack stared on.

"Hey, retard! Answer me!"

"Bran…" Marcus butted in, reaching out to Bran in an attempt to calm his temper.

"Back the hell off!" snapped Bran as he slapped away his friend's hand.

Bran stood sharply, and in turn so did the others. Marcus had never seen him like this before. He had seen him angry, sure. But not like this. Hate pulsated around him. His face was red and wet with nervous sweat. And to be perfectly honest, Marcus was starting to feel a little scared himself.

Bran launched forward, his steps charging through the smouldering firewood. He wasn't sure what he would do. All he knew was he wanted to hurt Jack. Hurt him in a way he had never wanted to hurt anyone in his wildest dreams.

A gunshot rang out. The violent burst of sound echoed across the lake, and startled birds fled in flocks from the treetops.

"Was that a gun? Was that a gunshot?" Marcus questioned twice. Concern overcame him as he searched from side to side.

Bran looked to the night sky, the sound slowly dying as the birds circled them overhead.

Bang! A second shot struck, breaking the flock from above and dispersing them from view. They again waited, certain that a third would rattle the air. But no third shot came. Bran began to relax, his breathing more under control. Just as he started to speak, loud footsteps crunched through the undergrowth.

The sound of tromping grew nearer. The shuffle of foliage. The snap of twigs. The rustle of leaves. It was all too much for Marcus, who froze solid, waiting for whomever was out there to strike. He felt vulnerable. He was prey being circled by creatures of the dark.

"Let's get out of here," urged Marcus, but his feet were firmly fixed to where he stood.

"Be quiet," Bran replied in an overly stern, albeit hushed, voice.

"We need to get out of here, we could be trespassing!"

"Will you shut it! I can't hear the –"

But it was too late. The footfalls had halted, sending a cavalcade of paranoia descending on both boys.

Torch light shone out from the treeline, its brightness blinding Bran as he lifted both hands to shield his squinting eyes. Branches swung forward and swiftly returned to their place as the steps again ceased.

"You know, you can hear you boys from the other side of Sleathton." It was a statement more than it was a question. And with that, the torch light lowered to the ground, and the boys' night vision gradually returned.

Gregory stood before them, tired and wretched. His head hung low as the heaviness of his rifle weighed on his shoulder. His clothes (from what could be seen) were thick with mud, his beard uncombed, his eyes carrying dark bags beneath them.

No one spoke. The boys were leery of the man who had followed them all this way, not to mention the weapon he happily carried.

"Not going to invite me to rest then?" Gregory removed the gun strap from his shoulder. "Very well. However, I will do it all the same." He slumped to the uncovered ground, regarding the boys while holding his outstretched hands to the flames.

Marcus looked to Bran, though his gaze was not returned. He was too concerned with how the old man came to be here.

"I guess a part of me didn't expect you boys to wait at the house. Thank goodness you biked it most of the way here. Otherwise, you'd have made it extremely difficult for me to track."

"You've been tracking us?" asked Bran.

"Yes, indeed," Gregory muttered, reaching out for the bowl of food that still remained untouched. "May I?"

Bran wasn't going to ask Jack if he cared to share, and simply nodded his head. He had no desire to cross the old man. Not right now.

"I suppose you boys are wondering why on God's green earth I'm here." Again, this was no question.

"The thought had crossed my mind." Marcus began to edge close to the fire.

The old man didn't answer. And without even asking for a fork, he tucked into the cheese-dripping pasta using only his fingers. He ate ravenously, like a desperate man who had not seen food in days. And at times, it seemed he wouldn't stop gorging even to breathe. He ate until the bowl was clean and then indicated he needed more.

A sudden movement caught the old man's eye, and he reached for his torch with a loud, dreary grunt. The beam shone directly onto the boy who stood furthest away, the only boy who had gone unnoticed.

"Wait!" he said, collecting the rifle that lay at his side, the light never leaving Jack's pale face. He cautiously approached the boy, as though the child himself would cause him greater harm.

"Have you any idea how long I've been searching for you?" asked Gregory.

He was on Jack like a predator. The light shone deep into the lad's widened eyes, as Jack stood pushed against the trunk of a large tree.

"What nice eyes you have." Gregory moved in closer, his nose and the light now only inches away. "Though… it's rather amusing, they're not at all as I remember."

Jack said nothing as he stared through the light at Bran.

167

Marcus almost interrupted. Though his ability to speak was unwillingly tied to the back of his throat.

"What's different?" Bran asked, purely playing along with the old man's fantasy.

Gregory scowled at the boy a moment longer before steadily stepping back. "Hmmmm," he hummed, turning away and retracing his steps.

"I said, what's different?" asked Bran again.

The old man crossed the fire, his back still facing the three. "Ah, young Bran. The leader of the gang, so to speak. Do you really wish to know?"

"Yes." The reply was slow and somewhat forceful.

Gregory stopped. He lowered his weapon and readied to fire.

"I'm sorry, boys. I never wanted this upon any of you."

It all happened so fast. The lit torch fell to the ground with a thud, sending light to trees in the rear. Gregory turned swiftly, his rifle raised high and the target locked.

No! Bran almost bellowed to protest, but it was too late. The third shot had been fired, the noise piercing his eardrums as short-term deafness lingered. Each of them could hear nothing. The world had fallen silent, the land dark. And all they could recognise was the potent scent of gunpowder.

Amongst the Mists

Chapter Twenty-Seven

A hissing noise dominated Bran's hearing. The natural reaction of covering the ears proved completely useless. He dropped to the ground, reaching for the torch as it rolled across the pebbles. There were no more shots fired. One was all it took. The old man casually rested the barrel of the gun across his chest, the stock balanced confidently on his wrist.

"Are you mad!" Bran shouted. At least he thought he yelled, though the words weren't heard by the elderly man beside him.

The old man ignored the torch light, his sight transfixed on the tree line.

The light shone momentarily on Marcus who was slowly regaining his balance.

"Marcus, you OK?" Bran yelled, and again he thought *He can't hear me!*

The light panned past Gregory, whose stance remained unaltered, before finally reaching over to Jack. He was now sitting contently in place, his back still resting against the base of a tree.

"Hey, Special, you alright?" Bran shouted as loudly as he could.

Jack didn't move. His body stayed rigid while his sight was fixed on Gregory.

"Hey... you alright?" Bran repeated as he walked toward Jack. The torch light was raised. Jack's gaunt expression glared through him.

Bran fell back, clutching at the ground as he scrambled through the dried-up leaves.

A single shot. One bullet to the head of his friend. The picture was sickening, as if Jack's very head had been stapled firmly to a post. Blood dripped down from the circle between his eyes, slowly falling onto his chest. It was the blood that caused Bran to fall. He retched where he sat, gagging on the gruesome sight and struggling for breath.

"Calm yourself, son." Gregory spoke as if the whole ordeal were natural. It was not natural, not by any means. It was without doubt the most unnatural thing Bran had ever seen.

"Run!" Bran screamed to Marcus, only now noticing the ringing in his ears had ceased and words again could be heard easily. He dashed past Marcus, grabbing him firmly by the sleeve and tearing the seam of his shirt. "Run, you idiot!" he implored.

"What?... Why?" Marcus retorted, shrugging off Bran's grasp which caused him to slip and fall.

"Are you deluded!" snapped Bran, the desperation on his face forced Marcus back all the more.

Is he blind as well as thick?

"He shot... He shot Jack! Look, you stupid idiot!" Bran pointed to the bloody mess that trickled down the tree.

"We... we gotta go!" screamed Bran.

"But he didn't shoot anyone!"

Bran's short sprint slowed until it became nothing. He turned to look at the two figures staring back at him through the fire. The forgotten torch light now masking the ghastly corpse beyond them.

"What the hell has got into you, Bran?" pleaded Marcus, now unsure of whether to stick by his travel companion or keep his distance.

"What's got into me? What's got into you?" The words came tumbling out as he tried to collect himself.

"Jack's dead! He shot him!" Bran exclaimed, pointing aggressively at the old man.

Marcus looked behind him, to where Jack sat limp and pale.

"He shot a tree, Bran." The words came out confused and slow, as if he were not wanting to cause Bran further distress. "We haven't seen Jack since Thyme."

What?

Bran's blood ran cold, a tightness captured his chest which he powerlessly tried to break. Silence took them all, as they waited for Bran to summon his words.

"He's… behind you!"

Marcus looked again. He felt like part of a pantomime show.

"There's nothing there, mate. Nothing but a bullet hole."

"But Jack… he's been with us all night. We've been talking to him, for Christ sake!"

"You've been talking to thin air, pal. I was getting rather worried. That was a nasty knock you took to the head."

Bran gruffly rubbed at his face and tried to pull together the memories that had seemed so clear, trying to think of anything, anything at all, that would make Marcus believe his story.

"The boat!" shouted Bran.

"OK… What about it?"

"Jack was screaming for help. We pulled him… you and me. Remember? We pulled him up from the water. He nearly drowned!"

Marcus looked back to Gregory, embarrassed for his friend. A great concern stirred within him. After all, Bran had not been the same since his fall. Bran had never acted so strangely before, and to be truthful, Marcus wasn't entirely sure how to deal with him.

"Bran, it was a bird. Nothing more than a drowned raven. It must have flown too low during the storm. By the time we got to it, it was already dead."

"So, who carried me from the boat?"

"I did." For Marcus the reply was all too obvious.

Bran couldn't believe what he was hearing. The body was right there. Right in front of them. Fresh blood still oozed from the single wound and covered Jack's face like a red silk mask.

How can he not see it? How could he not…

Bran shifted his crazed, maddened stare to Gregory, whose expression looked all too casual.

"You!" shrieked Bran. "You can see him. Tell him you can see him." He waved his tightly clenched fist at the old man. "You put a bullet straight through the poor bastard's head!"

Gregory frowned at the gesture. He was neither threatened nor intimidated by a mere frightened boy.

"What you going to do with that fist, boy?"

"I'll thump ya, you see if I don't!"

"I believe you forget yourself, son. I carry the bullets."

"It's your last chance," sobbed Bran. "Tell him you can see him, that you… that you shot him!" Bran's eyes began to water, tears blurring his vision before they ran down his cheeks, and his speech began to crackle. "Look back and tell me he's there!"

The old man shook his head without sympathy before turning to look back.

"Aye… I see him, boy. I see him as clear as I see you now."

Surprised, Marcus glanced over the targeted shot again, though he could see nothing, nothing but the shattered oak. The thought had crossed his mind that the old man was simply humouring Bran, in an attempt to gain his trust and calm his delirium.

"I told you! He shot him, Marcus," Bran continued, wiping the phlegm from his nose.

"I shot no child." Gregory held a finger in the air to ask for silence. "I simply shot a form that deceived you as one."

Bran smeared the tears across his blubbering face; the cuff of his shirt was soaked.

"What?" said Bran.

"I know how it sounds. I, too, had my doubts until I saw the spirits myself."

"Spirits?" questioned Marcus.

The old man scratched at his mud matted beard. He knew he wasn't explaining himself clearly, but this was difficult. No matter how he considered his words they all came out the same. He just needed the boys to understand.

"Come here, boy," said Gregory as he reached out to Bran.

The invitation stood for quite some time. Bran may not have been all that clever, but he certainly was no simpleton.

I think not, as he stepped back farther. Gregory allowed his hand to fall and his grasp on the gun to loosen.

"Have I yet given you any reason to distrust me, boy?"

"Well..." said Bran, looking back to the blood ridden carcass, its hands hanging limply at its side.

"Come, let me show you," said Gregory, "then you'll understand. You'll see as I do."

He knew he shouldn't. But something deep within Bran persuaded him to listen. He wasn't sure what it was. The desire for fear to end, no doubt, was part of it. His feet shuffled forward then back.

"That's it, good lad, good lad. You just keep coming."

The old man placed his arm securely around his shoulders, embracing him tightly to his side. The unwelcome embrace gave Bran the uncomfortable sensation of capture, as the old man's stench drifted strongly up each nostril. And although Bran wasn't willing, his hesitant steps were forced forward, retracing his walk to the bloodied corpse.

The night around them suddenly grew cold. Within only a few seconds a mist rolled over the ground, spreading softly above the camp floor and dampening the fire to a steamy hiss. The bark of the tallest trees glimmered in sparkling white frost. Their breath before them formed a foggy cloud in the winter's air. The boys were so enthralled in the dreadful scenario they didn't notice the abnormal change. But Gregory noticed, and he listened to the lake slowly cracking, forming thick bedded ice.

"Come, who do you see?" The old man asked him as they approached the dead boy. In fact, they were so close that the sickening sound of dripping blood was far too much for Bran to bear.

"Come now, who do you see?" Gregory prompted encouragingly.

"I… I…" Bran gave himself a second while he tried to push down the lump that was trying to make a permanent home at the back of his throat. "I see Jack."

Gregory's stare sent shivers up Bran's spine. The man reached down to his belt and retrieved a sharp edged blade with its hilt wrapped in something eerily reminiscent of human hair.

"Hold out your hand, boy." Gregory wrestled Bran closer, his time running short and patience wearing thin.

Footsteps ran frantically behind them. Heavy breathing rattled the air, distracting their stare from the dead. And then, the gun was cocked.

"Let. Him. Go!" yelled Marcus, aiming the barrel at the old man's chest.

Old Gregory immediately released his grip, allowing Bran to dash forward and stand alongside his friend.

"Now, young Marcus, let's not do anything rash," the old man stuttered, reaching out to grasp and lower the tip of the barrel.

"Back off, old man! We ain't getting bummed tonight!"

Old Gregory stepped back. A puzzled look crossed his face as he searched for words to say.

"Bummed? Surely you both don't think…?"

"Hell right, we do!" shouted Marcus. "We know your game. And my friend ain't getting any tonight!"

Marcus steadied the gun, his finger held firmly against the trigger. All he needed was an excuse, any excuse, to justify his shot. And he sincerely believed he would do it if it became necessary.

Bran leaned forward, tapping his friend repetitively on the shoulder, as Gregory stepped forward in exasperation.

"We have no time for such utter nonsense. If you wish to shoot, then shoot. I will not stop you."

Gregory walked back to the cooling corpse, readying himself as he took the sharpened blade to the palm of his hand. He sliced quickly. The cut was deep and smooth. Almost immediately, his hand gave birth to shiny red pearls. The blood beads raced down his wrist to the tip of his bony elbow. Stunned by the gory sight before him, Marcus's aim fell slack. He whispered to Bran, "Let's make a break for it."

"No. Wait," replied Bran, mesmerised by the scene.

With his one clean hand, Gregory lifted Jack's head by the scruff of his curls and dragged his bloody hand roughly across the skin of the young corpse's face. He looked back at the boys like a teacher would gaze at uneducated students. There was nothing more to be done. Stepping back, he clenched his dripping fist in pain and silently waited for the inevitable.

Amongst the Mists

Chapter Twenty-Eight

Marcus stumbled backward, dropping helplessly into a hard fall. Fear took up residency in his young eyes as they, too, could recognise the lifeless body of the friend he had thought home and safe.

"Jesus Christ!" His words cracked as he hit the ground, releasing the gun from his grip. The single shot that was fired into the air caused them all to flinch.

No matter how hard he tried, Marcus couldn't look away. The unnatural image of oozing blood stringing from Jack's weak jaw embedded itself deep in Marcus's mind. He closed his eyes and muttered persuasive self-incentives that only he could interpret. It was a trick he used often; a knack to escape his fears, burying them deep. Though he'd never in his life experienced a sight such as this. He lay back, reassuring himself the whole ordeal was nothing more than a sick and twisted prank or perhaps an absurdly disturbing hallucination.

He anxiously opened one eye. He squinted, which restricted his vision, as he peeked across the camp.

"No…" Marcus whispered.

Of course, all remained as it was. Every gory detail. Why he expected it to be different at that precise moment was beyond him. He would've given his left arm for someone to quickly pinch him right about now, to awaken him from such a horrendously gruesome dream.

Marcus knew well enough this was no dream; no dream he'd ever experienced. He sat forward, waiting for someone… anyone, to speak and break the silence.

"Bran?" asked Marcus, reaching for a hand to guide him to his feet.

"Quiet!" whispered Bran, waving his hand aside. His eyes quickly scanned the trees above them.

"What is it?" said Marcus.

"The gun," said Bran. His head still tilted to the darkened sky. "It fired, but no birds fled. Listen, can you hear it?"

"Hear what?"

"Exactly. There's nothing. Not so much as a flutter."

"Who gives a shit about pissin' birds! They probably all swarmed off earlier."

179

"You sure?" said Bran.

"No, but…."

"Marcus…"

"What?"

"Shut up."

"What? Why?"

Marcus stood, his knees shaking helplessly beneath him as his mind finally began to clear. He turned his face to the starry sky before catching a view that caused his palms to sweat.

Tall trees encircled them, each one stretching higher and higher to the crisp clear sky, giving the illusion the branches were desperate to touch the twinkling of the stars. It was then Marcus caught the intermittent twitch of tiny shapes, soon followed by more, and more, until he began to question if the entire forest was cursed and had come to life.

"What is that?" Marcus spoke hoarsely, straining his eyes to the simultaneous movements of tiny feet. His shoulders locked side by side with Bran, a form of interaction usually far too close for their liking. Regardless, they remained knitted all the same, if only for a little protection.

"It's birds," said Bran.

Bran was right. The branches above spread out, clustered with tiny eyes that observed their every movement.

"Did you see them fly back here?" asked Marcus.

"No, I think… I think they've been here the entire time."

It was the strangest sight. The tiny creatures looked like ornamental figures perched silently in their domain, intrigued by every move made below them. Bran didn't like this, not one bit. The more he paced and gazed up to the trees, the more the feathers were highlighted by the gloom of the rising moon.

"Get out of here!" cried Bran, raising his hands and loudly clapping them together in an attempt to drive them away. He continued until his hands grew tired, eventually allowing his claps to echo and fade while his hands throbbed with pain.

"It'll do you no good, young man," said the old man, his silhouette barely visible as he crept further out of sight.

"The hell it won't!" replied Bran as he marched over to the weapon left abandoned in the dirt.

"Go to hell!" He cocked the gun, hopeful that the chamber remained loaded as he turned to take his aim.

"Now see here boy!" yelled Gregory. His voice was low and stern as he began to step forward.

But it was too late.

Bang!

The gun fired, throwing the butt into Bran's shoulder with a violent kick. The weapon dropped to his side.

"Shit!" Bran mumbled. "That hurt!"

Marcus had covered his ears, predicting the shot was coming. Bran was no stranger to firearms. Well... pellet guns, and he would often try to shoot any filthy creature that tried its luck

181

wandering into his mother's garden. Saying that, he wasn't much of a shot. A terrible shot to be truthful. And from the look of it, as Marcus searched the tallest trees, his aim had not improved.

"Boys," hushed Gregory. He was ignored.

The birds remained still. Yes, all of them. Not one flew, shrieked, or fluttered. They did nothing but stare down at the strangers like vultures scrutinizing their next feast.

"All them targets and you couldn't hit one?" said Marcus with a push.

"They didn't bloody flinch," said Bran in astonishment. "Not so much as a quiver."

The same rolling mist brushed gently against Bran's ankles, giving the impression something lurked just out of sight. He kicked that chilling sensation away. He looked up again as the creatures above them began calling aggressively. It was a troubling sound, the kind of noise that caused Bran's heart to pound and adrenaline to spike.

What the hell is this? he thought, still aiming the gun at the haunting trees. The creatures' calls grew deafening, somehow disguising the pattern as one distorted cry.

It was a vile sound. He scowled, unable to tolerate the torturous racket.

"Why do they do that?" yelled Marcus, his face grimacing through the high-pitched whines that dove deep into his ear drums.

"I'll show them!" yelled Bran. His finger squeezed tighter around the curve of the trigger, and he held his breath this time to steady his aim.

The trigger released as he took his stance preparing for the gun to kick back again.

Click

Bran looked down at the gun.

Click, click, click.

No, it was no good. The chamber was empty, and he carelessly dropped the gun on the ground. The birds immediately ceased their distressing screams. As though intrigued, they perched themselves forward, their sharp beaks pointing like daggers to targets.

Old Gregory edged forward though his body remained cloaked by the dismal gloom.

"Why are they staring at us?" repeated Bran, his words heard clearly as they flowed through the humid air.

"They aren't staring at us," said Gregory knowingly and reached out to reclaim his weapon.

Marcus's skin turned pale. He felt his hair stand on end while he fiercely tried to rescue his voice from the black abyss of fear. Instead, he stubbornly grabbed Bran by the hand forcing him to meet the same certain fear. It took Bran a moment. He glanced quickly away from Marcus, determined to release his irritating grasp. However, there was no time to think about that. Not now.

Jack stood at an angle, his back arched, and his feet submerged in a floor of soft hovering mist.

His eyes rolled to the left, then wearily to the right, before crossing in the middle to observe the hole at the centre of his bloodied head.

"Jack?" whispered Marcus, taking a step forward to the twisted figure.

Jack grunted, his wide eyes lifting at Marcus's approach. A disturbing smile appeared from ear to ear as he noticed the old man watching.

"Hiya G…Guys!" Jack said, tilting his head curiously to the side. The bones of his angled neck cracked with stiffness.

Marcus stopped. The voice he heard was playful, yet rough. It was nothing like the sound of his friend. There was something wrong here, terribly wrong, and he turned to look for Gregory.

"It's not Jack, is it?" said Marcus.

"No… no, it is not," spoke Gregory holding out his wounded hand. Red ruby beads still ran smoothly from his twiglike wrist and dropped in teardrop forms on the dry curled leaves.

He moved closer, but never carelessly, as he measured his every footstep.

"Hiya G…Guys!" said Jack again. Only now his smile fell flat, and he watched closely as the oncoming hand of falling blood drew nearer.

It made a noise, a noise unlike anything they had ever heard before. A grinding, gurgling groan passed its scabbed lips, the tone constantly modulating from high to low and back again. It was an unpleasant sound, a despicable sound.

The boys watched as old Gregory trod on, pushing this… this *thing*… back with an invisible force, as his palm stayed rigid and narrow.

"Back to the fen with you," ordered Gregory, flicking the droplets aggressively from his tingling hand.

The figure fell back, slowly edging nearer to the lake's edge, its distress filled with anguish as it flinched away from the blood.

"That's it, get back to the stinking bog with you."

There was something different now. They both saw it. As the figure's foot scraped the water's edge, its neck strayed far from Gregory and quickly glanced over to the boys behind him. Then the likeness of Jack slowly began to fade, as *it* stepped back farther into the lake. The curly hair began to dissolve, the chubby shape of Jack's childlike face collapsed. And as it looked upon them one last time, the colourful eyes Jack carried quickly dimmed, stretching down into deep hollow sockets only to bare a bright reflective orb from within.

"Back you get now," shouted Gregory.

Any resemblance to their friend had evaporated. What stood before them was of no boy nor man. It was *a... a Something?* and something they never imagined a part of this world. It was something of evil, the purest evil. And if it hadn't been for this crazy old fool, it was likely they'd be dead.

The creature retreated farther into the misty lake. Its gaping eyes of bright reflecting holes bored into their souls. The human form it held had morphed, changing into a hazy shadowed mist.

The clothes it once wore were absorbed like ink into porous paper. And as quickly as it started, its mighty quarrel ceased, again bringing white noise to drift through the camp.

The three stood in fear on the pebbled bank, watching as the distance between them and the creature gradually increased. It was a frightening sight. The water never moved, never once made a sound as the dark shadow flowed bewitchingly through it.

It stopped dead at the lake's centre. Its giant eyes reflecting like warning lights on a stormy sea. It did nothing but watch them before slowly sinking beneath its misty bed.

Chapter Twenty-Nine

The old man fell roughly on his rump, sighing aloud about what would soon be another scar forged by his own beaten hands. Tearing a narrow strip from his stained shirt, he began to wrap it tightly around his palm.

"You're meant to clean it, you know?" uttered Marcus.

"Wah? Speak up!"

"You're meant to clean it. You're trapping all the shit in there."

Gregory gave a sarcastic grunt as he finished pulling the knot.

"It'll do," he said. "Besides, where would you suggest I clean it?"

Marcus gave a short, hard look to the lake.

Good point!

Gregory leaned forward, allowing his head to fall and his eyelids to close for only a moment. The task had taken much out of him, plenty more than he had remembered. He lay back watching as the mist began to thin, slowly drifting back to the darkened spots from which it came. Bran caught his eye while standing speechless, impatiently waiting for an explanation.

A huff of air escaped Gregory as he manoeuvred his weight.

"You OK, son?"

"What?" said Bran, his face scrunched with annoyance.

"I said, you OK?"

"Am I OK?

"Yes…"

"Hmm, oh yes, no concerns at all.

"So, you're alright then?"

"No! I'm bloody not!"

Marcus sat beside the old timer. He wasn't sure why. Maybe it was the scared child in him, or maybe he just simply feared for his own personal safety. Either way, he said nothing and only watched as Gregory began to reload the chamber of his gun. Bullets fell loose from his knee-high pocket, rebounding off his feet as he reached out to the ground. Blood from his cut already started to show through his poorly administered bandage, blotching his ammo in bright red markings as each bullet slotted into place.

The camp descended into a deathly silence as the campfire made the sound of a weak and calming crackle.

The gun barrel snapped firmly shut, and the old man stood, leaning on his weapon like a stick to support his weight.

"Grab your things, boys. Grab anything. We need to move."

"Move? Move where?" questioned Bran.

"Back to Thyme, of course. Once we're back on the road, I'll get you boys home. I knew I'd live to regret leaving you two alone. But Sleathton is no place for our kind. It never was."

Marcus began to gather his things, scrambling through the torchlight. Getting out of this predicament couldn't happen quickly enough.

"You should've taken us home in the first place," said Bran. "Instead, you left us at your scabby old house."

"It's a lodge."

"That's beside the point!"

The old man lifted his gun uneasily, aiming at the hidden paths around them while he calculated the quickest way home.

"What do you mean, taken you home in the first place?" questioned Gregory.

"With Jack. You deaf as well as senile?"

"Watch your tongue boy. And I never took Jack anywhere."

The regular clanking of background noise came to a sudden halt, as Marcus caught wind of the discussion.

With bag in hand, Marcus wandered over to Gregory. The thought that Jack really had gone missing now flooded his mind with worry.

"He never went back with you?" asked Marcus.

"With me? No, son, I never took him back to Bonhil."

"Then where the hell were you both yesterday?" Bran interrupted, his manner now far too confrontational for the old man's liking.

"Wind your neck in, boy," snarled Gregory, "before I do it for you. Yes, I can't say that I never saw him. That would be dishonest. But... but there is a perfectly reasonable explanation."

189

The boys remained quiet. It was the very way in which the old man used his words that somehow led them to believe he would speak without being prompted. And as he lowered his aim to the ground, the old man's tongue began to wag in riddles.

*

"Horseshit!" yelled Bran.

"It's the God's honest truth, son," snapped Gregory, unable to persuade the boy further, no matter what he said or how he wished to say it.

Marcus thought on the idea a little, piecing the story together like a drawn-out puzzle. He took his time, wanting to believe the old man. Yet he wanted out of this God forsaken forest even more.

"You really saw him? I mean... really, you saw him?"

Gregory had no time to speak, as Bran continued his rant.

"Don't give in to this crap! The old man will tell us anything."

A short pause stretched into a longer pause.

"Did you really see him?" Marcus again asked, staring at Gregory's wrinkled features.

He nodded softly in return. "Aye, I did. I swear it." Placing his hand firmly on his chest, he continued. "As I stood out back that night, I heard the house door swing shut with an unsettling slam. I thought you all had fled after the telling of my evening's tale. I mean... who would blame you? I grabbed my rifle, which over the years had become nothing more than a force of habit. And I

190

began to make my way to the front of the house. Lo and behold, who do I see but young Jack, crossing the long moist grass. Of course, I thought nothing of it at first. It was a peaceful night, and his actions were innocent enough. For all I knew, the young man had simply abandoned his bed for the pleasure of sniffing the crisp night air. It's common enough, I remember thinking as I stood by secretly. So innocent in fact, that I thought it best not to disturb him and leave the lad to wander."

A branch snapped loudly in the distance, causing their heads to turn in surprise and Gregory to rest the gun to his shoulder. They waited, but alas, all remained quiet, and the old man continued to speak of his recent memories.

"I would have left him. I was about to, when from out of the corner of my eye, the bushes parted revealing a dark path, and your young friend was striding towards it. I called for him. I called at the top of my lungs, so I did. But it made no odds. The young man looked up to the evening sky as though my warnings were nothing but soft whispers. And it was as the path consumed him that those reflective eyes glowed through the night, staring back at me like a long lost friend I could never forget."

The old man paused momentarily. His voice broke a little with emotion retelling the tale.

Awkward, thought Bran.

Things certainly didn't look good for Jack now. And the very thought about his whereabouts was far from encouraging.

"So…" urged Marcus.

"So what?"

"Well, what happened?" asked Marcus. The dreadful considerations raced rapidly about in his overactive imagination.

"What do you think happened?" replied Gregory. "I followed, of course. I followed all night and all day, but it was no good. I couldn't find the lad. Couldn't find him anywhere. And by the time I returned to Thyme, you boys were long since gone.

"At first I didn't know what to think. Had your fate been the same as poor Jack's? Or had you simply travelled further into the estate?"

"Fate?" interrupted Bran, though Gregory continued regardless.

"It was when I saw your bikes missing, I knew there and then there was still hope."

"What fate?" Bran spoke more impatiently, his steps edging closer to the group, now forcing himself to be acknowledged.

"So, I followed your tracks. Took me most of the day, so it did. The overgrowth can get rather thick and tricky to search through this time of year. But I knew I'd find you, Marcus… you and your big mouthed friend here."

Both glanced quickly over to Bran.

"I just wasn't expecting to find the company you kept," said Gregory.

It was an obvious remark, though a remark that neither of them could explain. One thing, however, was certain; they wanted as far away from *it* as possible.

"What the hell was that thing?" asked Bran. His body trembled when he turned towards the stillness of the moonlit lake.

"Not here. Not now. We must move, and quickly," said Gregory, as he held his head high on lookout.

Marcus packed in a hurry, forgetting items that took many weeks to scrounge for this long awaited trip. He no longer cared. The tent was unhooked and shoved haphazardly into the rucksack, the pots and pans emptied and stored without a thought of cleaning them.

"How did you know?" asked Bran, looking hard at the back of Gregory's head. "How did you know it wasn't him? Wasn't Jack I mean?"

The old man turned slowly as he looked down to the boy, his chest rising and falling uneasily.

"Hmm… detail, boy, the smallest detail at that."

He turned again to avoid further questioning and stood anxiously at the lakeside.

"What detail?" persisted Bran. "Looked like the spitting image of him to me."

"And you call yourself a friend, do you?" the old man muttered. Again, he tossed the young boy a shifty eyed glance.

"Well, what was it then?"

"His eyes, boy. Something as innocent as those bright coloured eyes struck me immediately. I noticed them the day we coincidently crossed paths. Quite unusual wouldn't you agree? The right, blue. The left, a shade of green. It was a feature I acknowledged instantly, and strangely enough stuck to my mind onwards."

Bran hadn't the foggiest notion what this daft old prune was leading to.

So what if he had odd coloured eyes? Many weird people do.

"So? That explains nothing."

"It explains everything if you'd shut your trap and allow this tired man to finish."

Bran bit down on his tongue, though he didn't really want to. He wanted to understand, to agree. Yet he was undecided about his opinion of the old man. *Is he trustworthy?* he thought as his glance panned down to Marcus. *No point asking him.*

He needed the truth, and as quickly as possible. It was the only way to decide if the old man was reliable.

"What about his eyes?" said Bran.

Gregory smiled knowingly, his facial wrinkles deepening in the dense light.

"You really didn't notice?" he spoke as though disclosing a deep secret.

"No, what?" said Bran leaning forward, the anticipated answer pushed him towards the old man like a strong gust of wind.

"They were mirrored, boy."

"Mirrored?"

194

"Yes, meaning to say they were opposite. A complete reversal of those colourful eyes I bumped into just days prior. That's how I knew, son. And that's why…"

"Why you pulled the trigger?" interrupted Bran.

"Yes, boy."

Jesus! thought Bran. *The old man took a shot at nothing but a hunch. It could have been any of us.*

Bran quickly weighed up the possibilities. The absurdity of noticing something as simple as an alteration of eye colour seemed preposterous.

I mean, how reliable was the old timer's sight after all.

"You could have been wrong!" said Bran.

The old man shook his head with conviction as he bent forward, his face getting closer to Bran's. "No, son. Once you are able to see past the form *it* chooses, you can see only the truest form itself."

"It?" Bran was astounded, his mind spinning continuously.

Whatever Marcus's shaking hands were unable to secure now spilled out from the sides of each rucksack. He knelt and hastily placed the twisted straps over his shoulders. The unbalanced bag forced him to lean dramatically to his side which allowed even more equipment to spill from the bag's sleeves. Gregory and Bran watched as the boy panicked and again regained his balance.

"Well?" said Bran, referring to what was left unanswered.

"All good questions," replied Gregory. "But now is not the time, boy. We must leave here and seek shelter until sunrise. I know a place. The walk is not too far, but a mile or two."

And so, without further questioning they grabbed their gear, leaving the fire and allowing it to smoulder. The boys stood waiting as Gregory took one last look at the still, reflecting water. A gurgling noise began to rise from the lake's centre. Its sound, weak at first, slowly built as the old man watched. The surface began to ripple when a struggling, childlike hand broke through from below.

"Drowning!" called a frail voice and the hand swept beneath the waves.

We need to leave! Thought Gregory.

Bran and Marcus watched while the upset man stomped up from the bank and shoved the boys towards the blackest part of the woodland.

"Move boys!" demanded Gregory with a push.

Bran's stride was quick for a boy of his age, but the land was not on his side. It was more difficult than he imagined to travel through the darkness. Looking back, he found his eyes were finally adjusting and he caught sight of Marcus slowly gaining on him. The old man wasn't far behind as he aimed his rifle to the sky.

Bang!

The night was alive with the cries of shrieking birds: the same birds Bran had so quickly forgotten.

"That'll give us some time," Gregory shouted from behind.

They walked quickly, forcing their blood to pulse rapidly through their veins. The fear of the hundreds of pursuers overhead spurred them on. The sound gradually faded, and in time only their own heavy breathing was heard as they clambered on through a darkened world.

Chapter Thirty

It seemed the trail continued for hours. Each step sent them off balance as the boys' inappropriate footwear could gain little purchase on the protruding rocks and roots. The night had grown quiet. *Too quiet.* Now, only the chirrup of crickets sung out intermittently into the muggy air. They were tired now, all of them. So tired, that rest was becoming more necessary by the second. The very idea permeated their aching limbs. But regardless of their situation, the desire to sleep was almost overwhelming. They all began to crave these comforts more and more, and they yawned aloud, forgetting what could be lurking behind them

"Quiet now." Gregory was undeniably agitated. "Stop your moping and move."

Easy for him to say, thought Bran. He looked back at the old man, who had only his own weight to bear and was assisted by his rifle-come-walking-stick.

It had been a hard day for them all. No, that was an understatement. It had been a tense day. Inky visions washed over them, the memories staining their minds. Nothing had felt right since the day they had crossed the estate border. Nothing! And now, the very events that had taken place felt like nothing more than a terrifying dream.

Am I dreaming? Bran thought to himself. *Still dreaming?* as he inspected the sky for the hidden moon. At any moment he'd awaken and be huddled up in his sleeping bag, far away from this strange, unsettling place. Or better still, he would be protected and back in the safety of his very own home. Reminiscing on such matters provided a gentle warmth within him, a particular excitement that continued to drive both legs forward. *It'll all be over soon,* he thought. And once this entire charade had come to a close, his young life would continue exactly as it had before.

"Hold it," whispered Gregory.

The boys turned around, thankful for even a short break to help them calm their overly exerted, trembling legs.

"What is it now?" asked Bran with a sigh.

"Silence, boy."

The old man stood exceedingly still on a small mound of earth and closely observed the area, searching for higher ground. He glanced in every direction, once, twice, then a third time. Closing his eyes, he waited for a slight breeze to brush calmly over his clammy skin.

"What is it, sir?" questioned Marcus politely, though past tightly clenched teeth.

The leaden bag continued to pull on his scrawny shoulders, the straps burying deeper into flesh. Gregory opened his eyes and stared kindly at the boy who looked like he was about to drop where he stood.

"Nothing, son, nothing. Just lost my bearings a little, is all. But we're quite on schedule. Just a little farther this way." Pointing indecisively northeast before altering his direction again to west. He then led off, leaving the boys to follow sluggishly behind at their own pace.

"How much farther?" asked Marcus, now beginning to suffer and becoming too weak to keep up with the old man's energetic pace. Only an uncomfortable pause was returned. The old man continued to plough through the thorns, causing a swishing sound in his wake.

"Hey! How much farther?" *you stubborn old git*, said Bran. He was tempted to verbalise his thoughts.

"Just a little farther now, I say," hissed Gregory, without returning so much as a glance. "Quit your infantile dallying and make use of those youthful limbs while you still got 'em. It's been some years since I came this way, that's all. But we're almost there. I can feel it in these old bones of mine. Now move yourself!"

*

A little farther, my arse. Bran was thinking the trek would never cease.

To make matters worse, the slippery path they had come to detest had vanished and had been replaced by high grass interspersed with countless stems of stinging nettles.

"Ouch!" Marcus flinched when the entwined nettles stung viciously up his uncovered legs.

"Trust you to wear shorts on a night like this," said Bran, only now imagining the discomfort his friend suffered.

"Ouch," he hissed again, rubbing firmly to relieve his stinging calves. "How the hell was I meant to know we'd be trudging through a torture pit?"

Enough was enough. Bran couldn't take it anymore. If they didn't stop soon, there'd be no reason to stop at all.

"Hey! Greg! You're killing us back here."

The old man turned, his eyes burning with irritation at the loud and careless outburst.

"Have you gone mad, you idiotic child? You'll see the death of us." He lifted his index finger to his puckered mouth.

"You'll see the death of us both if we keep pushing on like this. How much longer?"

"Soon."

"How soon?"

"Soon, I tell ya! Keep your damn voice down!"

"You've been pitching that all night. A mile or so walk, you said. We've been staggering on for three fuckin' hours! We must be close to the border by now!" said Bran, now gripping Marcus by the arm and trying to steady his balance.

The old man raised his brow. Shaking his arms to relieve the stiffness caused by clearing a path.

"We... we ain't nowhere near the border, boy."

Bran released Marcus which let the exhausted boy fall flat.

"What?" demanded Bran. "You said an hour's walk?"

"I did. But not to the border. We need shelter, do we not?"

"And this is the nearest place? We'll be dead come morning."

A strong gust swept its way between the trees, shaking the grass with a violent wave. Bran was losing it, the anger buried within him stirred, and he looked at the old man with spite.

Breathe, just breathe, thought Bran as his chest rose and fell in anger.

"If we get into any trouble, it'll be on your head, Gregory!" hushed Bran. His words were forceful but were uttered with an air of calmness. He shoved his hands deep into his pockets, clenching them tightly, as his rage began to grow.

"Hmmm," said Gregory with a smirk, lifting his head to the cooling air. "The only thing that's gonna get you into trouble is that smart arsed mouth of yours."

Gregory hadn't seen it coming. Nor would he have expected it. But before he had time to consider anything, his face was planted firmly in the dirt. He was about to regain himself when a series of blows were struck hard to his shoulder blades, causing him to gasp and groan. Gregory spun around, latched onto Bran, and pulled him to the ground while he regained his position above. The struggle didn't end there. Bran clawed and squirmed from under the old man's weight.

Reaching out determinedly, Gregory took hold of the rifle, placing the wooden butt flat against Bran's chest and restraining his upper body from movement.

"Get off me!" huffed Bran. Saliva dripped from the corners of his mouth in the hopeless struggle.

"Not so tough now, huh?" tormented Gregory, their faces only inches apart. "You need to learn some God damn manners, boy! Show some frickin' respect!"

Bran hawked, spitting into the old man's crazed eyes, and accompanied the insult with a swift knee up between the legs. Gregory cried out in pain, as he collapsed and was pushed by Bran through the wall of weeds beside them. Bran lay still for a moment, catching his breath as consistent moans from Gregory were heard coming from the deep grass.

Marcus waited back in the shadows. His rucksack had been abandoned, left neglected on the boggy ground while he contemplated fleeing into the night.

"Call yourself a friend?" said Bran while bending over to gag as the night air scratched the roof of his mouth like sandpaper.

Marcus shrugged, embarrassed by his own cowardly desire to run.

"I… I'm sorry, alright? I just… I didn't think."

"Damn right, you didn't," said Bran, firmly tossing the bag back to Marcus. Its weight threw him backward like he'd been kicked by a mule.

"It's an instinctive response, that's all," explained Marcus, placing the straps around his sore shoulders. "When in danger, leg it!"

"I'll have to remember that one the next time you're in trouble."

"Whatever."

The grasses beside them rustled, bringing the conversation to a short and bitter halt. The groans of pain soon mellowed, quieting to a discomforted sigh as the old man struggled to stand. Still concealed, the boys waited somewhat fearfully as the wall of weeds began to sway and part. Gregory stepped out. His rifle was held tightly but pointed at the ground. His other hand pressed tentatively and lightly against his aching groin. Beads of sweat trailed down his head, smearing as they hit the deep creases of his brow. Gregory looked up, stumbling where he stood. Adjusting his focus, he gazed drunkenly upward. He looked to Marcus, remembering the young lad instantly. A politely inquisitive boy, struck from his bike and taking a nasty bump to the head. He smiled without humour before the boy beside Marcus flinched. His addled senses wandered, and he stared over the child, observing him with great curiosity. His head bobbed frantically, resembling a man who had drunk his fill. Yes, he remembered this boy, too.

Smart mouthed runt, he thought. The words fell silently from his lips. It all came flooding back so quickly. The old man strode forward.

"You little shite!" yelled Gregory, forgetting the danger his rattling voice may provoke.

He launched forward swiping at Bran with frail shaking hands. But the young lad dodged and weaved, finding it almost too easy to evade the old man's strike.

A hand intervened, pressing firmly on the man's chest.

"That's enough," begged Marcus, but he was unable to persuade the old man to end his deadly stare. Gregory continued to edge forward.

"Please!" Marcus insisted. "This isn't helping!"

Gregory held back. The pressure against his chest eased as his attention transferred to the boy's hand.

"I… I'm sorry boys," said Gregory shamefully. "I don't like being out here." He looked around suspiciously. "Don't like being out here at all."

Marcus removed his hand as the man stepped back, sulking. This night had been hard on all of them. The boys were too quick to complain about their own needs and had not spent time considering those of a tired old man.

"I'm sorry for charging you… and hitting you."

Marcus turned, looking at Bran with a raised brow.

"OK, OK," replied Bran. "And for kneeing you right in the bollocks."

Gregory muttered, then smirked. "Hmm… lucky shot."

The bitter tenseness eased like a pitiful rant that had run its childish course. And although the quarrel was dead and done, each of them waited for the other to speak.

"So… where to now?" asked Bran.

"Well… I …" the old man hesitated. "The truth of the matter is, much has changed since I last trod these grounds, so much that I barely recall it at all."

"So, we're lost?" said Bran, rolling his eyes.

"Not lost… I didn't say that. Just a little off course is all." He spoke with a reassuring wink.

We're lost then, Bran tried to hide his disappointment behind a forced smile.

The old man fumbled about himself, rearranging his shirt and trousers before gazing past the woodland's upper reaches. The moon was at its highest, a thin cloud veiling its existence in a dreary glow as Gregory attempted to navigate their way. Deep in thought, he scratched at his beard. He was astounded at the very idea that he had lost his bearing.

"Any luck?" pestered Bran.

"Give me a second, boy."

"You actually know how to navigate from those stars then?"

"Well, of course I do. Ain't pretending, am I!" whispered Gregory. "I… well… I've just not exercised the practice in quite some years."

Bloody smashing, thought Bran, who was by now getting so tired, even the idea of sleeping on bare earth began to sound appealing. Leaving the old man to mumble, Bran walked away. Quietly leaning himself against the cushioned body of his backpack and breathing heavily, he rested. His eyes were losing the good fight to stay focused.

"Wait!" yelled Marcus, stopping Gregory in his tracks and causing Bran to jump from his near sleep.

He wandered off in the distance, peering through the grass where Gregory had fallen. "Get over here," he cried and beckoned them ecstatically, his flailing arm rotating like a turbine on a blustery day.

Old Gregory staggered there first, looking through the collapsed vegetation with a squint. He let out a joyful exclamation and immediately patted Marcus on the back.

"Way to go, son! That's a sharp eye you have." Gregory clenched his palm tighter on the boy's shoulder.

Hiding a sly smile, Marcus buried his mouth into his sleeve, embarrassed by the compliment but also feeling particularly proud of his find.

"Comin'," said Bran with a huff, carelessly dragging his bag across the ground and causing it to rip. "Oh, for fuck sake!"

He stopped but saw nothing. The darkness had seen to that. But the more he concentrated past the chaotic view of spreading ferns and trees, a pointed object caught his eye, peeking out of the distance.

"Is that a house?" asked Bran.

Gregory's smirk dwindled as he looked out to the unlit shelter.

"Was a house, yes," said Gregory. "It's the old Reservist Outpost. Wouldn't have been used since the searches." A loud gulp lingered until he regained his will to speak. "Still, it will see us safe for the night."

A spine-tingling howl twisted around the trees. The sound sent goosebumps crawling up each and every spine as they resisted the urge to glance back. The rural land lay quiet. The howl echoed into nothingness as the branches rustled overhead.

Let's get moving, thought Gregory.

One by one their bodies vanished into the thicket, determination pulsing through them, as they fought through pathless trails.

Amongst the Mists

Chapter Thirty-One

Thee entrance slammed violently behind them with a loud, shaking thud, loosening the door from its frame. Inside the hut was clouded in dust. It floated down from the ceiling's beams in a thick, snow-like flurry after the disturbance by the dramatic invasion. Heavy coughing filled the darkness as Marcus darted his hand into a pocket for his puffer, purely out of instinct. His mouth remained blanketed beneath his shirt for protection as a hacking cough took hold.

They looked around but couldn't see much. It was dark, not overly unsettling, but a dense darkness nonetheless. Clumps of dust specks began to settle, leaving only a musty sort of smell that spoke of disuse. Yet it was to be expected. It appeared that no one had visited here in many years, not even by chance.

The small rectangular room didn't hold much. Neither did it provide any means of comfort to its guests. Broken chairs and stools lay rotting on their sides. Cupboard doors left open displayed shattered shelves, in most cases hanging only by a rusted hinge. Fabric curtains hung shredded over small glassless windows, the material devoured by winged insects. A stone chimney arch stood solidly at the room's centre. The grate itself was filled with a collection of fallen birds' nests that had accumulated throughout the seasons.

"Least we can get a fire going," croaked Bran before beginning to choke. "I can't help but feel outside would be healthier," he continued, as the longstanding dust continued to settle on his lungs.

"Nonsense," said Gregory.

The old man barged past, deliberately swiping aside the clutter, and began to tap on the floorboards with the ball of his foot.

God's sake, thought Bran, watching the old man clear away the jumbled mess. The release of an inhaler disturbed his train of thought as Marcus sucked on his container like his life depended on it.

Bran slumped down beneath the glassless window, the cool air softly caressing his neck with each twitch of the ragged curtains.

A board loosened below the old man's feet. He knelt, digging his fingers deep into the cracks, and prised the plank from its place.

"Ah, ha!" he yelped with excitement, his hands diving deep into the filthy hole.

Scraping his palms along the ground below, the boys watched as he stretched to reach his target.

"Gotcha!" he cried and began to pull himself up.

A dark unlabelled bottle was clutched tightly in his cobweb ridden fingers, the top still securely sealed after years of abandonment.

"Always knew I left a stash here." Gregory was overjoyed with his find. His hands smeared a grey silky web along the breast of his shirt before again diving down to retrieve more. A lantern was lifted from its dusty grave, the handle flaking shreds of rust as the body rocked like a cradle beneath.

"Hmm…. out of oil," the old man said. "I'll snoop around. There's bound to be some hiding."

Bran and Marcus watched as the elderly man, still on his knees, moaned his way along the floor. Finding comfort against the wall, he held the bottle lovingly in his hands as though it were his only prized possession.

"Don't suppose you got any food stashed away down there?" asked Bran, whose stomach by now was beginning to cramp.

"No…" replied Gregory. "Though would you really want it if there were?"

Touché, thought Bran, finally resting his head back against the wall.

*

The night dragged on slowly. Despite their uneasiness about staying, the outpost, regardless of its filth, soon began to grow in comfort. Its four timbered walls shielded them from the strangeness of the murky woodland. Oil was carefully poured into the lantern from a red spouted can they found high on a shelf. Marcus had matches, thousands of them. Having no desire to wait, he handed the old man a box he kept ready at his disposal. A brief spark struck the head of the match, momentarily lighting the small room with a single flash of light. An unappealing bleakness followed as the lantern caught flame, slowly glowing brighter as it lifted the room from darkness.

"There we are," said Gregory. "Much better."

Bran looked up. Spiders and insects crawled across the wooden joists, and the orange light at his feet projected ghastly shadows onto the walls and ceiling of the hut. It looked like something from a horror tale, sickening Bran's stomach, as giant shadows crept unnaturally across the ghostly lit space. None of this appeared to alarm the old man, who sat back happily on his rear, impatiently attempting to access the contents of his beloved bottle. The shadows of monsters continued to hang and dance around him.

"You boys wouldn't happen to be carrying a corkscrew, would you?"

Marcus patted about his pockets, pulling out a small steel penknife he'd been eager to use since the journey started. "Here," he said, sending the knife sliding noisily across the warped floor. Bran stomped his foot. The vicious impact sent a howling racket bouncing off walls.

"Hang on a damn second," said Bran sternly. "You just plan on getting sauced? You owe us an explanation."

"Is that so?" replied Gregory.

"Damn straight you do," said Bran as he twisted the ball of his foot against the knife to draw it back. "That thing out there, what was it?"

The old man sank even farther, bringing his knees to his chest as he cradled the bottle between them. "I'm afraid I ain't been completely truthful with you boys." His voice was gruff. "But, how could I?" he asked himself shamefully. "How could I retell those stories, relive those times. The same memories, those same sounds that have haunted my every waking breath for all too long."

He held the bottle in his hand now, pressing the cooling black glass against his temple.

"Yes, you're quite right," Gregory continued. "I do indeed owe you both just that. But hear me now, boys. You will not gain the answers you seek until my mind is numbed."

Gregory held out his hand, his palm trembled uncontrollably in the flickering light as Bran slowly relaxed his foot. The man fiddled with the penknife desperately, yearning for the taste of that sweet fix to dance on the tip of his tongue. He swigged impatiently, guzzling back the long awaited pleasure before lowering the bottle and taking an exaggerated gasp for air.

"You'll tell us now? Everything?" asked Marcus, his body unmoved from the corner of the room.

Old Gregory took another long gulp and paused, slowly swirling the remaining spirit.

"Aye, I'll tell you."

"Everything?"

"Everything I wish to remember."

Amongst the Mists

Chapter Thirty-Two

It was never supposed to be this way. This was not what an adventure was supposed to be. And as time cruelly froze for Olivia, she couldn't help but consider what made her long to chase it. She was in no way a religious minded girl, except for grace before dinner, but that was different. And perfectly justifiable. If she didn't pray before meals, she simply didn't eat. It was a no brainer for her, and Olivia accepted this to gain exactly what she wanted. That and to keep her relatives' lectures at bay. The whole ordeal just felt far too pointless for her liking. To her, it was time that would've easily been spent doing something much more constructive. She recalled sitting hand in hand around her family table while her mother spoke thankfully to an almighty power, one which Olivia didn't believe existed.

How could it?

The dilemma had repeated endlessly in her mind for years, but no more so than now. I mean, how could this higher power truly exist? Wasn't the one true God supposed to look down on her, watch over her, make sure that no harm would ever befall her? She was a child after all, and an innocent one at that. She pondered the idea. Perhaps it was her lack of faith that stood against her. When all the family prayed silently, Olivia's

215

mind would wander, thinking of anything but what to be thankful for.

Yes, that would probably be it.

But as the cold wind swept over her uncovered feet, and the moonlight was weakened by the clouds, Olivia couldn't help but wonder if it was all too late. Had she had her chance to believe? A chance where she had epically failed? Maybe that's what led her here. Maybe that's why the Almighty had forsaken her.

For the first time in a very long time, her hands knitted softly together. She hesitated at first, glaring at the gesture anxiously, not knowing where to begin. Should she speak aloud or in her head? Would the good Lord hear her words, or by now would he look upon her as a fraud, still pretending to pray as she had done many times before. Olivia knew what to say. She had heard her mother repeatedly speak the same, memorised lines since she could remember.

Just get on with it.

Olivia's knuckle gently touched the skin of her lips. Both her eyes squeezed shut, her position unmoved, as she began to utter the words.

"Lord God, I pray for Your protection as I begin this day. You are my hiding place, and under Your wings I can always find refuge. Protect me from trouble wherever I go, and keep evil far from me. No matter where I am, I will look to You as my Protector, the One who fights for me every day. Your love and faithfulness, along with Your goodness and mercy, surround me daily, so I will not fear whatever might come against me. My trust is in You, God, and I give thanks to You for Your love and protection. Amen."

She opened an eye. Just one. Nothing had changed.

"What?" she spoke aloud. "Didn't you hear me?" questioning the sky above as she walked on through the cold. "OK, how's this?"

Her hands clapped violently together, sending the sound ricocheting back from the trees. She spoke the words in anger, making sure that this time the prayer remained unaltered. If it had worked for her mother all these years, by God it would work for her, too. She repeated the prayer.

Olivia's words fell flat, the final sentence disappearing into the coldness as she waited on nothing to appear. She kicked the ground angrily, stubbing her toe in the process. She cried aloud with the pain, feeling irritated with herself. I mean, what did she really expect? Belief itself was more than muttering a few magic words. And she knew that. But she was desperate, so desperate she had to at least try. But a trial was all it had been, a simple attempt to regain her faith, if she ever had any to begin with. Looking down at her foot, she saw the blood oozing from the edge of her split toenail while the pulsating pain caused her to grind her teeth. It was utter nonsense, every word of it. And she pledged right then and there she would never pray again.

Footsteps caught her attention; a clear sound of shuffling through fallen leaves came from behind her.

You can tell an awful lot about the way someone walks. The eagerness of these steps was clear. Olivia followed secretly, completely forgetting her injured foot as she weaved through the thicket. The footsteps stomped, and heavy panting fell on her ears.

A person!

She caught a glimpse of motion above the hill's crest, forcing her to scurry forward using her hands to guide the way. Reaching the top had been far from easy. Although not a steep incline, it felt like the hardest thing she had ever done. Supporting herself, the air alone seemed to sicken her stomach and caused her head to spin. It took her only a moment, but by the time she regained her bearings, the footsteps had already died.

"Hello?" Olivia called softly, half expecting someone was now watching her. No one was. At least, not that she could tell. The night again fell deathly quiet. The same forest floor was listening to her every move as she fought through her fears. It was less frightening on top of the hill. The trees thinned out considerably, welcoming the sky and permitting the moon to shine, should the clouds allow. It offered no more safety. Yet still, she felt all the safer for it. She wandered the higher ground, using the time to let nerves calm.

Maybe there was no one, Olivia thought indecisively. *Maybe I'm just chasing demons.*

She reluctantly knew all about demons. She had been taught relentlessly since the day she was born; if you didn't have strength to fight them, you would undoubtedly become one yourself. The full moon crept from behind a sluggish cloud, sending a spectacular glow to illuminate the forest floor in a chalky whiteness. It was quite magnificent: the most magical thing she had seen, as moonlight shimmered softly across her skin. A noise focussed her attention. The sound came from high above her and was followed by an unsettling and lingering creaking. The sound remained as Olivia dashed to find it, the loose earth burying deep between her toes. She looked up; her hair draped wildly over her face. There, in the whitened gleam, a man hovered. His elegant glide swung weightlessly. She crept forward slowly, desperate to see his face. Yet still, she could not. His features were masked by shadows, no matter how close she approached. A grunt burst from the man, followed by a desperate gasp as he kicked the open air. The figure twitched and squirmed. A frayed rope was tucked deep beneath his jaw, its length viciously shuddering towards the sky. She couldn't watch further and blocked the sight with her arm. The groans began to soften, telling Olivia that death was soon to come. Holding her breath, she listened as life escaped him. The tormented groans decreased into nothing more than gentle whispers.

Snap!

The break was followed by a lifeless thud hitting the ground. Her eyes remained covered, but she could breathe now and listen to the man who now began to weep more and more loudly until the sobbing terminated in a hysterical, maddened wail. She contemplated helping, but only for a moment. As quickly as she had the thought, the cries stilled and a voice spoke out in sadness.

"Grandchild?"

Olivia's arm dropped immediately, and she saw the knotted rope piled across the fallen leaves.

The man himself was gone.

Amongst the Mists

Chapter Thirty-Three

A heavy downpour fell over the land. The thunderous sound of rain echoed about the room with a tremendous clatter, accompanied by the uneasiness caused by a whistling woodland wind. Drops fell from the collapsing roof splashing like bullets to the boards below.

"So," Marcus began. "Where's Jack?"

The bottle fell roughly to the old man's side with a heavy *clunk*, the beverage swirling inside.

"You see… right there, son, you asked the wrong question."

"I did?" replied Marcus.

"Indeed," said Gregory with a brief yet certain nod. "The question is not where is? But who took?"

"OK… who took him then?"

"A Sprit, son."

221

"What the hell is a Sprit?"

"Just what we call them. A form of spirit if you like. Though not at all pleasant. It is a mirrored image of good, forged this way by the doing of mankind."

"So, why is it called a Sprit?"

"We couldn't possibly call it a ghoul or a goblin. It wouldn't have been fair for the children at the time."

For God's sake, here we go, thought Bran.

"Spirits, really? That's all you've got?"

"Did I stutter, boy? Hmm?" Gregory gave a harsh drunken glare toward Bran. "Yes, spirits. At least that's what we've been led to believe. Saying that, there is no proof, of course. However, there rarely is with this kind of thing."

An air of confusion was evident on the boys' faces as the old man spoke in ghostly riddles. And now only the sound of rain filled the room.

"Tell me, boys. Do you recall the story I spoke of?" asked Gregory with a belch. The bottle was returned tightly to his lips.

"Of Thyme? Yes, of course," spoke Marcus. He had remembered it clearly.

Gregory slouched a little farther in his position and gave an honest glance their way.

"There's much more to it than that. Much more." He spoke quietly, his humble voice fitting with the bouncing sound of rain.

"The night my granddaughter vanished, I consoled my wife. I held her firmly, rocking her. Oh, how she wept. The pain inside her bursting out in pitiful screams and sobs. I told her... I said I would find our sweet girl. Find her and bring her home. Then, and only then, would we leave Thyme for good. She buried her face deep into my chest, begging me to promise as her exhausted body shook with grief. I left her alone that night. Alone and sick with worry as I pounded on the doors of the town's folk, begging them as one desperate man to another to search by my side once more.

"Well, some men agreed, others cowered behind their doors. No matter how I pleaded their minds would not be changed, fearing what might happen to their already broken families. It was a reasonable decision by them. I see that now. Still, I cursed them all the same, screaming pitifully as they slammed their doors in my face. Good men held me back, persuading me enough time had already been lost. And they were right. We gathered what was needed with little time to spare. I don't recall much, wanting only to leave. The weather was harsh, I remember that part well. The day's gentle snowfall had rapidly brewed, churning into stinging sleet that grazed and cut my flesh. Just five men went with me, all fine men at that. Though we never spoke again after this. Maybe it was for the best.

"We made our way out of the village, watching as men who refused to help stood by, partially concealed behind the protection of their shabby curtains. I looked at them with hate, an emotion I have come to show all too often. But as we continued to walk, those same cowardly faces soon blurred and disappeared into the blizzard, and soon enough so did Thyme. Only the glow of the street lamps blinked dimly from afar, as thick clouds built across the rural landscape. The men called out for my grandchild as we spread out. At times, the men who scouted next to me would vanish, engulfed by the suffocating fog that trapped us in its maze. I painfully screamed out her name. The cold air stabbed my lungs like a dagger to the heart.

"Soon, we sheltered beneath the trees. The men fell down, already exhausted from the incline. I saw defeat in their faces, yet I said nothing as I determinedly pushed them forward. 'Stop,' one of the chaps shouted. Which man it was I couldn't be certain. But in his hand, dangling in the fierce wind, was a narrow blue ribbon. 'It's hers,' I yelled with sorrow. 'It's hers. We must move.' I grabbed the ribbon, wrapping it tightly around my wrist, blessing the cloth with the gentle touch of my lips. Yes, my granddaughter had been here. And with that thought, I pushed on purposefully deeper into the woodland and into the grounds of Sleathton.

"We walked on for miles. So far in fact, that I didn't know where we were, blinded by my objective and the promise made to my beloved. The snow had ceased, though frost spread fiercely across the mud and trees, giving all nature a glaze of white. It was the early hours of the morning when we thought our luck had changed. Each man had grown tired of his own voice, leaving only the sound of frozen ground as ice crunched beneath our boots. Our breathing was heavy, our minds dazed. And just as our sluggish pace began to halt, we heard a noise from the gloom of trees."

*

The lantern flickered on the floor boards, its light sending shadows dancing around the room, not at all welcome given the story being told. Bran looked up, watching the curtains as they blew overhead, revealing a glimpse of stars that gleamed past the movement of branches. He moved himself nervously, edging closer to Marcus, and sat at his young friend's side.

"What was the noise?" asked Marcus.

The old man was about to speak, but then suddenly looked at Bran.

"Something I'm sure young Bran here will be all too familiar with. It was a cry. A plea for help."

Bran tensed. And although he could not see it, he sensed the colour drain from his face, his memory recalling the haunting resonance of drowning screams.

"Cry for help?" queried Marcus. "Your granddaughter then?"

"No," replied Gregory abruptly. "Though how I wish it was." He looked away from the now very pale Bran.

"Our feet stood dead on solid ground, as each man stared at the next. At first, we believed we had imagined it. Ridiculous, I know! The very idea of five men imagining the exact same thing was unbelievable. But then as we began moving again, the voice echoed through the forest once more. 'I'm here!'

"The men were stunned. *Could it be?* I thought. My determination was driving me onwards, leaving the rest of the men to follow on. In that very moment, I had found a new reserve of energy. Adrenaline pulsed through my veins, my legs pounded through the undergrowth, moving faster than I ever thought possible. I called her name repeatedly until I was hoarse. I listened closely for her response, for her delicate voice to caress my frost-bitten ears and put my heart at ease. 'I'm here!'

"The sound was so clear, my head whipped from side to side in order to gauge its direction. Shortly after this, I realised I was alone. I had lost the others in my haste. Stopping, I listened. The panicked yelling of the men came from all directions of this strangely disturbing place.

"I felt like a stag caught in the headlights. As I glimpsed a movement behind a wall of spreading oak trees, I ran forward in anticipation. But there was only a distorted shape shadowed in the gloom. 'My dear,' I called sadly. 'Come… come home my darling, it… it's me.' But I was ignored, and the shape was absorbed back into the shadows.

"Again, I ran, my feet slipping beneath me. Reaching the oaks, the forest dipped and thickened. I stumbled and fell, the ground too challenging for me to keep my pace. A coldness bit cruelly at my feet. Before I realised it, my ankles sank down past the surface and into the soggy earth. The ground had become soft and boggy, slowly deepening into an unpleasant swamp. Still the cries went on. The further I went, the deeper the pool became. I'd heard of such a place before. From time to time the local hunting groups spoke of its borders over beers in the bar. It was a dark, troublesome place, they told me. A place to avoid, where strange things had been seen. Though I was never known to be an irrational man, and being typically logical, I shrugged off their stories as nothing more than idiotic folklore. Their humorous tale was fit only to terrify the most gullible children. Yes, I knew where I walked; it was the Brocton Swamp.

"Slowly I waded into the black water until it was at my knees. Shortly after, the curious voice ceased. Scanning the swamp for guidance, I called out to my men. But it was hopeless. There was nothing but silence. Needless to say, I was lost. Not only had I lost my bearings, but I was terrified. Afraid not only for my grandchild, but also for my fearful wife at home. At this particular time, dare I say it, I was considerably afraid for myself. Though I will tell you this. I was never one to be afraid of the dark, but there was something different about this place, something sinister. I could sense it in the air as I began to struggle in my exhaustion. Fatigued, I leant against a dying birch tree. The bark withered instantly at my touch. Giving myself a moment, I devised a plan. *Turn back,* I thought. Though at this particular time, I was unable to determine which direction would lead me there. The forest ceiling hung low, and the feeling of being trapped caused my heart to flutter as I scrambled through fallen branches. I was disoriented and fell head first into the slimy water. I gasped with shock as the coldness jolted my body. It was as I regained my balance, that an unnatural, albeit rather harmonic, sound rang through the night. I had never heard such a relentless static hum. Its tone rising and falling in frequency, making the water around my knees churn."

"Then what happened?" Bran interrupted Gregory in mid-thought.

"Well, if you shut the hell up, you'll find out," said the old man impatiently, remembering his place to continue.

"I walked on, of course. I mean, what else could I have done? But regardless of where I turned, no matter where I trod, the forest grew thicker and that dreadful humming closed around me. There were times I felt I was going mad, watching as silhouetted figures stood beside the line of trees, their existence nothing more than imaginary. Things seemed to go from bad to worse. A dense mist rolled across the swamp, concealing the murky water, soon completely engulfing me. I had never known a mist like it, not in my life, as the damp air struck my lungs with a deathly purpose.

"Well, boys, I thought my time was up. My aching bones swayed beneath me. The very idea of finding my way started to become all too doubtful. 'I'm here...' the voice called and nothing more.

"I yelled instantly in desperation. But unfortunately, the voice did not reply. A break in the wall of mist showed briefly ahead. And beyond it stood a line of rigid shadows. I discovered soon enough they were nothing but tall standing stones. I staggered forward breathlessly to escape the wretched swamp. At last, my hand held firmly against the surface of cold, mossy stone. A strange impression overtook me as though a hand rested on my own. I slapped it away with a frightened flick as I stomped my feet on firmer ground.

"By now, this infernal humming was resonating in waves around the stones. The touch to each rock vibrated up my arm as I waved my one free hand through the fog. My eyes watered from the sting of coldness, my head dizzy from the unsettling sound. Drowsily, I slumped on a filthy mound, watching as the mist climbed hauntingly above the towering stones. I felt hypnotised for a time, unable to turn my eyes away from the scene before me. Again I questioned my own sanity. My heart palpitated as my body shook with fear. With wide-eyes, I looked on into the unknown. Something stirred there.

"Rising from the filth, I stumbled forward. Each step slow and weak, I blindly pushed my way through. 'Who's out there!' I demanded. My courage was admittedly hanging by a thread. Footsteps pattered about the ground, weaving in and out of the swamp with quick splashes, sending my fears soaring. 'God, where the hell are you?' I yelled. Defeated, I could only weep.

'I'm here.' It hushed.

"I looked up. And in the blink of an eye my heart lifted. There she was. My grandchild. My sweetheart, looking so precious, so vulnerable, as she stood knee deep in the pool encircled by giant stones. She silently gazed at me with those beautiful eyes that I had come to love so much. 'There you are,' I mumbled, trying for a calm face. 'Come, hold my hand, and we'll go home.' I stepped into the freezing pool, holding my hand out to guide her. But she stood motionless, like she was paralysed. It was then my leg snagged against a hidden root, or so I thought. As I tugged to break free, I fell backward, flapping my arms like a mad man to stay afloat. The grasp around my leg loosened and bubbles rose to the surface. I cowered in terror at the horrifying sight of a small hand as it bobbed in the water before its body appeared. Struggling to stand, I tried to get away before an object blocked my path and sent me into another violent stumble. But this time, the waters did not catch me. I turned, afraid to see what lay slumped at the water's edge. Another body. I heaved at the image, bringing up the remains of a festively cooked meal. Gathering myself for the sake of my grandchild, I pulled myself up tall and strong and watched as the mist thinned across the swamp.

"Bodies lay scattered. Dumped disgustingly across the muddy swamp. Children from our village, their limbs plump and swollen from death.

Oh, how I wished I'd have saved them. I looked at their twisted bodies. Frost had tinted their skin in the darkness, and their eyes were still open and wide with fear. The mist slid over them like in a dream. A life's-worth of unshed tears rolled freely down my cheeks, the cold freezing them as they fell. The vision sickened me, knowing that this is what could have become of my granddaughter. My hand reached out once more, shaking as it stretched for her to take it. 'Come!' I demanded. The quiver in my voice was uncontrollable. But still, she would not budge. She held her ground, firmly gazing with untrusting eyes at the one who loved her most. She looked as though I was the beast that stole her. 'Please, darling.' I begged again, falling deeper into despair. 'Take my hand... please.' But I was too late.

"She shuddered as the hum deepened. A quake shook the land beneath our feet, forcing the trees to sway and lean as the devil pulled relentlessly on their roots. The fog thickened around her, hugging her, demanding she stay. But I wouldn't have it! I panicked, lunging forward through the greyness to reach her. And then it appeared. I had sensed it for a time, like eyes stalking us from the dark. Yet still I doubted my perception. It was a formless shadow. A shadow of no human that faded amongst the mist. It lingered in silence as it crept behind my dearest. The child sobbed aloud, feeling its presence, her tearful face buried deep into her tiny hands. I didn't know it would be the last time I'd stare into her eyes. Such stunning blue eyes. 'Get away from her!' I cried as the shadow grew over her and shrouded her in darkness. I stopped in my tracks as two hollow eyes watched me. Like torches in the night, their stare was cold and deathly and followed my every move. 'Leave her alone.' I whimpered, daring not to move. A transparent arm manifested from a cloud of nothingness and rested weightlessly on her shoulder.

"The creature let out a screeching shriek, its pitch high and distorted as its grasp held her firm. 'Stop that!' I screamed. The girl cried out in fear.

"The trees crowded in around us, spinning grotesquely like a fairground ride. The crackle of static, the land's constant hum, all filled my head with a pressure I couldn't bear. I looked into those big vacant eyes that stared blankly in return. Its unearthly scream continued from a mouthless face. It was now or never. I lunged forward to reach her. My jump fell short, and I slipped into the Stygian pool. The sound of the girl's scream was muffled through murky water. A small hand reached out to grasp my own and pulled on the ribbon, still wrapped around my wrist. Everything was quiet after that. And as my head emerged, the pull on my arm slackened and the ribbon was gone from my wrist.

"There was only silence after that. The events of the night drained away before me. The pool rippled with green foam, its thin layers of algae sticking to me as I pushed myself up from the bank. Spinning around on the spot, one thing was clear. She was gone. But not only my granddaughter, so was the shadow that bound her. The heavy mist began to clear, revealing the swamp as nothing more than the wasteland it truly was. The corpses of the missing lay still, the gentle nudge of the water rocking them slowly as though lulling them to sleep. Emotion overcame me as I let out a sound not even I could recognise. Orange rays of the morning sun shone in beams through the branches. The sensation of mild warmth washed across my face. Crawling to the standing stones, I wept. My broken heart was torn from my body while I bellowed in grief. 'Where are you!' I screamed, my inconsolable voice echoing through the empty land.

"Lying on my back, the garish light above blinded me as my head became weak and weary. 'Where are you?' I whispered, as my vision darkened, the pounding in my chest slowed. I was on the brink of passing out, or death. I couldn't be sure. But as my mind fell numb, and the familiarity of dreams overpowered me, a shallow voice pressed softly against my ear. 'I'm here,' it spoke. I… I don't remember the rest."

Amongst the Mists

Chapter Thirty-Four

Gregory's tale halted as he drained his bottle. The boys felt so very sad for the elderly man who for years had drunk away his memories.

"Sorry about your granddaughter," said Marcus, sincerely.

The old man nodded, acknowledging the sentiment as the bottle rolled across the floor.

"So… did your men find you in the end?" asked Bran. His arrogant persistence to know more was exceedingly dismissive of the old man's feelings.

"On the contrary," said Gregory with a roll of his eyes. "They most certainly did not. No one found me. I woke on the edge of the Brocton Swamp some days later with no memory of how I'd come to be there. In time, the trail brought me back to Thyme. Several villagers caught me wandering, their concerned expressions suggested

I looked closer to being dead than alive. They guided me back to the Lodge house after covering my frostbitten skin with fleece. When I finally reached home, my wife rushed eagerly to the porch. I knew it wasn't how I looked that broke her, but that I was alone.

"I ate in silence that afternoon; my spoon rattled uncontrollably against the bowl of hot soup. I pushed it aside as my appetite had vanished, and demanded to see the men who travelled in my party. I had much to discuss, and I thought only they would truly understand my state of mind. It took some time, more than necessary, but eventually, a man came rapping at my door: one of the men who'd refused my need for help. He was a lanky chap, in his late thirties…. early forties maybe… Anyhow, he insisted I sit while he spoke. His nasal voice wound on like nails to a chalkboard. His deep set eyes looked at me with great intensity. Regardless, I listened to the weasel as he spoke with grunts and stutters.

"See here, Mr Degg," he said. "You see, well the thing is. I mean… what I want to say is…"

"Spit it out, man," I said impatiently, though it made no odds as the man continued to choke on his words. "Ah, be gone with you! And make yourself useful. Fetch the men that were brave enough to search by my side."

"The man straightened his back, brushing his sweaty palms up and down his thighs.

"Well, that's just it, Mr Degg, sir. The men… well, they never returned.

"My grip tightened on the edge of my seat while my heart began to pound.

"None of them?"

"None of them, Mr Degg, sir." the man said in certain agreement.

"Then what are you doing here? You cowardly runt. Go... go gather the villagers and search the woods."

"My wife entered the room with a tray to offer the man a hot drink. The tray shook noticeably when she rested it on his lap.

"It will do you no good, Mr Degg," said the man before taking a sip from the steaming mug.

"Cowards! The lot of you. Nothing but a bunch of good for nothing –

"Now, Gregory! That'll do," my wife said. The warmth of her hand stroking softly against my forearm calmed me.

"We... we need to gather the town. There are good men out there, and God forbid anything should have happened to them. It was on my watch."

"The man said nothing. His eyes darted skittishly to my wife before returning to my own.

"You deaf as well as sheepish? Go gather the villagers I say."

"The villagers have already gone, Mr Degg."

"Gone? What do you mean gone? You mean hiding?"

"No, just what I said, sir," said the man sheepishly. "They have all left, every one of them."

"Yet you're still here?"

"Only in passing. My family is waiting for me at your gate. See for yourself."

"I stood quickly, almost forgetting the tiredness that numbed my shaking legs. He was indeed truthful. Beyond the frosty window, stood his wife and child... his remaining child. Waiting with luggage scattered around their feet.

"Why?" I asked, turning back to the man who looked ready to leave.

"Need you ask, Mr Degg?"

"No, I suppose not, but I would respect a truthful answer, nonetheless."

"The man didn't return to his seat but began to button up his winter coat while he spoke, leaving the tea bag in his mug to brew.

"We are only human, Mr Degg. We can't take any more of this. None of us. When you and your party didn't return, well... it made things so much worse. People were frightened, Mr Degg. They did what any family would do once their homes became unsafe. We are one of those families. And I, like you, have suffered greatly."

"So, when did they all leave?" I asked.

"The day before last. Most walked. I expect they found rides at the main road."

"I still call it cowardice."

"I wouldn't, far from it. I would call it bravery."

"Bah," I said with a stubborn wave of the arm.

"Then... call it fear, Mr Degg.'

"Fear can be beaten."

"In this case, I dare say it has beaten us already. Including you, Mr Degg," said the man with a questioning stare. "You are not the same man who caused havoc at my door some nights ago. I can see it in your eyes. Something happened to you out there?"

"Preposterous!" I muttered, avoiding the man's interrogation with a disinterested shrug.

"The conversation fell somewhat flat after that, as a blast of wind hit heavily over the rooftop.

"I must leave, Mr Degg," said the man, now reaching out his hand.

"I shook it. The firm grip of my shake caused him to stagger slightly.

"All the best to you then." I spoke with a disapproving tone as the man regained his balance.

"And to you, Mr Degg. And to you."

"And with those words he went to the door, stopping before he opened it.

"My son… Mr Degg. My boy. You remember him?"

"I do."

"If you should ever find him, would you do right by him? See my boy gets a proper burial? I can't bear the thought of him still lying out there in the mud."

"My mind shuddered at the vivid memory of the boy half submerged in the swamp. *A nightmare possibly?* I thought. However, I had neither the strength nor the desire to tell the man what I may or may not have seen.

"I shall," I responded, my head sinking low past my shoulders. The door closed gently in the hallway, and the sound of my wife's footsteps were left again to echo as she roamed the house. I watched from the corner window. The man rejoined his family, embracing them for a brief moment before gathering their belongings and beginning their walk. And just like that, within those few seconds, we were left alone. A tight hold wrapped around my waist to the sound of gentle sobs. My eyes didn't stray, though I cupped both hands over hers and squeezed her tightly.

"What do we do?" she whimpered, her voice partially muffled as she buried her face deep in my back.

"We stay, my dear."

"We don't leave Thyme like the rest?"

"No," I said, watching as the departing shadows disappeared down the woodland road."

Amongst the Mists

Chapter Thirty-Five

A bird landed on the rooftop, scurrying and hopping to the chimney, and making an ugly screech.

"If that thing falls down here, I'm eating it," said Bran, holding both hands on his belly as it began to rumble violently. "You sure we ain't got anything left?"

Tired, Marcus shrugged and leant forward. "It's worth a look, I guess." And he began to empty the bags.

An irritating noise accompanied the search. The sound rattled about the room like a fire alarm losing its juice. Old Gregory sat slumped with his chin pushed forward into his chest, crushing his windpipe as he let out the most disturbing snore.

"Reckon he's alright like that?" said Marcus with a nod of his head.

"Yeah," said Bran, whose eyes were getting heavy. "He's just hammered."

"How can you tell?" asked Marcus. His attention was again distracted from the bags and over to the slouched, drooling figure.

"Experience," said Bran, with a playful wink.

"Bull crap! You've never got wasted... have you?"

"Me? Nah... but my dad's not one to shy away from a bottle. I know that snore all too well. I practically grew up with it."

"Well, I can't stand it."

"You'll get used to it. I personally find it rather soothing," Bran said sarcastically.

Gregory snorted aggressively, disturbing his rest and causing the boys to jump. He uttered nothing but gibberish as he moved his head to rest back on the wall.

"See, told you. He's absolutely bladdered." said Bran waving away the stench of alcoholic fumes.

"Forget about it!" said Marcus as his arm plunged down to the bottom of the bag, quickly pulling out wrappers that rustled in his fist.

"Marathon bars! You bloody legend!" said Bran in excitement as he snatched the bar and ate it in under a minute.

God that tastes good!

It wasn't much, but it was certainly better than nothing and much better than the bird that continued to squawk overhead. There was nothing left to do now. Nothing but sleep. That and eagerly wait for daylight to arrive. The rain had found a way to calm the atmosphere. The outside world no longer provoked their fear and worries, and the aftermath of the showers landed as droplets falling from the tallest trees.

*

"*Psst*, you awake?"

"Wah?"

"I said, you awake?"

"Well, I am now, aren't I?" Bran manoeuvred his weight in hope of finding a more comfortable spot. "What is it?"

"I can't sleep, that's all."

"So, you've woken me up to tell me you can't sleep? Jesus, Marcus. Count sheep or something."

"I've tried the whole counting thing, not sheep mind you. Though it never seems to help."

"Oh, really?" said Bran sarcastically. "Here try this,"

"What is it?" asked Marcus, watching Bran's hand move towards him.

"It's my bag of fucks, Marcus."

"Bag of wah?"

"My bag of fucks. Here. Take it and count how many I have to give."

A childish snigger crept out from the corner of the room as both sat upright.

"It's too dark in here," said Marcus panning around the place.

"It usually is at night."

"You reckon we can get that fire alight? There's plenty of junk about this place to burn."

"Matches?" prompted Bran, just as a small box rattled closely beside his ear.

It didn't take long to get the fire going, the fallen birds' nests turned out to be the perfect kindling for the boys to light it. They grabbed what they could, anything really. It was all disposable, nothing but discarded objects belonging to people that were long since forgotten. Before long, they had gathered enough to keep the fire going until dawn. A deep orange radiated outward, painting the room from floor to ceiling in a heart-warming glow. There was something pleasing about it as they sat there watching the glimmer of light flash against the cobwebbed walls. The gloominess of the room was dispelled, and it now appeared completely harmless; and dare they say it, even comforting, as Gregory continued to ramble in his sleep. The old man certainly wasn't all that bad. They would've been completely screwed without him, that's for sure.

A stack of dusty papers stood piled at Bran's side as a handful at a time were thrown randomly onto the grate. They were old and dated, now serving more of a purpose to the flames. He held no interest in their content, only in crushing them into round paper balls. The light dimmed and a brisk wind spiralled down the chimney, sending the pile to scatter.

"Christ's sake!" whispered Bran while he clambered across the floor to collect them.

It was then a particular image caught his attention when the dull light spread weakly across the page's crinkled surface. Bran carried it by the corner's edge, trying not to tear it, and lowered its words carefully to the chimney arch.

Child Missing
8-year-old girl. Last seen in Thyme village.

A portrait was printed below, though time had certainly taken its toll; the black ink on cheaply processed paper had gradually turned to a smudge-like blur. Regardless, Bran could make it out. The black and white poster displayed the likeness of a small girl. Bran didn't recognise her, nor did he need to. Within this one dusty print he bore witness to a face that showed a childlike innocence. It was a happy, yet innocent emotion he felt. Something he'd lost some years ago. The girl cast a smile back at him, as Bran's stare wandered curiously to Marcus, who had continued to repack both rucksacks. Her hair was fair; A ribbon fell innocently from her head, camouflaging itself in her shoulder length curls. And beneath her straight cut fringe, wide, adventurous eyes.

So, it really was true.

The old man shifted positions in his sleep, catching Bran off guard as he carefully folded the paper into his trouser pocket. Why he acted in such secrecy he didn't know. To spare the old man's feelings perhaps? Or maybe, it was to conceal an item which in reality was no business of his. Either way, he had no intention of showing Gregory, or Marcus for that matter. This whole ordeal had been stressful enough already. No, he would keep this to himself for now, trying his best to forget, like it had never occurred.

"What are you up to?" asked Marcus who was still rummaging around in his bag.

"Uh? Nothing."

"Well, stop watching him sleep. It's weird!"

Marcus was right. God knows how Gregory would have reacted to find him standing over him like this.

Bran sat back down next to Marcus, resuming the role of keeper of the fire. He had grown drowsy now as the warmth softly forced his eyelids to close.

*

His mother called him. She sounded pleased to see him. And, in this instance, he was glad to see her.

"I've missed you." She spoke as her arms wrapped tightly around him. It all seemed so real: the touch of her hands, the smell of her clothes as his head pressed into her shoulder. He had never considered the aroma of fabric detergent before. It was odd that he recalled such a thing now. She held his arms, pushing him away to observe the expression on his face. She smiled gaily, the happiest smile he had ever seen.

"Where have you been, Branny?" she asked while playfully scuffing the top of his head. "I've been waiting for you."

He tried to speak, tried to explain, though for some odd reason he could not remember. His mind was blank as the woman he knew so well stared inquisitively back at him.

"Where have you been, Bran?"

Again, he searched his thoughts. His memory held no clue as to why he would feel so homesick. He couldn't explain his sadness.

"I... I can't remember, Mum," he said.

"You can't? Well, that's OK," she said, rubbing at his wrists with her softened palms.

He looked around him. The sun shone down on his family home. The lawn on which he stood was a vibrant green of freshly cut grass, sending out a recognisable scent to stimulate his senses.

"Where's Dad?" he asked.

"Who?"

"Dad. You know, that guy you married."

"I'm not quite sure."

"Oh..."

She gazed deep into his eyes, her smile never weakening as he allowed his arms to fall.

"Would you like to play a game, Branny?"

"Not really, Mum. I'm not five anymore."

"I know that. It's just a bit of fun. Please?" she asked, guiding his hands to his eyes.

"Now, tell me. Think of the place you've always dreamed of visiting, and I will take you there."

"What?" he said, forcefully pushing away his hand.

"No! No, Bran," she said. "No peeking!"

He held his hand over his eyes. The sun's rays penetrated his hands and caused a red glow to seep through his fingers.

"Now count to three," she giggled childishly. He had never heard her make such a sound.

"Why?"

"Because, it's all part of the game, isn't it?"

He closed his eyes regardless, counting aloud the numbers down to zero.

"Now what?"

A quietness followed as the warmth of the sun fell flat.

"Mum? Now what?"

"Open those eyes, son," she said plainly.

Something was different. It may have been the way she spoke, or maybe it was only his desire to keep his eyes closed a moment longer. Either way, as his hand pressed firmly to his brow the sound of sobs assaulted his ears.

"Don't be upset, Mum," he said. "I'll do it properly."

Again, he counted down from three. This time thinking of the place he wanted most of all. He let down his hands, but still his eyes clenched tightly shut.

"Ok... I'm gonna open them."

Though this time she gave no answer. Not even her loving touch reassured him of her presence.

"Mum?" he spoke, finally allowing his eyelids to split.

She was not there. No one was there. More importantly, this was not the place he wished for. A thick forest surrounded him, its trees and vines colliding as though preparing to collapse from above.

"Mum?" he yelled for the final time.

The sun had perished, and a dusk-like atmosphere shimmered disturbingly over the grounds. He realised he knew this place. He rubbed his arms in an attempt to chase away the chill. Someone stood between the far-off shadows. A small someone, yet he couldn't see a face. The vision was elusive, fading in and out of sight. The land began to shake beneath him, making the forest frantic as trees mysteriously circled his path. Even though he tried, he was speechless. He tried to move, but his limbs turned rigid. The small figure drew nearer. Leaves rustled as it floated towards him, filling the air with fear. He watched it closely. The creepiness of its motionless body sent him closer to the edge of insanity as he struggled to free himself from invisible bonds. The image stopped. And soon, so did his battle. A crisp white light settled at his feet and coalesced into a body.

It was a girl. A young girl. Far too young to be roaming alone out here. She was pretty, in a completely innocent way. A well presented child at that. A nightgown of the purest white hung from her shoulders. The breeze tossed her long, curly hair around her neck... She looked back at him blankly before turning to glide away. He had seen this girl somewhere. Where exactly, he couldn't quite remember. But he knew he had seen her all the same.

He finally found his voice, "Do you need help?" he shuddered as he spoke.

The child stopped and weakly turned her head as her eyes again found his. She smiled joyfully as he began to speak, but the question brought an emotional reaction. Her eyes grew wide, and she allowed a few tears to flow.

It was then he remembered her. That very same smile. Not in passing, nor a dream, but in memory. The missing child from the poster.

Chapter Thirty-Six

A heavy jolt struck Bran's arm. The unexpected shock forced a grimace on his face while he wavered between a dream and reality.

"Oi," a distant voice echoed.

Another jolt smashed against his side.

"Ouch!" said Bran, rubbing at what would soon become a very tender bruise.

"You let the fire go out," said Marcus with a scowl.

Bran sat up, his hand pressing firmly to his side as he grabbed the stash of papers, throwing them swiftly onto the hot ash.

"I fell asleep, you moron! What is it with you?"

The papers' centre began to glow, quickly bursting back into a violent flame and allowing Marcus to again rest easy.

"I just had the strangest dream," said Bran, as he smeared the cold sweat along his brow.

"It's understandable after the past few days."

"No, this was unlike any dream I've ever had.

"Really? What about?"

"I'm not actually sure. My mum was there, I remember that much."

"That doesn't sound so strange."

"No. But she seemed really happy to see me. Normally she doesn't give a toss."

"Ah," said Marcus and paused. "Still, I've had worse."

Bran laid back, the heartbeat of disturbed dreams still thumping loudly within his ears. He wasn't quite sure what the dream meant, or why it chose to happen. Gosh, he couldn't even recall the last time he had a bad dream. Such things were for kids to worry about. And considering he wasn't a kid anymore, why did it worry him so?

"There's more," said Bran. He, too, was now eager to keep the light from fading.

"Go on?"

"Well... I was lost in the woods... these woods, at least I think it was. Everything went cold, and out of nowhere appeared this girl."

"What girl?"

"That girl from the poster."

"What! What poster?"

Bran bit his tongue, remembering the scrunched up image that rested secretly within his trouser pocket.

So much for keeping it schtum.

"Well, what girl?" insisted Marcus. His attention seemed to increase by the mention.

"Ah... No one," he stuttered, beginning to pedal back his words. "You know, that redhead from those stupid cassette commercials."

"Oh yeah, she's a right corker. Anything else happen?"

"No. Nothing else," said Bran, the blatant lie sending his skin to a beetroot shade of red.

"Ah, shame that," said Marcus. "Well, it's certainly a weird one, pal. I'll give you that. I'll look after the fire for now. Get yourself some sleep. You look like you need it."

Despite how tired he was, Bran was opposed to the suggestion. He was unable to shake away the girl's face from his mind whether his eyes were open or closed.

"No, it's fine. I can't sleep now," he groaned. He looked away from Marcus and watched the floating ash rise calmly up the chimney.

Marcus had lowered his head, and his eyes shifted rapidly from left to right. He made the odd noise, the odd grunt, and soon he began an irritating whisper.

"What are you doing?" asked Bran.

"Reading."

"Huh? Reading what?"

Marcus stopped for a second and lifted the small, leather bound book above him. The orange light bounced off its smooth but weathered surface.

"So, you abandoned half our food stash but decided to bring a poxy book."

"I thought it could be useful?"

"It's utter gibberish, Marcus," said Bran impatiently. "Trust me, you'll find nothing to help us in those worn out pages."

"Actually, there's good reason why its pages are worn," said Marcus. "And I guarantee it's not because they're useless."

Bran stubbornly folded his arms and sighed heavily. Whether he liked it or not it was inevitable Marcus would recount his findings. He could either accept it or let the story fall on deaf ears. Neither one seemed pleasant. And with that thought, he reluctantly decided to lower his guard.

"Go on then, Sherlock. What have you found?"

*

The book lay open between them, allowing the pages to flutter intermittently in the gentle waves of heat. Marcus leaned forward, his finger pressed heavily upon the printed words while moving his hand for guidance.

"This is it, right here," said Marcus, pushing the book away from him.

Bran picked up the book and rested it comfortably in his lap. Marcus watched in anticipation, waiting for Bran to close it and arrogantly toss it aside as he had done before. Instead, he didn't. Bran cocked his head and slowly turned the title page. He spoke not a word for the next few minutes while he lifted the book higher and higher to the burning light. For Marcus, the time went by slowly. He remained quiet as he watched Bran's interest grow with the turn of each and every page.

*

The pages slammed shut as Bran's thumbs gently caressed the wrinkled spine and gold printed lettering. He wasn't quite sure what to think. If what he read was real, it would certainly give cause to worry. But it was nothing more than words on paper. Anyone, yes, anyone could have written it.

"So, what you think?" asked Marcus

"Err… I'm not a big mythology fan."

Marcus snatched the book in a childlike huff, passionately skimming the pages to find the passage that caught his eye. "Here," he prompted, shoving the open pages directly below Bran's nose. "What about this then?"

The page displayed an image, a sort of charcoal representation of a darkened woodland setting. The trees stood black and twisted, as though burnt from the roots up. The talented use of shading had been created with the simple smudge of a finger. Bran had learnt the technique in art class, and it was the only way he knew of incorporating a hazy texture in his amateurish work. It was an unsettling picture, that was all. There was nothing else to see.

"Do you see it?" asked Marcus, shoving the yellow stained pages closer, now forcing Bran's sight to blur.

See what? thought Bran, as he bitterly gazed at the smudges.

Yes, he saw it now. It was so clear. Between the twisted branches stood something concealed. A silhouette, camouflaged by the thick fog and cluttered brambles. It was an uncomfortable find. The creepy shadow seemed to lurk shyly in the distance. It stared out at him, watching him. Its head followed Bran through the sketch of claw-like branches and out of the page.

"That's enough!" Bran was exhausted from thinking about it.

"There's a poem underneath it," said Marcus, preparing himself to read.

"I hate poetry with a passion," uttered Bran.

Nonetheless, Marcus was determined to read it. He cleared his throat as his eyes prepared his tongue. "Ahem." He was about to begin, when a voice they knew began to speak, alarming them both. Their eyes stared out across the smoky room. A strong deep tone filled the hut with a grand hall echo. The boys tensed, forgetting the old man's slumber as they listened to a haunting rhyme that imprinted itself in their minds.

> "Amongst the oaks the shadows stride.
> The shallow pools reflect the eyes.
> You hear the cries and voices call,
> haunting, taunting, escape to stall.
> The whispers at the Folklore Stones
> will guide you to their forest home.
> And when you grasp this tale so true,
> woodlands will wail at skies of blue."

Gregory's words were slow and calming. He took his time and allowed the lines to roll off his uneducated tongue. It was an unnerving poem, or possibly it was only in the way he recited it, letting the final line fall into a sinister silence. The crackle of flames again began to crowd the dingy room. No one dared speak for a time as an awkwardness seemed like an accompaniment to the poet's dramatic words. Marcus looked down towards the pages. *He was right*, he thought as he cast his eyes over the faded font. Every word of it was right.

"How, how did you know that?" asked Marcus, combing his greasy hair back through his fingers.

"I wrote it. More importantly, young man," hushed Gregory, "where did you come to find that book?"

Marcus's mind felt numb as he searched for ways to explain. He had never wished to make a habit of stealing, nor becoming a liar for that matter. But if he didn't tell the truth now, he would rightfully be accused of both.

"I found it."

"Where?"

"Your place."

"I see. So, tell me. When did you plan on returning it?"

Marcus shrugged. The thought of taking without permission was beginning to make him feel very small, indeed.

"I would have given it back..."

"I'm sure," said Gregory.

Bran stood up, his mind now quite uneasy.

"Forget the book!"

"Forget the book?" mimicked Gregory.

"Yes, forget it. It's just a bunch of mumbo jumbo anyway."

The book was passed back to the old man's hands, the cover lightly patted as he fanned out the bleached pages.

"What's happening in this place?" asked Marcus.

"What's happening?" said Gregory, slamming the book shut with a single hand. "Nothing that hasn't gone on for many years. It's all here, written down in ink."

"We don't have time for that!" exclaimed Marcus, placing his hands stubbornly on his hips.

"Very well," said Gregory. "I'll tell you. But we must make haste. Soon, the sun will show and we must rise with it. We have a long day ahead of us and not a moment to lose."

"Where are we headed to?" asked Marcus, curiously.

"To find your friend, of course."

Chapter Thirty-Seven

"There are reasons why this sea of trees remains uninhabited and untouched. For the few folk who decided to wander its overgrown trails, almost all have claimed to have sensed the unknown. It goes back many, no… hundreds of years: when the hills and valleys of the surrounding lands were also a part of its magnificent estate. Times were different then. There was not so much hate in the world as we have grown accustomed to. But still, people sensed it all the same. It all began on the brightest of summer days, apparently. A typically normal day like any other. It was the most playful of calls through the woodlands that distracted a single passer-by, a young farm boy, as he pulled his wooden cart to the nearest village. Now, what exactly these calls spoke I have no idea. But what I do know is these calls were purely innocent, playful cries for attention. The boy, as you'd imagine, was scared out of his wits at first, though over time grew more curious about the voices that continually summoned him.

"He bolted home, so they say, excited to inform his townsfolk of such a peculiar experience. Over the following days people soon dragged families to witness the phenomenon. And in turn, they escorted nearby locals. The voice was said to be tireless. Yelling out day after day, night after night, to whomever should step beneath the shade of sheltering treetops. After several weeks, the local population didn't know what to think. Many were now beginning to find their inner courage to step off the path and into the undergrowth of Sleathton. Many searched throughout the remaining summer months that soon led to a damp and dreary autumn. They searched the forest floor, each and every one of them desperate to uncover the truth of the mysterious woodland secret. They followed the drone for hours until finally reaching their limit. Whether it be when they finally reached a river, stream, or swamp, the voices would noticeably fade, leaving them with an enigma and confusing thoughts. It's said that as the searchers turned to make their journey home, a mischievous laughter would always be heard from behind them, echoing around the trunk of every tree, playfully mocking their failure.

"The strangest thing is, and this will surprise you both, nothing bad ever happened to them. They returned to their villages amused and light-hearted, telling such stories about what would soon be known as the Sleathton Ghost and the pranks it played."

"Wait," said Bran with a motion of his hand. "So, you're saying it's a ghost?"

"I'm not saying it's a ghost or otherwise. I'm purely stating what is told."

"So, if it's not a ghost then what the hell is it?"

"Look, son, the land on which we walk holds many old stories, this is simply one of them. Some are nothing but fables, childish tales to teach we idiotic mortals right from wrong. Others hold an undying essence of truth, a lesson to be learned and respected. But if anything can be said of this particular tale, it is that some legends are so much more than ghost stories."

Marcus gave Bran a gentle nudge, immediately followed by a hardened frown. Bran recognised the look right away. It was an unspoken caution for him to wind his neck in. Bran gave a nod, sat quietly back and closed his eyes to listen.

"Well now," said Gregory, speaking slowly to himself. "Where was I?" He scratched firmly at his scruffy red beard in thought. "Ahh, yes," he said with a yawn.

"And so, that's how it was. Day after day, week after week, month after month, the voices continued to spread across the forest. Calling out to anyone in hope of tempting them to play its harmless game. Though very soon, and like everything else in this world, the magic would shortly fade. The voice still called, of course, though people lost interest in the mystery, and in time not even so much as a head would turn as they walked along the narrow dusty paths. It remained this way for years, until eventually the villagers moved on, the voices were forgotten, and the forest land fell silent.

"It was an eternity. So much time, in fact, the roads and pathways located around the estate had vanished, hiding away any evidence of its settlers and unusual past. It was again a wild place, an unforgiving place, very much like you see today.

"It happened to be on the 20th February, 1921, that a military group recorded passing through the area after falling off course from the Claymore River. They reported hearing the sounds of terrified screams for help from within the woods. Honouring their oath of duty, they followed the cries for many miles, some say even days. Yet they found nothing. Not so much as a single clue did they find. It was reported back to their superior. Unsurprisingly, the story itself had become intriguingly popular between their units. Within days, patrols in the hundreds marched outward to Sleathton. Their purpose, to uncover the truth behind the so-called enchanted forest. For days the men searched, fighting their way through the brambles. When it got dark the men grew ill-tempered and tormented, listening to the sounds chuckling back at them throughout the night."

"So, what did they do?" asked Marcus. His heavy breathing quickened as he listened to the old man's every word.

"They did what all mankind does to things they don't understand. They started to destroy the forest."

"But why?" said a confused Marcus.

"For control, of course," said Gregory. "But little did they know what circumstances were about to befall them. The trees toppled like falling dominos. And in the distance, bellows of grief could be heard with each snap of falling timber.

The calls of mischief that were once heard had merged and now pierced the humid air with sounds of deep and unrelenting sorrow. Many trees had been felled, denuding the once thriving forest and creating fields of logs. And by the time a full week's work had passed, the voices that had echoed across the land were hushed.

"Well, the men were joyful at first. They couldn't leave this uninhabited place soon enough. As ordered, they scouted the remaining woodland. Interestingly, several of the men never made it back to the camps after their first search. It caused no true concern, you understand. People always happen to get lost in rural places like this. And with no map or markings to guide them, it would have been as easy as losing yourself in a corn field. The morning finally dawned, and the last remaining unit started to search the darkest patch of land, ordered to find the men who had recklessly gone missing. Splitting up, the small troop divided the area equally, which would at last see them safely to the other side of Sleathton and thankfully closer to their awaiting homes. The men quickly drifted apart. The tramp of their heavy boots was still in sync as they trudged their separate ways. Of all the remaining units, only one young lad made it to the other side. He was hardly older than a child himself, much too young to be called a soldier. He alone made it through the estate and over the valleys, back to his reporting officer. Oh, the things he reported to have seen would make your hair curl, boys."

"What? What'd he see?" Bran was now captivated by the history.

Gregory cleared his parched throat, letting out a gruff growl and firmly patting his chest.

"He reported seeing something that simply should not exist. They say he was level headed. But even the sanest of minds can be tricked. He had walked for many hours without food or water, and fatigue was getting a stranglehold on his body. His attention was captured by the sound of water smashing against the mossy rocks. With his mouth parched and his mind weak, he roamed in search of what would quench his thirst. He found the fast-flowing stream of fresh, clear water and fell to his knees. He immediately removed his jacket and tags and submerged his face in the current. The young man drank his fill, before resting against the bank, watching his own gaunt reflection as beads of sweat fell freely from his brow. Sitting there for quite some time, he became almost hypnotised by the glimmer on the water. It was so intriguing he almost failed to notice a slight tint of red flowing across his field of vision. The colour was diluted as the stream twined and twisted around jagged rocks. The man rubbed his eyes ferociously, leaning over to take a closer look. The colour grew stronger, patchy at first, before turning to a vibrant bloody red. He placed his hand in the water and allowed the liquid to run through his fingers. It was warm and thick and embedded itself deep beneath his nails. The trickle had turned to a stream of blood, surging towards him, following every dip and turn of its ghastly trail.

"Another soldier from his unit sat hunched over on a rock that rose up from the grass. Although he faced the man's back, he was very familiar with the uniform. The young lad watched suspiciously as his comrade viciously delved his arms into the steady flowing stream. He looked again at the water, annoyed with his sluggish reaction in helping his fellow soldier who was obviously hurt, probably by gunshot. Yet he heard no gunfire that morning. The day itself had been as silent as a graveyard in the depths of winter. Caught up in the emotion of the moment, he sprinted up the bank, forgetting his bag and rifle that still sat hidden beside a tree. Calling out to the soldier as he ran, he was out of breath when he reached the stone. His brother-in-arms continued to drown his blood-soaked wrists. There was no way for the young soldier to know exactly what had happened, but a nervousness churned within his gut as he wordlessly crept beside him. Later he said he recognised the injured man as a bunkmate from his hometown whom he had known quite well. His black hair was drenched and flattened against his face. Concerned for the injured man, he spoke but received no answer from the soldier who stubbornly continued to cleanse his hands. The colour of the stream was not fading but growing more intense, blending now to a dark shade of red wine. He was desperate to know the source of such a devastating loss of blood: the loss of a finger or even a hand perhaps? Nothing could have prepared him for what he was about to see. The comrade's arms now remained tense and stiff, almost as though he was purposely fighting to keep his hands from rising. The lad looked down, letting out a horrified gasp. He fell to the ground, heaving on only the dryness of the air. The soldier pushed down hard, shaking his hands in anger. His grip clenched the neck of another fellow soldier who had been sentenced to a most horrible death. Blood spilled out from the body beneath the surface, from where exactly he couldn't see. But as the lad gazed upon the victim's face another shock rocked him. The figure who pushed down on the corpse looked to be the same as the corpse himself. They were identical in every way, one and the same.

"The lad, he stepped back, his skin pale and his body loose. He said nothing, retracing his steps sluggishly and trying to go unseen. His heel struck something hard, sending him off balance and causing him to fall clumsily on his back. Surprisingly, his fall did not cause any harm. Instead, he happened to land on something soft. It reminded him of the lumpy mattresses supplied at the headquarters, that was if you were lucky enough to receive one. He lifted himself, pushing off the cushioned ground. It was soft, yet hard in places, moving freely under the pressure of his movement. Lifting a hand, a stain of clotted blood smeared his palm. Anxious, the boy checked himself to see if he'd been hurt. He wasn't, but as he moved a putrid stench rose around him. It was an odour so vile. This smell he knew. Bodies lay beneath him. Several of them in fact. All were men who set out on that morning's search. Their limbs spread unnaturally across the uneven grass, resembling a collection of cheap, discarded toys. The young boy let out an involuntary shriek, clambering over the bodies of his fallen friends. He had no time to think. He had no time to run. A hand grabbed desperately at his ankle, its fingernails digging deep into his skin and piercing his flesh. He cringed in pain, catching sight of the figure who still remained perched upon a rock. The figure stared back at him blankly. His eyes all but gone, a white glow inhabiting their sockets. The figure smiled at him. A dark and twisted smile, as its arms tensed aggressively and continued to strangle the dead.

"The lad stumbled, the fall sending him tumbling to the bottom of the bank. Life became a blur and the descent seemed never ending. He collided with a tree which sent him splashing into the stream. He pulled himself from the water, crawling upward to escape the gushing blood. He looked down. His uniform remained clean with the exception of a heavy sweat stain. He glared at the stream. The rippling current was now as clear as when he first found it. There was no explanation for it, nor at that point could he have readied himself for one. His heart beat wildly in his chest while his jaw tightened and locked. Terrified, he surveyed the land above him. The figure was gone. Vanished like magic, without a trace. The bodies of his comrades had disappeared, too, also leaving not even one clue, not even a drop of blood, to mark the ground where they laid.

"Needless to say, the young man made it out alive. And thank goodness for him, too. Otherwise, this written account would never have made it to paper. He finally arrived back to his unit, refusing to speak to anyone but his commanding officer."

"And did they believe him?" asked Marcus.

"They believed the lad had lost his mind," answered Gregory. "He told them everything, leaving nothing out. Not even the smallest detail was kept secret. He wanted them to believe him. He needed them to. And in time, even the lad himself began to doubt his own story. Isolation can be a very funny thing. It can play tricks on your eyes and your brain to convince you something really exists. His superiors departed, leaving him resting on an old infirmary bed. A tender sting itched at his ankle, and he pulled up his hospital gown. Five nails had torn his skin. The marks were still evident. The wounds were seeping pus, and the sensation of fire surged up to his knee. He closed his eyes, clenching through the pain. He was unable to escape the memory of that day. Yet, no matter what thoughts passed his mind, the love of his wife, the memories of home, all reverted to that one day in the woods and those bright reflective eyes that shone back at him. They stared deeply into him. Even while he slept, they peered past his flesh, watching the soul that got away. He would never forget the expression that accompanied those empty eyes; the cruel smile that would shatter all bravery in a heartbeat. It warned him that one day his soul would be stolen. No matter where he ran, no matter where he hid, he would be found."

Chapter Thirty-Eight

The bright morning sunshine burst through the curtains, its shimmering path sending a narrow gleam to the far-off corner where the old man lay. Gregory awoke almost instantly. He raised his hand to block the glare and smacked his lips together. The aftertaste of last night's drink was offensive. Gregory was thirsty, his throat as dry as dust. Clumsily rising to his feet, his hip stiffened from sleeping on the floor. He was no spring chicken after all, and over the past decade he had started to accept the consequences of such decisions. The boys lay silent, as they had done through the twilight hours, making it difficult for Gregory to tell whether they were asleep or awake. He made his way to the door with an involuntary hop as he walked.

Stepping outside, the vibrant colours of the woodland and the morning's warmth hugged him as he carefully stepped off the porch to relieve his bladder. Each step created a disturbingly loud crack from somewhere inside his body.

"God, I'm getting old," said Gregory with a disappointed sigh.

Everything seemed to be an effort these days, even the simple need to piss.

May as well be pissing dust, he thought, irritated. He pulled up his zipper and lifted his face to the sky. It was still early morning but they had missed the planned departure at first light.

Blast!

Gregory knew it was irresponsible of him to drink so heavily. But the decision to stop was almost impossible to make. He had acquired his love for the drink so long ago now, that as time flowed on, and without his realising what was happening, his thirst for it grew stronger. So strong he no longer denied his dependence on it. The desire had grown unrestrained, morphing from its effects of a calming comfort into the most unpleasant monster, forever sitting on his shoulder and taunting him endlessly. He didn't want the drink, he needed it! And without so much as a shot, God only knows what torment he'd be in. Regardless, he needed to keep his wits about him. If he somehow came to misplace the boys due to his own drunken stupidity, this entire venture would be pointless. He couldn't remember the last time he'd come across young folk. He'd be damned if he was going to let those poor boys slip through his fingers. He sat peacefully for a moment and listened to the subtle noises around him: the hypnotic buzz of hovering wasps, the innocent whistle of birds nesting high above the ground, all accompanied by the freshness of the summer morning air. Yes, this was his favourite time. There was something about it, something tranquil perhaps? It was nature at its finest. And it pleased Gregory greatly to behold it, to capture it. The world felt like his own. It was bliss.

*

Breakfast was sparse, though they all had come to expect it. The boys had woken tired and groggy, disturbed by a thumping racket outside the cabin walls. They ventured out with heavy eyes, wanting nothing more than to curl up again and go back to sleep.

"Morning, boys." Gregory beckoned them over with a wave of his hand.

The boys did not reply. They had no desire to. It was far too early to encourage chit chat, especially pleasant chit chat.

"You boys hungry?" asked Gregory. "Here. I made us these." He handed out two wooden poles, freshly cut from branches of a nearby sapling. Two metal clips were twisted into the base, followed by several rounded hooks spread evenly up to the tip. An almost invisible wire wrapped tightly around each handle, carefully threaded through each hook and purposely left to dangle.

"Fishing rods?" Marcus was puzzled as he recalled his own abandoned rod.

"Indeed, son. Not my best work but it will surely catch us a bite to eat."

Marcus took the rod, weighing it up in his hand and pretending to cast.

"It's great," remarked Marcus. "But where did you find the kit?"

"There's plenty of scrap lying around here. I just gathered what I needed."

Gregory tossed the second rod to Bran whose slow and clumsy reflexes allowed the pole to bounce off his face.

"I thought you said we had no time to lose?" said Bran holding the side of his face. "How is it we have time for this?"

"You wanna starve, do you?" Gregory asked.

"No but…"

"Then we must get moving, and fast. The closest river runs short of a mile north. Whatever we catch will serve us well over the coming days, as long as the fish stay cooled."

"Days?" asked Bran. The thought alone exhausted him.

"Yes," said Gregory without hesitation. "We have miles to go, and time is of the essence."

"And what about Jack?" asked Marcus. "You think he'll be alright?"

The old man exhaled and knotted his coat tightly around the waist. "I hope so, son, but hanging around here does nothing for no one."

Marcus said no more but hurried back inside, his feet still tender from last evening's excruciating walk. He collected his rucksack, throwing a single strap around his shoulder and made his way to the door.

"So, what are we waiting for?"

*

Looking back, the cabin seemed to dissolve, fading from sight behind the evergreens. It was strange to think they'd never see it again. Though their stay there hadn't been exactly pleasant, the boys still found it difficult to look away. Would they find it again, even if they tried?

Probably not, thought Marcus.

The walls had served their purpose and would slowly deteriorate into nothing more than a collapsed heap. The thought was disheartening, but Marcus felt somewhat special. His footsteps would be the last to walk the cabin's floor. Gregory never looked back. He focused his thoughts on only the journey ahead as he lifted his knees high. Marcus doubted the man would ever consider coming back here, not after all he'd been through. And to see the cabin in such a sorry state must have driven home all the memories. Even so they trod on, making a turn which led down a steep and slippery slope. They slid down it, almost falling at times, the earth was too loose for them to gain a foothold. Reaching the bottom, they laughed while they playfully scraped off the heavy mud that stuck to the soles of their shoes.

"Come, let's not lose ourselves," said Gregory, striding off ahead. Bran followed. His steps quickened as he attempted to resume his pace. Marcus watched for a second, taking in the sights and smells about him as the others fell from view. He wanted a moment, just one. To see what it would feel like to be truly alone out here. He held his breath, allowing only the forest's sound to be present.

"Oi, what you playing at!"

Marcus exhaled as he gave a casual thumbs up to Bran, who stood impatiently waiting.

"What's wrong with you?" said Bran angrily.

"Nothing. I was just fastening my laces."

Bran raised his brow. Marcus may have been a loyal friend, but he was a terrible liar.

"Come on," said Bran hastily. "You know what the old sod's like. He doesn't wait about for no one. It's like he's got bionic legs or something."

Marcus nodded as he began to jog forward. He turned back while running, taking one last look at the past before forgetting. The cabin was no more.

Amongst the Mists

Chapter Thirty-Nine

The river flowed peacefully like an endless stream of glass. Its water was clear and refreshing as it splashed against their skin. The mid-day sun had peaked, sending an unwelcome wave of heat to warm the ground below. It was hot! There was no other word for it. And despite the gloominess, there was no relief, not even in the darkest patch of shade.

"It's like a bloody oven down here!" said Bran, waving his shirt like a fan.

"This?" asked the amused old man. "This is nothing, son. You should have seen the heatwave of 1979. It would have melted your eyeballs straight from your sockets. Couple of acres went up in flames, too!"

"Right now, that doesn't seem like such a concern. I'm sick to death of trees."

Marcus went to the river, casting out the line and wrapping it neatly around its handle. Fish jumped playfully from the shallows, thriving on the insects that floated on the surface. Marcus's face turned sour. He hadn't the time or the patience for this. The old man sat beside him, watching as the young boy struggled.

"You boys take a break," said Gregory. "It's been an odd few days."

He took the rod from Marcus, switching places while keeping close to the water's edge. The boys seemed not to mind, resting flat against the dirt.

Marcus woke, wondering if he'd slept at all. He trudged to the riverbank. The old man faced away, reeling in the wire, his faded shirt blotched with an ever-growing sweat stain. Next to him was a sight that made Marcus's mouth water: three large fish that were perfect for dinner.

"How did you manage that?" asked a very surprised Marcus.

"Just some old tricks."

"What kinda fish are they?"

"Brown trout. The best you'll ever eat." Gregory stepped away from the water and gave a pleasing wink.

*

The aroma of grilling fish permeated the air. The remains of unwanted fish innards were slopped messily in a pile as the old man cleaned his blade.

"Rest assured," said Gregory, "a fox will be grateful."

Tugging two sticks from the ground he handed each of the boys his own deliciously tender trout. The taste was heavenly. *If only there was more,* thought Bran hungrily chewing fish off the bones. Marcus looked around him. The forest had been still that day. Calm. The tranquil sound of water babbled softly behind them as he lay under the open sky, letting his thoughts flow freely.

"Are we safe here?" asked Marcus,

"No safer than this morning," replied Gregory, pulling at a missed bone wedged between his teeth. "It's always watching… at least I think it is."

"So, what's the plan?" Bran sat licking his fingers.

"Plan?"

"Well, if we find Jack, how do we end this thing?"

"End? You mean kill? You can't kill a myth, son."

"Why not!"

"You just can't. Ain't no one ever done such a thing."

"You managed to keep it in check the last time. Can't you just shoot it?"

Gregory looked down at the rifle sitting across his lap.

"No number of bullets would ever do what you're suggesting, son."

"Then why the hell did you even bring it?"

"I couldn't find my stick."

"Seriously?"

Marcus sat up to listen carefully to the old man's explanation.

"If it wasn't for the gun, how did you do it?"

"Simply with this."

Gregory lifted a hand. His palm was still tightly wrapped in a dirt covered and bloodstained cloth.

"I don't understand," said Marcus.

"It's blood, you fool," said Bran. "Blood is the weakness."

"On the contrary, boys." Gregory shook his head. "Blood doesn't discourage this beast. In fact, you'll find it yearns for the stuff. No, it's what hides beneath this cloth that holds its weakness."

Marcus and Bran gazed closer, as though the germ riddled bandage would somehow provide them with the answer.

"The scar?" said Marcus shrugging.

"Not the scar," replied the old man with a twist of his wrist. "The sacrifice. And the smallest sacrifice at that."

His hand dropped to his lap, gripping the gun firmly before attempting to stand.

"A sacrifice?" asked Bran nervously.

"That's right. But don't you worry yourself, young man." The old man's words were calm and collected. "This is not the sacrifice of another but of one's true self. This little slit to my hand here is just that. It proves my loyalty to the cause."

"What cause?"

"Valuing my own life much less in an attempt to secure your own."

"That's a bit steep," said Bran. "I mean, I'm thankful and everything. But what you have there will barely be a graze this time tomorrow. Hardly what you'd call a sacrifice."

Gregory's frown deepened, protruding veins pulsed along his forehead.

"A sacrifice is a sacrifice, boy. No matter what the case."

"So, what are you saying? If we see this thing again, we all just go knife happy?"

The old man placed his bandaged hand to his head, rubbing furiously, his patience beginning to run out.

"I don't expect you to do anything of the sort," said Gregory. "If any one uses this blade, it'll be me and me alone. Are we understood?"

Bran gulped loudly with a hesitant nod, thinking of a thousand things to say while knowing he shouldn't voice any of them.

"Alright," said Marcus in agreement.

"Good!" said the old man, relaxing his shoulders. "That's settled then. You boys are too important. I'm nothing but an old man, I can take the burden."

"How so?" asked Bran.

Gregory delayed his response, anxiously cracking his knuckles before beginning to roll up his sleeve. The boys gasped in horror when they saw the tanned, elderly arm that held the marks of torture. From wrist to elbow, a crisscross of scars disfigured his sagging flesh. The wounds spread unevenly from top to bottom, giving the impression a single cut had not healed before another cut was made. His skin had thickened over time, healing while the arm remained swollen and plump. Gregory rolled down his sleeve, fastening the cuff with a shameful stare.

"Now, are we in agreement?" asked Gregory.

Marcus and Bran nodded.

"Good. Then we'll speak no more about it."

Chapter Forty

O livia's feet hit the ground running. Her legs moved like never before, all the while she watched the path ahead. For a time she forced herself to remain calm, but that couldn't last long. A bitter cold spiked within her lungs, causing a high-pitched whistle that cut sharply into the night. Where exactly she was headed was no longer important. All that mattered was escape. To flee and hide.

My new existence. She looked back as she raced the unknown. The trail looked to be clear, but tricks had been played on her before. This time she was not going to be fooled. This time she would not stop. This time she would run and keep running. She would not stop until her body quit.

Spasms speared her abdomen, a sharpened point prodding deep within her side caused her to stumble. Olivia fell down on all fours; pain and a desperate need for breath enveloped her. She gasped violently, heaving on the biting air which tightened around her windpipe. Bile drooled from the corners of the young girl's mouth; her stomach far too empty to produce anything else. Both hands dug deep into the loose earth. She clenched her fists tightly and allowed the muck to squeeze through her fingers. Olivia's breathing returned to normal, and she could finally close her eyes and rest. The ground was comfortable. Much more than she anticipated. And with both eyes tightly shut, the sensation of a feather pillow blanketed her brow. Of course, she knew none of it was real. The pillow and soft mattress she laid on were only wishes. They were just desires. Simple, unadulterated desires, remembered from what seemed to be a previous life. Those were only dreams that floated in her mind. The memories didn't relinquish their hold until she opened her eyes. As quickly as it began, it ended. The comfort and the memories were gone. They had been bagged and tossed into a bin somewhere very far away. She didn't need them after all.

Shadows terrorized her soul with snippets from her old life; the life she thought she hated. Reflection can be a powerful thing, especially when all you crave is the home where you felt most trapped. Chains of isolation bound her. If only there were others here. Real people, just like her. Someone who she could depend on, who would look after her. Even someone to share her fears would do.

No one is coming, Olivia thought.

"They're not even looking for me."

She spoke humbly but all too calmly of a world she knew she'd lost. The very reality of this place had become her torment. Now, all she needed to do was accept it.

She wept aloud, sobbing in misery as dry eyes failed to form a tear. What would she do now? Simply remain here, in this very spot, waiting until sleep would finally take her? Perhaps she was trapped for eternity. Her only desire was that her cries would be heard in heaven. Her pale arms embraced her body, the last human touch she would ever know.

Olivia lay resigned, staring out into the twilight as her whimpers began to wane. The trees whispered softly against the gentle breeze, soothing her mind as she listened to nature's song. The eerie, dark green forest dwindled to a blur as trees dressed in shadows stood to watch her rest.

Amongst the Mists

Chapter Forty-One

The sun drowned in the horizon, painting the sky in an array of pink and yellow. Its rays gleamed in the dusk as a faint moon peaked shyly from beyond a wall of cloud. Camp had haphazardly been made. They carelessly assembled the tent that immediately collapsed drunkenly on its side, though none of them had the strength to care. Poles and pegs had vanished, left behind in Marcus's incompetent rush to pack. Still, the waving canvas served its purpose well enough. The night was cold and damp, a considerable change from the blistering heat of that scorching summer's day. Darkness soon engulfed the twilight dimness and a stillness fell across the land.

The meal left them dissatisfied. There was space in their bellies, and they grumbled loudly in protest, hoping to have more.

They didn't keep the fire going overnight, a precaution the old man demanded as he scouted the camp before they rested. Gregory settled down against a rotting stump whose roots had been pulled up from the earth: fingers reaching from a shallow grave. Still, the old man seemed happy enough, accepting the kind gesture of a sleeping bag and leaving the boys to share. A coldness invaded the tent as Bran and Marcus looked down at the one remaining bag.

"Wanna flip for it?" asked Bran.

"We could share it?"

"We'd be very close, wouldn't we?" Bran nervously eyed the narrow bag.

"A little too close for my liking."

"We'd undo the zipper, you prick!"

"Oh…"

"Yeah, believe or not, I'm not overly keen on sharing it with you."

"You better be! I wouldn't have offered mine to that old goat otherwise."

A deliberate grunt filtered through the blowing canvas.

"I may be old, boys, but I certainly ain't deaf!" Gregory's voice was as clear as day.

"Sorry!"

*

In spite of the cold, the boys slept soundly, undisturbed by the incessant flapping of the tent. Morning had broken, the weak light shining through the paper-thin wall of the tent. Marcus stirred, moving his body to shade his eyes from the glare. Bran's morning breath blew directly at his face. If it weren't for the snores that would inevitably follow, he would have punched him.

Great, now I gotta piss.

Marcus was determined to sleep. He tossed and turned in an attempt to delay the growing urge that would force him to venture outside the relative warmth of their shelter. He couldn't take the feeling much longer, convinced that if he didn't move he would surely burst. He unzipped the tent. Rain had fallen during the night, dampening both the ground and Marcus's mood as he stomped barefoot across the untamed grass. Gregory lay still, his head hidden from the elements, his position unmoved from the previous evening. Twigs snapped loudly under the heels of Marcus's feet, projecting a startling crack that echoed up into the heights and alarmed the birds as they woke to the day. A grove of trees hid him, perfectly camouflaging Marcus completely, as he crouched to drop his kecks.

"What you doing?" a voice called at his side.

Marcus reacted with a startle, struggling to pull up the trousers that lay scrunched around the knees.

"Jesus Christ!" shrieked Marcus staring toward Bran. "Trying to give me a bloody heart attack? You idiot!"

Bran stepped back looking slightly flustered. His clothes were all creased and faded, the pocket on his right breast still dangling loosely from their fight some days earlier.

"I saw you creep off, that's all. Just wondered what you were up to."

"Up to? I'm trying to do my numbers! Hardly mischievous, is it?"

Marcus waited, hopeful that Bran would take the hint and sulk off back to the tent.

"Hey, you gotta check this out!" said Bran dismissing the gracelessness of his squatting friend.

"Later." Marcus tried to dismiss him with a wave of his hand.

"Come on, you're gonna want to see this."

"Bran, I've got a turtle head poking out right here. Whatever it is, it can wait."

"But…"

"Piss off, will you!"

Bran began to walk back, then stopped mid-stride and kicked the ground with an irritating sigh.

"We won't get the chance to see it again," said Bran.

Marcus clenched his eyes tightly, his trousers for a second time stopping at his thighs.

"See what?"

"Bones."

"Christ! What bones?"

"I stumbled across them yesterday. Just before we settled for the night. Didn't want to say anything, mind you. Not in front of the old man."

"What? Why?" asked a confused Marcus.

"Because... he'll change the route. Make it twice as long as necessary, of course. The old fart's got a habit of doing that."

Marcus held his position and convinced himself that Bran's find would only take a moment.

"Fine, but hurry up," Marcus stood up and zipped up.

Bran shifted quickly through the saplings, heading back toward the path they were on yesterday.

"This way," whispered Bran over his shoulder. "It's just through here," pointing off the trail.

Marcus began to follow reluctantly, his bare feet slowed his pace to a stop. The ground was rough and sharp allowing twigs and rocks to stab sharply at his soles.

"Wait a minute." Marcus lifted his foot to pick out the embedded stones. "Just let me get my trainers. I'll be right back."

"It's only around this corner," said Bran eagerly. "The old man could wake any second. Come on!"

Turning back, Marcus judged the distance to camp.

"I'll be just a second. I left my boots outside the tent."

"Wait... we need to check this out now."

"Hang fire," whispered Marcus as he darted off back towards the tent, leaving Bran to stand and wait.

The ground sucked at his feet as he trudged briskly through the long, wet grass. Droplets sprayed into the air in a cloud-like form, leaving his trouser cuffs glued against the skin of his legs. Gregory had altered his position some, yet still remained sound asleep. The only movement was that of his sleeping bag, rising and falling with each breath he took. Marcus sat on the ground with a groan. Tired and weak, the usual sense of adventure had truly escaped him as he slipped on the heel of his shoe. The figure of Bran could be seen in the distance anticipating Marcus's return, now beckoning him to hurry, accompanied by a long hard glare of annoyance. Marcus ignored him, of course. He put on the second shoe slowly and secured both with a reliable double knot. He was only half way through tying his second lace when something made him stop. Perplexed, he looked back at Bran who still stood waiting at the woodland's edge staring directly back at him. A blank expression was painted clearly across his face. Immediately, a gust of wind blew across the campsite, causing Marcus to turn away from the force. The tent's door flapped freely: the zip left fully open, just as he recalled.

Jacket, he thought, placing his arm through the gap of the door and feeling his way along the floor.

"Bloody thing. Where is it?"

He crawled inside to grab his coat. The hair on the back of his neck suddenly rose and his mind went blank. He was paralysed by the sight before him. Bran lay comfortably wrapped in the sleeping bag, deep in sleep and snoring loudly. A shiver clawed through him as he watched his friend peacefully slumber.

Breaking his trance, Marcus turned to look at the woods, afraid of what he might see. The wood lay bare. Silent as night. Not even the sounds of the wildlife making their presence known. And as he looked to the place where he thought Bran stood, all that remained was a colourful hat. Its fluorescent colours caught his eye through the tall green grass.

His hand delved deep into his pocket. His chest became tight and constricted. The symptoms he had come to know all too well throughout his childhood presented themselves, and he lifted his inhaler to his lips.

A hand grabbed Marcus firmly by the shoulder, followed by a prompting squeeze. A sound moved past his lips. A sound he had not heard before, yet felt little embarrassment for. Falling backwards his head hit the wet earth, his inhaler rebounding quietly from the ground. He looked up. Gregory stood above him. It was obvious by his expression he was clueless as to what had caused the young boy's reaction.

"You OK there, son?" said Gregory. "For a moment there, I could have swore you were struggling for air?"

The old man lowered a hand down to Marcus, helping him up with a strong and sturdy pull. Marcus looked around him, avoiding the question and collecting his inhaler. He made sure it was undamaged, pressing the container down and sending dry power to fire suddenly into the breeze.

"Won't you waste it? Doing that, I mean?" asked the old man.

"It's fine," replied Marcus, trying to get over the shock.

The old man frowned, watching as the young boy was still trying to survey the distant tree line.

"You sure everything is OK, boy?"

"Hmm?" replied Marcus bringing the inhaler to his mouth for a third time.

"I said, you alright."

Marcus didn't answer. Was he alright? At this particular time, he wasn't entirely sure. Images of what had just occurred bounced about his mind. And with this, in his very soul there lived the lingering knowledge of eyes following him from afar.

Movement in the tent broke through the uneasiness as Bran sat up to yawn and rub the sleep from his eyes. His hair was standing on point.

Gregory looked to the morning sky, stretching his upper back.

"Best get a move on, boys," said Gregory, walking back to his rifle.

"What? Before breakfast?" Bran decided to resume his position in the sleeping bag.

*

The morning was warm and pleasant and not nearly as hot as the previous day. It was still early, and despite the old man's eagerness, the boys took their time to pack. The tent was folded neatly, allowing space for their jackets. Marcus was quiet, far more quiet than usual. He tiptoed around the camp, jumping at any noise, not to mention the sight of his own shadow.

"What's with you?" asked Bran.

"Nothing."

"Something's with you. You've been on pins all morning."

Marcus scowled, quickly looking over at the old man who also eyed him suspiciously.

"Nothing's with me. Just a bad dream, that's all." Marcus placed the colourful hat upon his head.

"Hey! You found it!" said Bran.

"Found what?"

"That stupid hat. I'm sure I watched that vile thing float off down the river."

Marcus tightened the cords on his backpack, ignoring the interrogating glares from either side while he looped the straps around his shoulders.

"Ready?" said Marcus, still dismissing their questioning stares.

The old man stood and walked past Marcus without a word. His rifle led the way, sinking into the ground with every given step. Bran began to follow, casually strolling past Marcus, whistling a familiar tune that was popular well before their time. Marcus's stare lifted from the ground. Evidently, time had slowed for only Marcus. A dizziness shook his head, and his vision blurred into one continuous loop. He was struggling to regain his focus, but staring at Bran's checked shirt caused the pattern to jump out at him. There was something different about it. He knew there was, but the more he studied the shirt, the more his feelings intensified.

"Bloody thing," said Bran looking down at the loose pocket bouncing about his chest. He grabbed at it, giving it a good hard yank. The stitching tore effortlessly from the shirt, ripping a larger hole beneath.

Marcus gazed at the torn pocket, his memory searching back to what had occurred that morning. Then it hit him. The memory belted him like a brick to the face. Bran's ripped pocket was on the left.

Chapter Forty-Two

They were closer now. The old man could feel it coming. Those same feelings that absorbed his senses for what felt to be a lifetime were returning. He hated the thought, the memories. However, his footing stayed true, never straying from his chosen path, moving forward as his past became the present. He never gave so much as a flinch as he repeatedly looked back to make sure the boys stayed close. He could hear them. It was impossible not to. Young folks today seemed to do nothing but bicker, despite holding the most desirable friendship. Gregory couldn't understand it, but it was quite obvious this generation of youth was miles apart from what he had known. Marcus and Bran continued their quarrel. Each voice raised in volume in a feeble attempt of one hot head to pathetically out voice the other.

"What's your game, boys?" Gregory slammed the rifle stock on the ground.

The boys stopped their sparring session, frowning deeply at each other and refusing to answer the question.

"Well?"

The silence persisted as the old man folded his arms to wait. "We shan't be moving until the matter is settled. I can't be listening to you both quarrel like that."

293

The boys again exchanged glances. The stubbornness in their eyes was beginning to soften.

"Well," said Marcus bashfully, "you just look kind of tired, Mr Degg. I'm…I mean, we were just a little concerned about your health, is all."

The old man raised a single brow, preparing himself for what might come next.

"Go on," he said humbly, allowing them time to speak.

"Well, we were just talking. Wondering, I suppose. If anything should ever happen to you out here, how the hell we'd get you back."

Marcus paused for a moment, struggling to swallow back his words.

"I mean, you're no young man anymore, sir."

"No need to remind me."

"How old did you say you were?"

"I didn't," snapped Gregory. "And never you mind."

"Look, Greg," Bran confidently stated. "All I said was, with this being Marcus's trip and all, if you so happened to drop down dead, it would be his responsibility alone to drag your bony carcass back to Thyme. That's all."

"Charming," muttered Gregory. "How very decent of you."

"Yeah," replied Bran. "But I was only having a laugh. It's not my fault the poor sap takes everything so seriously."

The boys' quarrel started again. Not even the old man could delay it.

They pushed and prodded, eventually rolling to the ground, grasping one another in some kind of strange entangled hug.

So, this is fighting these days, thought Gregory with a pitiful glance.

Bang!

A single report echoed through the woods. Bran and Marcus disengaged and lay flat on the grass, prostrate from the adrenaline of confrontation.

"There'll be no more of this," directed Gregory. "Do you understand me?"

His tone was reminiscent of the speech used by a parent, something which had been sitting dormant in Gregory for decades.

"Are we in agreement?" Gregory leaned forward as he repeated his question, trying to intimidate them by size alone.

"Yes."

The old man accepted the answer graciously, knowing it was coerced. They didn't have to like him or even respect him. But he had to rely on discipline. Maybe it was nothing more than a badly acted play, but there had to be discipline. He had learned for himself that to get what you wanted in life, sometimes a little pretence could go a long way. This was not one of life's big secrets. Everyone did it. Well, almost everyone. It would just take a person like him to admit it. He looked back down at the boys and brought his thoughts back to the discussion at hand.

"Shall we continue then?" asked Gregory, holding the barrel of his gun straight in front of him.

"And... you'll be alright?" said Marcus, his voice filled with concern. The idea of having to carry the old man was more than he wanted to consider.

"Indeed I will, son. There's still life in me yet."

*

The old man was determined to cover more ground. He swung his arms as he took giant strides across the land.

Where does he get the energy? Marcus was in no mood for conversation and filtered to the back of the line. Apparently no one else was wanting to talk either, and the trek fell quiet. That suited Marcus just fine.

The comfortable morning temperature had dissolved into another hot day in the forest. The heated air rose and shimmered. Marcus was getting dizzy, and his temples were starting to pulse.

When was the last time I drank anything?

He couldn't recall.

One day? Maybe more?

He walked on blindly, closing his eyes and allowing the summer breeze to help guide him. If only it was just another peaceful day. If only all of this was the trip he intended. If only.

He listened to the sounds ahead. Bran's footfalls brushed the knee-high grass and his laces sounded like whips when they struck the greenery.

He listened more closely and could almost detect the sound of the rifle as it clunked under Gregory's weight. As he continued to concentrate on what was audible, his mind began to drift to memories. They hauntingly played over and over: a play whose curtain would never fall. He knew it was embedded in his mind forever.

Marcus opened his eyes, surprised to see the view had radically changed. The forest opened up around them, stretching out into a field that was noticeably unshielded from the sun. Dead yellow grass stood on end, hissing in the breeze as though begging for water.

How long were my eyes closed? He was a bit bewildered and even wondered if he might have been sleepwalking. He couldn't deny that he was tired. He felt insecure and vulnerable. Was he experiencing a nervous breakdown? He asked himself that very question

I'm being ridiculous, he thought, unable to remember the last time he sensed fear during daylight.

Maybe I'm going insane?

It was possible. According to his history books, people had been declared insane for far less. They would get locked up and the key would be disposed of. They would never be seen nor heard of again. Could that happen to him?

Bran and old Gregory stopped ahead, their figures swaying in the heat haze as they slumped down to their knees. Marcus tried to catch up, but his efforts fell short and his legs began to wobble.

The sound of flowing water gave each of them the push they needed. They all knelt down by the stream and lifted cupped hands to dry mouths.

Gregory sat upright gasping for breath. Drips of water paraded down his face, and the heat of the afternoon dried his forehead in seconds.

"Fill your boots, boys," said Gregory while returning to the stream. "It'll be the last clean water you'll get."

The youngsters were far too consumed by an unquenchable thirst to hear what he said. A large cloud came to shade the ground, cooling and calming the air. They continued to drink, and soon tiredness caught up with them. Dry grass rustled beneath them as they sluggishly rolled onto their backs.

"No time for this, boys. We must move, right this second."

The boys climbed to their feet and groaned. The sense of thirst was never far away. They started to walk, following the brook downstream.

"And where are you both headed?" called Gregory. "We continue north I'm afraid, through here." He pointed across the stream.

Bran's eyes followed the man's shaking finger to the opposite side of the brook. A fortress of white oak blocked all paths, swallowing the land.

"Through there?" asked Marcus.

Gregory nodded, stepped over the shallow water, and walked towards the large protruding roots reaching out from the earth.

"I don't like the look of this." Bran stared past the trees.

"And you're right not to," replied Gregory.

"Can't we just carry on this way for a while?"

"No, our path lies ahead, I'm afraid. And no amount of whining will make it otherwise."

"But why?" continued Bran childishly. "How can you even tell where you're going?"

"I'd have thought by now that would be perfectly obvious."

The old man turned away, admiring the colonnade of trees towering overhead. He remembered the forest clearly now. It had changed some over the years, but the unwelcoming sense of emptiness was still there.

Marcus stood watching him scout beside the tree line. *He's lost his way*? And again Gregory backtracked. *He's afraid perhaps*? That would be the more understandable of those two options. After all, why wouldn't he be? Maybe coming back here was just a bad idea. Maybe it was all too much for him.

A memory flashed through Marcus like a bolt of electricity, and he remembered the night at the hut. He looked wildly around as he recalled events that seemed so long ago. The same rhyme was written in the book that Gregory carried. He asked to see it with excitement, then flicked through the pages to find the poem. When he found it, he flattened the pages and cracked the spine in the process. The first line jumped at him in the daytime sun.

Amongst the oaks the shadows stride.

Marcus looked up to Bran, who by now was dawdling next to the old man.

"Amongst the oaks the shadows stride," said Marcus softly beneath his breath.

It's a map!

His feet almost flew, barely touching the ground as he leaped over the steady flow of water.

"It's a map," yelled Marcus, waving the book in his hand. "You wrote it to remember."

"What… what is?" asked Bran.

"The poem! I was clueless before, but I see it now. Here, take a look for yourself."

Marcus tossed the book to Bran, but his gaze remained on Gregory.

"A sharp eye, Mr White. I like that." The old man clearly approved. "Though I assure you I was not concerned with remembering."

"Then, why write it down, if not to remember?"

"That's simple. To be warned."

*

With the book handed back, Marcus carefully wrapped it, covering it tightly and tucking it safely away in his rucksack.

"Thank you," said Gregory, watching the book being neatly tucked away.

"You're welcome. I should've took more care of it."

"Just words on paper, son. That's all it is. And when this is all over, I'd be happy to see the back of it."

"So would we!" interrupted Bran, slouching against the trunk of an oak tree.

The wind shifted direction and shook the tree, causing a few leaves to fall.

"So, what now?" Marcus was almost afraid to ask.

"Now? Now we end this, my boy," said Gregory.

"And you sure you know where you're going? I don't like the look of these woods." Bran was being a bit patronising.

Gregory surveyed the stretch of woodland, sighed deeply, and spat before he spoke. "Regrettably, I know these woods all too well. Nothing ever changes. Though I will warn you, this is a challenging place."

The old man thought for a second, rubbing on the back of his neck before finally making a suggestion. "Maybe I should do this alone, boys."

Marcus and Bran exchanged glances, not sure of the reason why.

"You have done well, boys, honestly you have," continued Gregory. "But perhaps you would be safer here. If I'm not back by morning, make your way home. You can contact the authorities from there. Be sure to tell them everything."

"Not a chance!" Marcus was adamant as he stood tall and prepared himself for whatever challenges were ahead.

"Now, boy, see reason, will you. I…"

"No, it's our friend! We're going!" yelled Marcus.

"I'm happy to wait here." Bran regretted the words as soon as they were uttered.

Eyes as sharp as daggers glared back at him. He realised that he should learn to think before he blurted out anything in future.

"What?" said Bran, ready to swallow his words. "You don't even know if he's in there!"

All three turned to the bleakness of the grove.

"He's in there alright," said Gregory. "I bet my soul he is."

"Then that's enough for us," whispered Marcus. "We're coming, Jack."

One by one the three merged with the jumble of branches. The boys first, followed shortly by Gregory who looked back one last time to catch a glimpse of the sun. His eyes glistened with sadness as he looked down. Although his lips were visibly trembling, he never let out a sob. His features twitched and his mouth fell slightly agape as he slyly drew in a breath. He hid his face as he walked.

Chapter Forty-Three

Olivia awoke from the same old dream. A sense of despair overcame her as she welcomed back the blackness that had engulfed her life. Frustrated, she let out a deranged scream. There were bruises over her arms and legs from hitting the hard ground, and her head filled with unstoppable images as the tears began.

Olivia shuddered and wiped the tears and sweat from her face, recalling the demon's haunting voice. And the smell of those damned pumpkin cakes! It was so real that she was sure it would linger here in this world. But there was one thing for sure; she'd never taste one again. That idea left a dull ache swirling in her gut. Despite her desire to vomit, she was hungry. She had looked at so many plants and leaves, wondering if any were edible.

Would they taste good?

Olivia tugged on the leaf of a nearby plant and inspected its texture and colour in the moonlight. She thought it didn't look poisonous, but how could she be certain?

Doesn't smell poisonous either.

The remark, even if just to herself, seemed rather stupid. Olivia pulled the plant up from its roots. She opened her mouth, took a large bite, and cringed at the foul potent taste. It was strong and assaulted her taste buds. Both shoulders scrunched in disgust.

Chew, God dammit, chew! She was unable to force her jaws to obey. A loud crunch finally could be heard when she bit down on the stem. She shook in revulsion as the vile thing slid slowly down her throat.

"Not too bad." She exhaled and prepared for the second course. She bit down hard and quick, but the taste never faded no matter how fast she chewed.

One more bite. Just one. She tried to convince herself and placed a rolled-up morsel gently on her tongue, dwelling on the lengths she had gone to trying to survive.

The night remained unchanged, a picture-perfect setting for a living nightmare. Everything was motionless for now. The solitude was comforting as she remained camouflaged by the surrounding ferns. Slightly emotional, she reminisced about the day she doodled innocently by the spring.

My notebook! she thought, wondering if someone, *anyone*, had found it. Olivia leaned back to conserve what little energy she had left. A coldness came up from the earth, but she hadn't noticed the goosebumps forming on her flesh. Her eyes closed, knowing that sleep would not come easily. A branch snapped in the distance, putting Olivia on edge. The forest was still. Just what she was hoping for. The woodland silhouette defined the land and reminded Olivia of those popup books she owned as a toddler.

Looks clear.

Convinced, she prepared to hide. And that's when she saw it.

There was only one. At least, that's what she thought. A girl no older than she emerged from the trees. The small body was draped in a grey tattered gown, her blonde hair plaited with a bow illuminated by the moonlight. Olivia watched nervously as her vision faded in and out from lack of sleep.

Please go away, she thought, her nose now just above the ferns.

The child stood as still as stone, gazing at Olivia through soulless, white eyes.

"Shoo! Get out of here!" commanded Olivia while she frantically waved her arms.

She searched the surrounding area for a quick and easy exit. There wasn't one. Instead, more figures materialized near the tree line. They all stood rigid and watched her from afar.

They were children. Innocent children, just like her. Something had happened to them, something terrible. Olivia could sense it. She could see it in their faces. Their eyes screamed out in torment as their bodies remained locked in place.

"Leave me alone!" Olivia screamed, her voice trembling, a flush of tears rolling swiftly down her cheeks. She had no idea who these children were. She didn't want to know. But she was certain she had no intention of becoming one of them. Footsteps rustled across the forest floor; childlike whispers stirred the echoes from another world.

Yet still the shadowed children observed her. Olivia slowly retreated, shuffling her feet backwards through the tangled shrubs. She stopped when she stumbled against something far too soft, turning in terror to be face to face with another. Olivia screamed again, staring up into eyes that looked down at her. It was a boy, slightly older than the others. His skin was pale and chalky. The clothes he wore were far too large, hanging loosely from his lanky physique. His hair was pasted down to his scalp, and water dripped continually from his forehead and seeped into his eyes. It was his eyes that caught Olivia's attention. They were not like the others, lost and ghostly. His eyes still bore a soul, shining vibrantly and filling the night with colour even though they were sad and desperate. They reflected a fight she knew he'd lost. Is this what would become of her? Destined to suffer these haunted grounds, wandering endlessly until her existence faded from memory?

No, she would not allow it. Not now. Not after all she had been through. The boy's bright eyes looked down at her, his expression dull and vacant, as she struggled to find her feet. The shadowed figures shrieked violently. The noise invaded her ears and shook the forest ground. She looked back at the boy whose dripping hand reached out for her to hold. But Olivia would not take it. Instead, she kept her distance and did the only thing she knew. She ran. Her feet smacking the ground as she fled, never looking back into those bright eyes.

Amongst the Mists

Chapter Forty-Four

The afternoon heat evaporated into the damp and eerie evening. A chill enveloped them, and the unpleasantness of the day's scorching heat somehow escaped their minds as they tensed their muscles and harshly rubbed their flesh for warmth. Hours had passed while they trudged relentlessly through the deep and dark jungle. It was otherworldly to them. Vines hung down from the trees like thickened ropes. The ground was thick with vegetation that wrapped around limbs and cut their path in every direction.

"Are you sure this is right?" said Bran, looking back at the old man.

"Yes." The reply was sharp.

"Well, I don't like it. Not one bit."

"Me, neither," said Marcus, holding back to wait for the others.

"I feel the same every time, boys," replied Gregory.

"Every time?"

A squelching noise drew Bran's attention. A wet and mucky sensation seeped through the leather of his trainers, soaking the soles of his feet. He stepped forward and his other foot sank deep in the mud. It was like quicksand that fed on his limbs and pulled him deeper into the muck.

It was a fight to break free, as Marcus soon learned, following the footprints left behind by Bran.

"What the hell is this place?" Bran asked in frustration while he tried desperately to stay upright. He fell in spite of his efforts and coated his clothes in a greenish brown sludge.

"It's exactly where we needed to be." Gregory pulled Bran up with the barrel of the gun.

"And that is?"

"This, my boy, is the outskirts of Brocton Swamp.

*

There was no telling how far they had come. Nevertheless, the three marched onwards. The swamp became deeper and trickier to navigate. Mud covered their clothing, weighing them down and numbing their legs. A thin mist crept across the stagnant surface, obscuring their footing and slowing their pace all the more. The old man stopped, his knees visibly buckled from under him as he sucked in humid air.

"Sorry boys, I'm no spring chicken anymore. This didn't seem so difficult the last time."

He coughed violently, spitting out mucus while thumping harshly at his chest.

Marcus didn't speak but looked all around. He considered how the height of the trees blocked out the reality of the normal world and buried him beneath. It was an unbearable thought. Now he understood why the locals avoided this place and why Gregory had suggested they stay behind.

Pull yourself together, thought Marcus. *We still have a job to do. Besides, what good would the old man be on his own?* He looked back, watching as Gregory hunched over and fought to catch his breath. *No good, that's what!*

It was then Marcus noticed the mist around his feet begin to thicken, slowly rising to envelope the bottom half of his body. A fog sank down from the sky and merged with the mists into one thick blanket. It had come out of nowhere, encircling them while all they could do was watch.

"You gotta be kidding me, right?" Bran fanned his hands in front of his face. "I've never seen a fog like it."

"What does it mean?" Marcus could barely see Gregory standing beside him.

"It means we're near," Gregory's voice was hoarse as he continued to choke on the fog.

"Near to Jack?"

"Aye," he coughed, placing a hand on the boys' shoulders. "But don't relax yourselves just yet. If Jack's still here, evil will be close at hand. It always is. Please remember, your friend will be trapped in its claws now, boys. Hidden away in a world unlike our own."

"How do you mean?" asked Bran.

"The mists, boy. I have come to understand it is the opening between two worlds. While the mists lie thick, its domain will not close. Beyond this door I have no answers. Only that there is more than death."

"Is there suffering?"

"I don't know," said Gregory. He hid his teary eyes from the stares that searched his face.

"We need to keep moving. Staying put will only weaken us."

Something brushed Marcus's arm. The movement was followed by the sound of heavy footsteps slopping behind the wall of mist.

"Listen out for my steps, lads. And please, keep close."

It was harder than expected. The mist became impenetrably dense. Time and time again they fell to the water's stinking slime. With each fall the footsteps halted while the others waited patiently for the fallen to re-join the march. It was exhausting work. The boys were so fatigued that their steps began to drag. They desperately held on to the hope that the end of their ordeal was near. Bran muttered to himself, frustrated by his constant stumbling. Up in front, Marcus struggled to breathe, the damp air drowning his lungs as he let out a deathly wheeze. He was concentrating so completely on the task at hand that he didn't notice his breathing. Their surroundings suddenly turned silent.

"Why we stopping?" asked Marcus, finally fishing out the inhaler from his pocket. He gave three solid puffs, exhaling, and his symptoms were relieved in seconds.

Gregory didn't reply. And with the fog blinding Marcus's senses, the old man appeared to have vanished.

"Old man! What's the hold up?" shouted Bran, bumping clumsily into the back of Marcus.

310

"Quiet!" whispered Gregory. His voice was soft and wary as the mist concealed him.

"Quiet? Why?" asked Bran.

"Can't you hear it?"

"Hear what?"

Goosebumps marched up Marcus's arms, spreading wildly until his entire body was covered. A faint hum pervaded the air. It was faint at first then grew gradually when the three stopped to listen.

"What is that?" Marcus reached out to tug the old man's shirt.

"Stay… still." Gregory's tone was stern. "Don't… move."

The sound of humming distorted to a static-like crackle, pitching high and low before finally syncing in time. A thunderous noise trembled through the darkness, forcing the swamp's floor to rise and shake. The boys gasped sharply. Shadows weaved from either side. Black forms twined through the mist like hovering ghosts. The three made no sound, watching intently as the dark sinister forms floated gracefully into the distance. It all happened so fast. From behind them, a voice called out. The boys pulled and scrambled, climbing over each other to take the lead. Marcus had no recollection of what was said. Panic overtook his body, and adrenaline gave him the energy to race through the fog, smacking into several trees along the way. Bran kept driving forward and managed to keep his pace.

Gregory shouted from far behind them. "Don't run, boys. Don't –"

A single shot fired from a distance letting a single spark spread through the thick grey cloud.

Marcus stopped and listened to Bran's feet charging through the murk. There was silence behind him. Water rippled around his knees. Fear took hold, followed by guilt as he got closer to Bran. The old man was gone.

Chapter Forty-Five

No matter how hard she screams, or how fast she runs, the forms of children are near her. They do not grab or chase, but remain still, simply watching from beyond the treeline as Olivia's legs merge to a blur across the forest floor.

The pain is now tearing at the soles of her feet. She doesn't care. She clenches her teeth and bears the pain that she knows so well.

"Who are they?" Olivia asks breathlessly. *Where do they come from?*

One by one the figures seem to emerge from nothingness; the sadness and trauma on their faces are far too intense for Olivia to handle. She sees a straight, narrow path in the distance, giving her the impetus to move faster, using all the concentration she has left to focus on the dangers ahead. Her body tenses with each advancing step, the colour drains from her face and changes her complexion to a clammy shade of grey. Her heartbeat pounds in her ears as she struggles to guide her steps.

Don't stop.

The same two words repeat in her mind over and over again, pushing her forward and convincing her that rest is not an option. Olivia's impetus starts falling short as weariness takes its toll. Her legs begin to feel like jelly as she tries for a few more strides. She stumbles to her side and hits the ground with a violent thud. Her head lifts but her body is too numb and weak.

Gunfire erupts in the distance. Havoc rolls through the forest as voices call in despair. Olivia's mind begins to wander, her fragile body too exhausted to acknowledge the distant haze of screams. Her hair falls in clumps around her neck. She clenches her fists and pounds the earth. It's the only way she knows to display her hatred.

The gun fire shortly dies. Again, the screams for help and the sound of stomping boots travel across the land. Bodies collide in panic. Then the steps of many turn into the steps of only one. Olivia begins to shake in anticipation as the sound draws closer. It takes all the strength she can muster to rise to a kneeling position. She brushes her hair from her face and looks up.

A man stumbles before her, his boots grind as he runs. He looks troubled, *scared,* as sweat flies freely down his temples. He wears a uniform. An old uniform with epaulettes drooping from its shoulders hangs on a boyish frame. He wears no cap, perhaps fallen behind him in the panic, though Olivia can tell he owned one; his hair squashed flatly to his head, spiking up only around the curves of his ears. He displays no badges or medals on his chest, only the look of horror painted across his face. Olivia calls out, already accepting the cause will do her no good. The man doesn't see her, doesn't acknowledge her. He looks her way as though she is nothing more than a ghost. Maybe that is exactly what she has become?

She looks out across the woodland to the children still standing there and watching. They look directly at him.

Can they see him? Can he see them?

It is an impossible question to answer. She is struck by the revelation that maybe her soul has passed to the afterlife. Maybe what she sees is the living.

Olivia pleads silently for a different outcome. She wishes hard. But the one certain thing is this place, *This Hell,* is not a part of the world she knew, the real world. No, this place is part of something far more wicked. This is a world where innocence is feasted on, where strength is drained, where a life is left to rot and a soul yearns for freedom. There is more. She knows something else thrives here. Olivia can feel it. Always has. Whatever it is exactly isn't clear to her. But its presence always lingers, feeding on the sorrow of suffering victims involuntarily trapped here and forced to roam for eternity.

*

The young soldier circles the ground again and again, his hands grip wildly at his slicked back hair, pulling it out by the roots. He mutters words through tightly clenched teeth, though Olivia fails to hear them. There is something in the air now. She feels it. A thick, unsettled atmosphere encircles them both, ready to be sliced with a knife. The man jolts back, gasping silently and almost trips on his own two feet. He knows where to look: back in the direction from where he came. Back to the sound of voices.

"Lost!"

The man hears it too, and whimpers aloud like a lost child. The haunting sound sends a shiver up her back and makes her bottom lip quiver uncontrollably. Somehow, she finds her feet. That same voice taunts her, reminding her of how little she's managed to achieve since that day. Sickness overwhelms her, and she realises there will be no escape. Olivia turns back to the soldier, who for the first time appears to gaze fearfully into her eyes.

He sees me! She wonders why the man looks so troubled as he sprints towards her.

The sound of the man's footfalls grows nearer and rapid, forcing her to try to protect her small body. Olivia tries the only way she knows how; she reaches out her arms to stop the impending collision. Though no impact ever comes. Instead, a bitter chill flows through her, a sensation she can only describe as walking headlong into an icy blizzard. She lowers her hands and looks at her surroundings. But the man has vanished. Even his boots failed to leave their marks.

She looks down at her ragged clothes and pale, bruised skin, feeling like she is wrapped in an icy blanket. The eyes are still watching. Behind her, the shadow of the man still runs and soon disappears into the wilderness.

"Wait!" Olivia yells desperately.

She turns to follow, somehow managing to keep him in her sights. His arms move frantically while a limp slows his pace on challenging ground, giving Olivia an opportunity to close the distance between them.

She is hot on his trail by now. The sound of his panicked breath becomes louder and louder. Still, he doesn't look back, doesn't acknowledge the fearful child who follows. Suddenly, the ground becomes boggy and slick, forcing Olivia's heart to sink as she surveys the mushy land ahead. Within a matter of seconds her progress is slowed by the ground itself. Every step feels like twenty. The sucking sludge holds her feet in an attempt to make her stay.

"Hey! Wait!" She cries in despair to the man upfront. "Don't leave me!"

But it is too late. His body fades from view, leaving only the sound of his sloshing steps that also soon fade into the night.

Olivia loses her balance, falling to one knee and punching the water's edge in frustration. She begins to sob and mutters the same words over and over, wishing that someone, *anyone* will hear.

"Please… don't leave me."

Amongst the Mists

Chapter Forty-Six

Regardless of where she looks, everything appears the same. Olivia regrets her decision to find her way back here to this watery and desolate wasteland. She now sees no point in continuing. In any of it.

If only she could sleep. Sleep and be at peace. *Now, that would truly be heaven.*

The idea swims around in her head like the water she pushes aside. *To sleep and be free from nightmares*: those hideous dreams that force her back to reality and cause her to cry out loud in terror to the crisp night air.

She knows what she is experiencing is not living. She also understands much more. This is nothing more than a feeble existence that claws away at the youth she no longer owns. Olivia was a smart enough girl; that's what she had always

319

been told. She is smart enough to realise why she feels this way. Pain circulates through her body: a pain no child should have to bear. The regret is tough and debilitating, but nothing comes close to her crippling hunger. The hunger for it all to end.

The swamp's surface slides up to her waist, its bitter kiss stinging her flesh as she wades amongst the floating foliage. She thinks of stopping, to cry aloud one final time, but that ship has sailed. For now, all she longs for is relief.

*

A cascade of hanging moss drapes down from the arms of withered decaying trees. Disturbed, the insects fly buzzing about the air, then land on the intruder who wanders below them. Olivia clenches her eyes, waving away the vile pests that swarm and settle on her face. She coughs viciously in disgust, heaving on bugs that crawl past her blue tinged lips. She panics. Thrashing through the water, her senses become blind to this dank and secluded world.

"Get away!" She attempts to scream, spitting the words through her teeth.

An object impedes her path. Its form is tall and hard, causing Olivia to graze her brow and fall backwards. She looks up. A tall stone towers over her. Its shape is intimidating, peering down as though it were looking at a forgotten friend. Olivia stands and grasps the rocky surface. For the shortest time, imagination takes hold and she fondly wraps her arms around her mother's waist. Olivia feels her presence, every bit of it. A love like no other. A love she desperately seeks. The smile on her face, the fragrance of her skin. All the little things she thought she'd lost. It was all still with her. She would never forget.

"I love you." Olivia whispers the words with an innocent sob. Loosening her hold, she gently touches the cold solid stone.

If only I could hear her voice. Olivia thinks. *Just one last time.*

Soon, walking becomes easier. The depth of the water sways to shallows and permits the glue-like muck to harden. Olivia's knees lift high, her legs as light as feathers. Yet she feels no joy, no sense of relief. There is only one course, *one choice.* She must continue walking, never stopping until she treads her last.

The desolation engulfs her presence. Olivia mumbles discreetly and hesitantly murmurs tunes of childhood to keep her mind distracted. Standing stones follow a snake-like curve, appearing to weave behind clouds of floating steam as they come into view. She brushes each one as she paces, never forgetful, recalling the ground she had walked. Olivia halts mid step. She listens hard, tilting her head to a sound trailing softly through the breeze. The hum of nature's song. It calls to her. There is comfort in its tone, the settling riff plays kindly to her senses. Even so, she follows willingly, each step chasing the last. She is terrified that the sound will cease and the tune lost forever.

The tune grows through the blackness, its sound now so loud it hurts her ears.

Where is it!

Olivia's head twists frantically from side to side: her attention focuses on a wall of rocks lying huddled upon a mound. The circular wall is tightly knit, feeding together like a drystone jigsaw with only two colliding stones for its entrance. The tune turns discordant, violently vibrating the ground and the stones. She peers inside the gap, both hands firmly clamped on her ears.

"Hello?" she yells, fighting through the noise. There is no reply.

Of course, there isn't.

Olivia bends down making sure to protect her head, the silhouette of her body unites with the shadows.

*

Emptiness entombs her. Olivia's nails scrape harshly against the rocks' rough and slimy surfaces as she guides herself around the inner walls. The sound that lingers fades to soothing silence. Little light enters this space. A pool of water swamps the centre, black and eerie, reflecting a shimmering ray from a pearl lit moon. The drops of water from the weeping rocks echo on impact, falling flatly to the pool with a defining *plink*. A heavy breath exhales, looping around the room, its mood cold and cruel.

Olivia freezes, scurrying to the ground for a weapon. Her hands find a long stick. She grips it stiffly and prepares to swing.

"Come out then, freak! Come on! Where I can see you," Olivia screams. She practices several heavy blows by sweeping cleanly through the air.

"What's the matter?" She gulps. "You a coward?"

The breathing deepens, crawling across the walls and surrounding her every turn. Olivia swings again and again, the stick striking nothing but stone.

"What are you waiting for?"

A cloud lifts from above the roofless structure, shining an icy light softly on her skin and illuminating the ground where she stands.

Olivia's knuckles clench, wrapping tighter around her weapon as she brings it up to the light. It is a stick like none she has ever seen. It is strong, bowed. The colour reflects a chalky shade and its shape widens at the end.

A bone!

Olivia gasps as shock sends spasms to her hands, and the club spirals to the ground. A rattle spreads around her, the noise ending in an abrupt splash.

Olivia's head bows down, her eyes bulging as she stares at the ground.

Bones. Thousands of them, an array of large and small, piled like garbage. There is no organisation to where they lay as she sees the toppling skulls with their empty eyes and slack jaws. She shrieks a sound unlike anything she has ever made before. Olivia jumps back, whacking her head against one of the stones.

Following the room's curve, she slides desperately to escape. Olivia steps lightly, though the sound of crunching bones beneath her feet cannot be helped. The sound penetrates the silence and makes her physically sick. Shapes merge into view, and before she realises what is happening, they sit on the floor beside her.

Olivia studies what is in front of her, something no one should witness. Bodies of wanderers long since passed are heaped side by side. Their remains are only bones, but the skeletons are still draped in tattered clothes. They look so small, helpless. Olivia cannot resist the thought that, by their appearance, they are no older than she. Her eyes pan over them, trying to count the deceased. One body stands out amongst the rest. Its tiny shape layered in a muddied white gown and curled up into a ball where it rests. A tear falls down Olivia's cheek, the overwhelming emotion too troubling for her to bear. She knows it's impossible, yet still she feels its suffering, its pain.

She kneels and strokes the smoothness of its skull in one swift movement. The body's hand is tightly fisted, concealed by only the baggy gown. Around the wrist is a loosely wrapped blue ribbon, holding on tightly for possession.

Olivia stands wiping the streams of tears from her face. She understands the irony of their suffering. Their torture in life has ended, but the torment of the soul continues. Another body catches her eye, somewhat different from the rest. Its form, larger. Its teeth jagged and chipped. The body rests painfully on its side; half submerged by the pool's murky depths. A skeletal arm reaches out on the bank, straining for what is out of reach: the white gowned girl. Olivia looks deep into the skull's cracked sockets, seeing the relief but also the desperation of its final living moments.

What happened to you?

A deep prolonged sigh envelops her and holds her where she stands. The smell was unpleasant as though left to fester for hundreds of years. She freezes, her head locking in place. Across the pool two eyes float, peering back at her. Their glow intensifies as her heart begins to skip. Olivia is trapped with nowhere to run. Her only exit is lying behind the creature that stands close by. She hears it move, though its eyes remain blankly fixed.

"What are you?" Olivia whimpers. Her words tremble as she attempts to repeat them.

The world vibrates above and beyond her as screams echo with the suffering of trapped desperate souls. Olivia cannot escape them, and each howl infests like a parasite into the deepest corners of her mind. She collapses to the floor; the sharp carpet of bones violently breaks her fall.

"Lost…"

The voice is faint, yet feels so near.

The shadow floats forward, holding out a faded hand and beckoning her to take it. But she will not. Olivia scurries back, burying herself between rock and bones.

"Lost." The creature repeats the word, hovering at the edge of the pool. Its eyes glow white.

Olivia looks around, unable to imagine the suffering that took place in this very spot. She thinks of the fear, the innocence, and the beauty. The thought in the back of her mind is suggesting maybe, just maybe, not all is lost. Olivia takes one last look at the adult skeleton reaching from the pool.

Is this my story, just a different time?

She surveys the pile of bones surrounding her.

Is this what will become of me?

She can't help but think of the children in the forest, their souls never to be granted freedom.

"No!" Olivia shouts, standing tall and strong.

The creature watches on, its arm held out for hers. But for the first time Olivia feels no fear. No longer will she hide, run, or scream. No longer will she allow the beast to control her, to make her the victim of its wicked deeds. No longer will she be a part of its game.

Olivia steps forward, closer and closer to those blinding eyes. Though now, she feels nothing. A numbness confines her, spreading throughout her limbs so that not even the pains in her body can overcome it. She stands at the edge of the pool, watching as the shadow grows in stature.

She reaches out, straining to take the creature's claw as her body leans forward and the water bites hard at her toes.

They are close to touching. So close, she can feel the shadow's icy breath of death smear across her face.

"Come on! You want me, don't you?" Olivia taunts, waving her palm up front. "This is what you've been waiting for!"

The creature tries to grab her, but she is too far.

"Almost there," she strains.

It leans further, ready to aggressively snatch her hand. Olivia knows it's coming. Whatever sick twisted plan this thing holds is only a blink away. She takes back her hand with a swipe but does not run and instead stares blankly at the eyes that so want her.

"You can't have me."

Olivia puffs up her chest and draws in the deepest breath she can. She jumps, sinking into the lightless depths of the pool.

*

Water pushes in from all directions. The more she struggles, the more disorientated she becomes. Up down, left right, nothing makes any sense anymore as she kicks her legs. Olivia cannot see, for the world has gone black around her. She knows what she must do, though time is no longer on her side except for these precious seconds. She thinks of her greatest love as the cold tightens her chest. There is no need to search her mind. A particular memory is not what she seeks. All Olivia desires is a picture. A picture of her mother's face.

The image of the lady who stands before her warms Olivia's heart. Wearing an ordinary dress and with her curly brown hair pinned up, still allowing a strand or two to fall neatly to the sides, the woman smiles at her. Her polished white teeth match the glint in her bright blue eyes as she begins to speak softly.

I'm so proud of you, sweetheart.

Olivia yearns to talk back but knows it's impossible. She wants to cry but understands there is no time.

You are so brave my darling... Just one last thing.

Her mother's words are so very gentle and full of love as she reaches to touch her daughter.

Oh, I love you, my darling.

Olivia's lungs lie heavy, burning with the need for air. Regardless, the time has come. She can no longer hold the pressure, as fluid fills her lungs. A muffled wail penetrates from above as she gives into the darkness and allows the water to take her.

Olivia's mind turns a blur. The sound of her own heartbeat drums loudly and wildly in her ears until it gradually beats its last. She can no longer tolerate it, nor does she have to. Words of prayer loop tediously around her brain, fading away to the sound of each thump.

Lord God, I pray for Your protection as I begin this day. You are my hiding place, and under Your wings I can always find refuge. Protect me from trouble wherever I go, and keep evil far from me...

Lifeless, she drifts downward, accompanied by the final sound of her mother's voice permeating through the blackness.

I love you, darling.

329

Amongst the Mists

Chapter Forty-Seven

The boys' panting resounded through the forest. The mist was at its densest. They felt it climbing over their faces, its thickness seeping down their throats.

Bran leaned forward, peering over Marcus's shoulders. He anticipated that Gregory would be walking behind them.

"Where's the old man?"

Marcus didn't reply. He didn't have the words. Not at the moment anyway.

"Marcus! Where is he? Where's Gregory?"

"Gone."

"Gone? What the hell do you mean, gone?"

Marcus placed his hands to his face, desperately trying to overcome the fears that have overtaken him.

"Well?"

"Don't start, Bran, – just don't."

Bran lunged forward and grabbed Marcus's collar with his trembling fist.

"Where is he?" Bran yelled.

"Gone." Marcus grit his teeth, smacking the hand that held him. "He's gone, alright? He told us not to run, but we did it anyway!"

An undeniable sense of guilt nestled on Bran's shoulders, forcing him to dismiss the possibility that the old man was alone and wounded.

"He could be OK. You don't know."

"No, didn't you hear him? He yelled out for us, but we just kept running... we didn't stop!"

"I didn't realise, alright. I was too busy –"

"Trying to save your own skin? Yeah, I got that. You were jumping over branches like Seabiscuit back there!"

"Well –

"Face it, Bran. We screwed him."

Bran said nothing. He could no longer think of what to say or how to justify his cowardice.

"I turned back," Marcus continued. "The man yelled out again and again. That was before going utterly gun crazy. He didn't make a peep afterwards. Whatever we fled from, it must've found him."

"That Sprit thing?"

Marcus nodded his weary head. Bending over and cowering into a ball, he began to weep quietly.

Bran huffed, and slowly knelt, resting his hand on his friend's shoulder.

"Come on, pal. We don't have time for this."

But his gesture didn't help. His friend's arched back jumped with each of his sobs.

"We'll get through this, I promise. Don't break on me now."

"Sure," stuttered Marcus. "Until you bail on me, too! Leaving me out in this shit hole to rot."

Compassion showed on Bran's face for the first time in years. He reassuringly patted his buddy firmly on the neck.

"That'll never happen, you hear me?"

"You swear?" bawled Marcus, slowly raising his head and sniffing loudly.

"Look at me, buddy."

Marcus looked up, glassy eyed. It was evident they shared the very same terror.

"I swear it."

They remained crouched side by side, quietly watching as the fog mimicked shapes out of the corners of their eyes. None stayed too long, each time dwindling back to a cloud-like form and soon drifted from sight.

"I can't wait to get home," Marcus muttered, his tears finally ending.

"Won't be long now," replied Bran poking at the small air bubbles that floated along the surface of the swamp.

"We'll both be back home before you know it."

"And Jack?"

"Yeah… that's what I meant. The both of us… and Jack."

"Oh. Okay."

Phew.

The light faded, the temperature dropping to a frosty chill. Still, they did not budge. They waited, holding the same positions, until the pain shooting up their thighs from their knees forced them to stand. The prolonged dampness had soaked their clothes, the fabric becoming soggy to the touch.

"We can't just stay here," said Bran trying to stand. His legs buckled beneath him.

"You're suggesting what exactly?"

"Well, to be truthful… I was kinda waiting on the old man to show up. At least he'd know the way out of here."

"I already told you, he's gone," hissed Marcus as he assisted Bran to his feet.

"I know, I know, calm down! But… there was always that chance," said Bran. "Now quiet! I'm going to take a peek."

Not in the mood to argue the point, Marcus sat impatiently waiting for a report.

"See anything?" Marcus whispered.

"One sec."

"What…?"

"I said one sec –"

"What…?"

"Christ sake, Marcus! Will you give me a bloody second!"

Bran stretched tall. As he wrapped himself around a small tree for support, its trunk creaked and groaned. Although he expected it to fall, it held his weight while he shifted his focus.

He fell back, sliding down heavily to Marcus's side.

"Well... see anything?"

"Nope."

"Nothing at all?"

"No. Not a soul."

"Try and climb a little higher, then."

"You fuckin' try and climb a little higher! There's nothing to see."

A few moments passed, giving time for them to collect their thoughts and for a sharp screech of a passing bird to warn them both of danger.

"So... any ideas?" asked Marcus.

"Yeah. We get out of here."

"But you have no clue which way. Don't even begin to pretend that you do."

"True," replied Bran "But moving somewhere, anywhere, is surely better than staying here!"

"I dunno..."

"Look! We can't stay. You know that! We'll freeze to death... without question. Look at us. We've barely sat here an hour already... I can't even feel my bollocks."

"No... me neither."

"So, get your arse up and move."

Marcus stood, aided by a branch that gave way to his grasp and showered them with crisp, dry leaves which spun and came to rest in the water. They didn't discuss a plan; there was none to discuss. Instead, they simply walked, single file, and no more than an arm length apart. Deeper and deeper through the fog.

*

The swamp was thick like day-old porridge. Night rolled over them like the flick of a switch, leaving little light to penetrate the ceiling of treetops. Every now and again overgrown brambles crept out, seemingly from nowhere, their razor thorns scraping like a wall of broken glass.

"Piss off, will ya!" Bran bit, turning to smack a bush clinging effortlessly to his shirt.

He tugged himself free, gaining an impressive new scratch that ran down the length of his arm.

"Well done." Marcus pulled his foot from the muck that was trying to swallow him whole.

"For what?"

"I'm just saying... you sure showed that plant who's boss."

"Oh, get lost!"

"No, seriously, what you gonna do next, headbutt a squirrel? Drop kick an owl?"

"No" snapped Bran. "But I just might smack you in the f–"

"Quiet!"

They both froze. While their feet sank slowly in the sludge, they both heard a familiar sound. The same sound had forced them both to run and had caused the fears that left a man to perish.

"You hear that?" asked Marcus, looking to the obstructed sky.

"I ain't deaf, 'course I hear it."

The noise enshrouded them and reverberated off the fog like perfectly tuned acoustics in the grandest theatre.

"Leg it!" instructed Bran. His feet were already coursing through the mire.

Marcus followed immediately, half expecting to be left for bait, the white smoke grabbing and pulling him back. He readied himself to shout, to curse aloud the selfish sod he followed. Bran splashed nearby, his silhouette visible, water foaming in waves at his sides. He paused before continuing to assure himself that Marcus was still at his tail.

"Come on!" Bran yelled back. "Don't stop for nothin!"

They ran hard despite the hindrance; the water slowing every single step. They got nowhere fast. Everything was a panic, *everything*. And soon, they no longer had the will to question the matter. Running was the only thing that made sense now, the direction was irrelevant.

The trees grew thicker ahead. Their shadows reminded Bran of a gathering crowd waiting for them to pass. Yet, all stayed still. Their forms were not like the other trees from the swampland: limp, rotting, and ready to fall. These trees were straight, tall, and strong and covered in a heavy padded moss from top to bottom. It was soft to the touch, crumbling in their hands as they grabbed and swung for leverage. The sound grew stronger, continually at their backs, like the chase of a mangy mutt, snarling and nipping at their feet.

Marcus looked back. *What is that?*

Something stirred just beyond his view. A faint dark shape swept creepily through the clouds with a *swoosh.* He didn't have the time to think. In fact, he didn't want to. The shape shifted from behind to his left, then right. *swoosh… swoosh… swoosh.* The movement was swift and faint but undeniably as visible as the mist he ran through.

Mind games. It's just mind games, thought Marcus as he ran into Bran, who now stood still in the water.

The two smacked heads with a cringe-worthy *thump,* throwing them dizzily to the mud.

"You gone blind or something?" yelled Bran, covering one eye.

"Blind or something? Are you for real?" replied Marcus sarcastically. "I can't see an inch in front of my pissin' nose!"

A rumble shook the swamp, followed by a prolonged hiss through the waving branches above. Bran and Marcus cowered, finding themselves tucked away beneath the roots of a fallen tree. They drew a deep breath, their backs pressed tightly against the hanging roots.

"Is that why you stopped?" whispered Marcus.

"What? No, I stopped for that thing."

"What thing?"

"That thing!"

Bran pointed over his shoulder as Marcus scuffled, clearing the curtain of roots aside. Bran joined him, and both watched the distant scene.

"Can you tell what it is?" asked Marcus.

"I dunno. At first I thought it was people."

"No, it's definitely not people."

"Well, I can see that now, can't I!"

The mist grew weaker as shadows towered up from what looked to be solid ground. The shadows solidified into large, tall stones.

"If that's what I think it is, I could kiss it," said Marcus, leaning himself back to rest.

"Kiss what?"

"Dry ground."

"Oh," replied Bran who was now on all fours with his head protruding from their hiding spot. A piece of paper dropped freely from his rear pocket. The paper was wet and fragile but was saved when Marcus swiped it from further harm. He shook away the droplets, delicately opening it out. Reading the text silently, his attention drifted when he observed the image of a young girl.

Blood drained from his face. Unable to budge he held his breath while his heart pounded in his chest. He could not divert his attention from the girl smiling back at him. He was mesmerised until the picture was snatched from his cold, wet hands.

"That's mine," said Bran with anger.

"Where did you get it?" asked Marcus.

"That dump of a cabin we stayed at. It was among all the clutter, that's all."

"Then why did you keep it?"

Bran grew speechless. "It's personal."

"Bran?"

"Ok! You remember that dream I told you about? The one with my mum?"

"Yeah…"

"Well, that little girl was a part of it. The same one, in this picture." Bran continued to point at the picture.

"Seriously?"

"Yeah. It's strange, some part of me just couldn't let it go. So I pocketed it. Funny really, I forgot all about it until now."

"It's anything but funny." Marcus was now turning a subtle shade of white.

"Why?"

"I never told you."

"Told me what?"

"On that day… the day we reached Sleathton, do you remember?"

Bran nodded his head, intrigued. *Of course, I do.*

"Well, we were racing for the lead. You darted off in front as usual, leaving me and Jack to chase. I recall it so vividly. I saw a girl, this girl," Marcus gestured to the paper, "watching us from the woods."

Bran looked down at the crinkled image.

"Impossible. This girl has been missing for years!"

"I can see that! But I'm telling you, it was her."

They both stared at the paper.

"It's the same smile, the same eyes," continued Marcus. "God, it's all coming back to me. I remember thinking, what was a girl that small doing out in the middle of nowhere?"

Bran shivered. A cold sensation brushed the back of his neck, causing the paper in their hands to tremble like jelly.

"What happened? And why didn't you bloody well mention it before?"

Marcus shrugged.

"Nothing happened. She was there, smiling at me. Then the world went black. I woke up on the ground, my bike turned over, and a hammer pounding at my head. The rest you know."

"Still doesn't explain why you kept it to yourself."

"There wasn't the chance."

"Bullshit!"

"Look, by the time I knew what happened, she was gone. I kept my eyes peeled for days. You would have thought me crazy. Don't deny it!"

Shaking his head, Bran leant back.

"If I'd have told you," Marcus continued, "it would have ruined everything. You would have found any excuse not to proceed with the trip. I couldn't risk it."

"Exactly! And by doing that you helped Jack's disappearance. We wouldn't be hiding in this slop right now if it wasn't for you."

Marcus didn't know how to respond, but anger stirred within his gut. He knew what Bran said was right. He could do or say nothing, he had to accept it.

The ground rumbled again and branches fell around them. They crouched down, edging out from their sinking refuge.

"Reckon we can make it to those rocks?" asked Bran.

Marcus looked to the stones, judging the distance.

"On the count of five?"

"Okay."

Bran counted down, his voice loud yet distant while preparing himself for the sprint.

For Marcus, his world became dizzy, a feeling that everything was happening in slow motion as he tried to listen to Bran shouting at his side.

"Four!"

He tried to pull himself together. But nothing made a difference. The world slowed.

"Two!" Bran warned, grasping Marcus firmly by his sleeve.

Marcus readied himself.

I don't know how much more of this I can handle.

"One!"

Bran tried to run, but Marcus was pulling him back.

"What are you playing at? Let go!" cried Bran without looking back.

Marcus didn't answer. He could not. Shock took hold of him, making it impossible to speak. He felt something. Something cold, blunt, and unyielding pressing into his scalp. Turning slowly, the object slid from ear to temple. Beyond the cold, solid metal was an old man, his finger ready at the trigger.

*

Terrified, Marcus did not move a muscle. He was frozen in place, watching his life flash before his eyes as he stared up the barrel of the gun.

"You!" gasped Bran.

The old man tightened the gun to his shoulder, his glare hard and aim steady.

"I warned you not to run, boys. This could have been so much easier. I promise you; you wouldn't have seen it coming.

"Seen what coming?"

The old man jolted. The rifle butt hit Marcus's head with a *crack*.

It all happened so fast Bran didn't have the time to react. He just stood there staring, mesmerised by his friend lying flat on his belly, air bubbles rising to his ears. The rifle's aim was shifted to Bran.

"Turn him over," said Gregory. "Unless you fancy him dead?"

Bran fell to the surface, turning Marcus over and exposing his front half which was now painted with mud. He put a hand on his chest and an ear to his lips.

"Still breathing?" asked Gregory.

Bran nodded, relieved.

"Hmm, good. I have a use for him."

A piece of paper brushed against the old man's ankle. He retrieved it, opening the fold with a flick of his hand.

"Ah, my darling girl. How beautiful you are."

Gregory's voice was soft and caring, his gaze sinking deep into the somewhat blurry print.

"Your girl?" asked Bran, still at Marcus's side.

"Quiet!" spit Gregory, allowing the paper to fall and his aim to rise.

Bran was stuck between a rock and a hard place. Should he stay, he believed it likely he would die. If he ran, any means of escape involved the abandonment of his friend.

"So… what now?" Bran looked up at the old man. "I guess I'm getting the same treatment?"

Gregory let out a false chuckle.

"On the contrary, Mr Lampshire. Who would I have to haul this body if I was to be so generous?"

Bran didn't answer but simply looked down and watched Marcus's shallow breathing.

"Come, up you get now," instructed the old man. "Don't forget the baggage, too. I won't risk anything being found."

"Where are we going?"

Gregory swung his gun to a one-armed point.

"To the stones, my boy. To the stones."

*

Marcus slid across the dirt. His body resembled a boy on the verge of death.

"Get a move on!" yelled Gregory.

Bran did as he was told without any questions, grasping Marcus's slippery wrists and heaving backwards. He quickly looked behind him and judged the stone's distance. For a moment, he wasn't sure he could make it. Two rucksacks hung heavily on his back, swaying him off balance. Sweat poured from this hairline: his face blotchy with redness. He heaved back again. His grip on his friend's wrists was hampered by the wetness of Marcus's skin. He lost his hold and dropped into the grime.

"You're slacking!" accused Gregory, swinging his rifle in an upward motion.

"I'm not! I swear!" Bran cried, overcome by his emotions.

"You are! I know you are!"

"The ground's too slick… and there's too much weight," said Bran, wiping the cool mud on his forehead. "I could make two trips? I'll carry Marcus first, then come back for the bags."

Gregory shook his head without even a mild consideration of the suggestion.

"Nonsense," said Gregory, directing a one-eyed stare. "Tell me, do you believe me a fool?"

Bran held his tongue, giving himself any opportunity to rest. The longer he kept the old goat talking the better.

No, I consider you a complete mental case!

"No…" replied Bran.

The old man gave a patronising grin that revealed black and yellow teeth hanging loosely from his gums.

"Then get to your feet and carry him."

"I can't!"

"You can, and you will," the old man growled. "Heed my words, boy. If you should fall again, a bullet could make its way to your leg. Fall a second time, and one may just make it to your chest. Now… how's that for an incentive?"

"You're bluffing!" whispered Bran.

"Oh, am I?"

The old man stood straight and tall and turned towards Bran. His stature was intimidating, but Bran exchanged a hate filled stare. The rifle was tossed from one hand to the other before the tip of the barrel was pressed firmly to Bran's kneecap. The trigger pulled, followed by a loud and defining *click*.

"No, no, no! Wait... please wait!" Bran shrieked desperately. "I'll walk, I'll walk, I swear it. I'll walk!"

Gregory twisted the end of the barrel, bending forward to torment him before he moved.

"Up... you... get!"

Amongst the Mists

Chapter Forty-Eight

Collapsing to hardened ground, Bran's fingers cramped. A sense of invisible needles stabbed at his ligaments, as he quietly sobbed and loosened his grip from Marcus's bruised flesh.

Exhausted, his head lay flat in the soil as he sighed in relief, his vision an unsettling blur. For now, Gregory had vanished, wandering aimlessly between the elements. Yet, Bran could still hear him, the sound of heavy boots never straying far.

Bran looked up; the weight of his head too heavy for his neck to handle. He was overcome by weakness when he tried to move. Now, he had no choice but to listen not only to the sounds of the forest but also to the crazed old man who hummed along with it.

"Your gun…" yelled Bran, still breathless and interrupting the old man's song.

"Aye, what of it?" replied Gregory.

"All this time... the gun. It was never for the beast, was it?"

The old man said nothing but simply looked down at the vintage weapon.

"It was only ever for us, wasn't it? We've been nothing but sitting ducks, waiting for you to take aim."

The old man groaned as he knelt.

"Right you are, Bran," replied Gregory, giving Bran a playful scuff on the head. "A little slow perhaps. But still, right you are all the same."

Marcus uttered a dream like mumble beside them, delirious to what awaited. His words faded again to whispers, then to nothing.

Gregory regained his bearing, his attention focused intently on the fog, as though waiting.

"So, what now?" shouted Bran, pushing himself slowly from the ground, scooting himself back with a *huff* against the closest stump.

"We wait, boy. We wait and be patient."

*

The old man paced from left to right, squirming under his collar and leaving a slimy trail in his path. Too much time had passed by the look of Gregory, who now appeared to grow increasingly agitated.

"Where is it!" He yelled, rubbing the back of his neck. "It's supposed to be here! It's always been here."

"Why have you led us here, Gregory?" asked Bran, his voice dry with thirst, his body lifting up from the rock.

The old man clenched his fists in frustration and whimpered with emotion.

"For her, of course. It's always been for her."

"Your granddaughter?"

The old man nodded in agreement, his eyes focused on the distances.

"I don't understand?" asked Bran.

"What does it matter, boy! You won't be around much longer anyway. Neither will your friend here. Not that he'll be aware. Best way to go I say, wouldn't you agree?"

Bran gulped, sensing his skin turn pale. "What are you going to do?"

"Me? Nothing... I've done my part."

"Part?"

"Bringing you here. That's all I've ever needed to do."

"Just to kill us!"

"It must be done."

Bran hid his face with both hands trying to mask the terror as Marcus twitched at his side.

"I have no choice," explained Gregory. "This thing, all of it, is far beyond my control."

"But you can change," pleaded Bran. "Do not become the very thing you despised all them years ago. You were good once. Do you remember? You tried to stop all of this!"

Gregory's head hung low. "I never."

A pause hung in the air, as though time itself had stopped. The trees stood still; the soft breeze broke, leaving only a lingering coldness.

"What are you saying?" mumbled Bran. "That you lied... about all of it?"

"Oh, come off it, boy." The old man scowled. "Don't be so damn gullible."

Gregory stood, going back to his markings on the ground, the gun swinging carelessly up and down.

"Those missing youngsters... it was me. All of it! Don't you see, boy? I took them from their beds, from their play. I swiped them from their families, marching them through the deepest, darkest wood. It was me. They all screamed. They all cried when they disappeared from this life."

Bran didn't realise it, but his muscles were as tense as steel.

"But why?"

"Because it asked me to. It calls to me, always has. Ever since I can remember."

Anger raged within Bran, though he knew he must stay calm. He sat still, waiting for the right moment.

"You're nothing but a monster."

"How so? I did only what needed to be done."

"Luring your own flesh and blood? Your own grandchild!"

Gregory stopped abruptly, slamming the gun's stock to the ground.

"No! Never her!" shouted Gregory. "I confess, yes, I took those children. And many more throughout the years. Leading their tiny legs to this very spot like innocent lambs to slaughter. I gave that demon everything. Everything it ever asked of me… but it took my darling anyway!"

"Then why do this? Why bring us here?"

"Because…" Gregory hesitated. "As long as I obey its demands, her beautiful soul will remain a part of this world forever. Maybe one day she will even return to my arms."

Gregory stomped over to Bran, settling himself against the same stump, their shoulders almost touching.

"I still see her. I see her all the time, you know? As clear as I see you now. She appears in the shadows when I least expect it. It's not much, but as long as I sense her, I have no choice. Many more must perish."

Bran sat back, for the first time allowing his eyes to rest.

"We don't deserve this."

"None of them did," said Gregory. "But I already told you," whispered his gravelly voice. "Our kind took from the Sprit without reason. Perhaps now, all it desires of us is what purely matters most."

*

"Wake up!"

The sound of the old man's command rang through Bran's dreamless sleep like a living nightmare.

"Up! On your feet!" Gregory grabbed the back of the young boy's shirt and pulled him upright.

The old man pushed him forcibly, making him trip and fall. Bran could taste blood as he grasped loose dirt in his hand.

"Up!" Gregory yelled again, laying a kick to Bran's side.

Somehow, Bran found a way to stand and walk. The tip of Gregory's gun dug sharply into his spine.

"Hold it there," said Gregory.

Bran stopped, looking down at what appeared to be a murky pool and a crumbling ring of stones that marked its boundaries. He wasn't sure what he was looking at, but dreaded what may be its only purpose.

"Now what?" asked Bran, tilting his head to the old man.

Gregory did not speak: he only looked down at the gloom.

Glowing eyes shone out from the water's surface and watched them from the edge. The mist grew blinding, like steam from a boiling pot, clouding their senses where they stood.

"It's time," said Gregory.

"Time for what?"

"Get in the water."

Bran turned to face the gun head on. "No!"

"Don't be foolish, boy. Get in the water, and make sure young Marcus there gets a respectable end."

They both looked at Marcus whose body disappeared in the fog.

"Why should I believe a word you say? You're a liar, Mr Degg. A good for nothing snake! I trusted you. We all did. Even Jack!"

Gregory's aim faltered. "Ah, I was never dishonest about Jack. I rather liked the lad. He is exactly where I promised you. And closer than you'd imagine, too. You'll be reunited with him soon enough."

The trickle of disturbed water found its way through the fog, playing hauntingly on their ears.

The rifle was lifted through the waves of air, resting delicately below Bran's blood-stained chin.

"In the water with you… please, boy. I shan't ask you again."

Bran frowned hard. "I won't do it."

Gregory sighed, pressing the rifle into his shoulder.

"Have it your way then."

Bran closed his eyes and accepted his fate, awaiting the scream of gunfire to pierce and shatter his body. He always thought life would flash before him under such circumstances, just like in the movies. Instead, there was nothing. Not even a memory.

This is it, he thought, counting down the space between seconds.

"Hey!" A voice weak and confused, shouted out from the distance.

Marcus!

Distracted, Gregory glanced over his shoulder, allowing Bran the opportunity to hurl the gathered dirt from his hand.

"Take that, you psychopath!"

Gregory screamed in agony as Bran made a run for it, using his last ounce of strength to escape. Fighting the blindness, the old man swung his rifle frantically, swiping through the air and striking his prey. He felt the impact rebounding up the length of his arm with a judder, as his body fell down with a *thud*.

"Play games with me, will you!" screeched Gregory. "I'll show ya."

Squinting past the dust he swept the ground with his boots. He found his trophy, nudging the body with a cruel, sturdy kick.

Rubbing at his eyelids, Gregory let out a sinister laugh and estimated his aim to the victim.

"It's just you and me now, young Marcus."

But no reply was returned.

"Step out from hiding. The mist is not your ally here."

He watched and waited, the hovering fog slithering over his face and eyelashes with its dampened touch.

Marcus emerged from the dreariness; the crunch of his footsteps intensifying with every step. The boy held something. What exactly wasn't clear as Gregory's weakened eyes bulged like a night owl.

"What have you got there, my friend?" asked Gregory.

"You're no friend of mine," replied Marcus coldly.

"Ah, sure we are. We've been through so much, you and I."

Gregory glanced down. His rifle's barrel was gradually disappearing into a blanket of soft flowing cloud that concealed the body below.

"Come closer, young man. I have something to tell you," Gregory whispered, enticing Marcus with the curl of his bony finger.

"I've heard enough from you!"

"Is that so?"

"Yes…" said Marcus holding his object with a shaky grip. "But I know something you need to hear."

The old man smirked, his round shoulders jumping with humour. "This should be interesting."

Marcus edged forward. Not too close, far enough for safety, thankful he was only a single step away from concealing himself.

"The girl. The child you love most. I've seen her," shouted Marcus. "She speaks to me."

"Hold your tongue! How –

"She is unhappy, Gregory. She has always been unhappy. Her existence is one of pure misery. An existence that you have forged by these horrendous acts."

Gregory's finger tensed, constricting around the trigger, his teeth gritting.

"How dare you stand there and speak of her!"

"She says she is tired and wretched, that she is never permitted to sleep. That she wanders an unknown world, praying for only death to take her."

"Preposterous!" screamed the old man with a fisted hand.

"She speaks of you, also, Gregory."

The elderly man's shoulders eased. His mind yearned for the words he'd waited a lifetime to hear. "And... what does she speak?" Gregory mumbled.

"That you are not the man you once were. The man who kissed her nose goodnight. The man who comforted her in front of a blazing fire on the coldest winter's night. She says you are lost, Gregory. Just as lost as she is."

The gun shook violently in his hands.

"I am no lost man! All I have done... Everything! It was all for her."

"And in doing so, you have brought misery to so many. All those children, Gregory. They all had families, they all had names."

Worry radiated from the blackness of the man's eyes.

"Yes," whispered Marcus. "She knows about everything."

"Everything?"

"Yes. Everything. Every child you've taken, luring them into the darkness. Every lie you have shamefully told to the people who trusted you most."

The tip of the rifle barrel moved, indicating Bran would soon wake.

"Enough!" spat Gregory.

"You have waited all this time and now you wish to silence her?" questioned Marcus confusingly.

The old man hesitated, his tongue delaying his speech. "Will... will she come back to me?"

Marcus shook his head. "No... Never."

Marcus closed his eyes, feeling the mist flow past his face.

"She is close," continued Marcus. "Closer than she has ever been. Yet, the love she treasured has gone."

Sadness clutched at Gregory's thumping heart. He heard crying, as his head shifted left to right.

"Convince her." The old man pleaded. "Tell her to come with me. I swear I can change."

Marcus paused to listen. "She says it is too late for such things. She says that she would rather die!"

A tear fell from the saggy skin which hung below Gregory's eyes. Grief consumed him that soon evolved into anger at the boy who tested him.

"It's over, Gregory. Stop all of this."

The old man twisted his gun, gently pushing down on the body he pinned to the ground. He looked to Marcus; his eyes alive with madness. "If that's the case, I truly have nothing left to lose, do I?"

Marcus's chest froze as he began to bravely charge. He would wrestle the man if need be; he would do whatever it took to disarm him.

But it was too late. A gunshot echoed like cannon fire throughout the swamp, throwing back Gregory's wrist with a kick, sending a reddish cloud of fresh blood into the air. The sound of shallow breathing was heard faintly from the ground as Gregory stared blankly at Marcus. They both exchanged a look, though Marcus couldn't find any words. He was frozen where he stood, mesmerised by the fool who stared back at him.

"That's one down." Gregory grinned from ear to ear.

He watched Marcus closely, expecting him to run. *To do something!* Yet, the boy remained unmoved. Instead, Marcus acted out a sympathetic smile, the mist curling around his limbs.

Confusion baffled the old man's mind, but his vision was improving by the second. He attempted to speak, then stopped and watched as something appeared behind Marcus.

A smudge-like form neared, the identifiable shape of moving legs and arms grew through the haze. Gregory was stunned, hypnotized, as the shadow walked forward, opening the curtain of fog. He stepped back, his mouth ajar, and deepening lines furrowed his brow.

Bran stood beside Marcus and placed a reassuring hand on his arm. They both did nothing but simply observe the old man.

Gregory was stunned. The cogs in his mind spun in overdrive until they seized. He slowly knelt, wafting away the white blanket that spread thick like cotton wool across the ground. Gregory gasped as the mists momentarily parted.

A small girl lay scrunched on her side, her hands clenching fiercely at her stomach. She breathed rapidly, her eyes staring only at nothingness. Gregory screamed in heartache, placing his hands gently upon his granddaughter.

357

She shivered wildly at his touch, as though feeling the harshest cold. The old man tried to move her, though she was rigid, her legs stiff up to her chest, as blood began to soak and stain her muddy gown.

"No!" screamed Gregory, looking to the boys for guidance "Help me!"

As the girl coughed and spluttered, a fine line of blood seeped slowly from the corner of her mouth.

"Stay with me, please," whispered Gregory in despair. "What have I done to you!"

The sound of breathing slowed to short agonising gasps, accompanied by the faintest murmur slipping past dry flaking lips. Her widened eyes glared up into the night before, at long last, focusing on his. He attempted to smile through his shame and guilt, stroking the clumps of hair from her face.

"All will be fine. You'll see. I won't lose you again."

Grasping her red painted hands from her wound, he held them both tightly and watched her drift away. Gregory's head rested upon the girl's chest, feeling it rise for the very last time.

The boys stood by quietly, listening to the smothered sobs that were muffled by the lifeless body. Gregory pulled desperately at his granddaughter's clothing, his body trembling from the shock.

The old man looked up, his eyes filled with loathing.

"You!" he cried past gritted teeth, pulling himself to his feet. "You'll pay! Both of you. You'll both pay!"

The rifle rose effortlessly as it was firmly tucked into position. It pointed directly at Bran as the young boy scampered. But there was no escape. Not this time. No matter how much Bran ducked and dived.

Gregory squeezed the trigger, his head low to the barrel.

It all happened so fast. Bran heard Marcus scream from behind him, his voice merging with his very last thought.

The trigger was pulled.

Click.

Click? Thought Bran, half expecting the delayed *bang* to follow. It did not. He turned to observe Gregory, who by now was examining the rifle in puzzlement.

"Blasted thing!" The old man muttered as he quickly checked over the weapon.

Marcus could hear Bran in the distance.

"Run, you idiot!"

He heard it again.

Run... yes, run, he repeated the words several times over, willing his legs to move. He looked down to the object he held.

The black book weighed heavy in his hands. His sweating thumbs rubbed across its leather surface with anticipation, leaving a moist print on its binding.

Gregory leaned on the rifle, rattling it vigorously in anger, struggling to open the chamber.

"You stay right where you are!" Gregory warned Marcus.

Click, click, click, went the trigger before the chamber was forcibly closed.

The voice returned again from afar. *Run, you idiot!*

It was now or never. Marcus released the book and sent it flying through the space between them, creating a worm tunnel of fog in its path. It landed true enough, catching Gregory's hand on the trigger *Bang!*

The old man was forced backwards but remained standing. Dazed, he looked at Marcus and then turned his attention to the girl. His knees buckled before slowly dropping to the ground.

A dark dot on his shoulder began to spread, covering his shirt in the matching colour to his loved one.

"I…" He struggled to speak. "I…"

He pressed firmly, tending the wound with a painful shriek: the shriek of a child, scared and alone.

Marcus approached, standing over the man who now appeared weak and frail.

"Now you know, don't you?" asked Marcus. "That feeling you sense. They all felt it."

The old man whispered, "I… I was good once." His face turned a ghostly colour.

The rifle was kicked across the ground, spiralling until it hit the water's surface. It would soon be lost forever. Bran stood beside Marcus, as the old man stared into his eyes.

"Forgive me," moaned Gregory. weeping like a child as his vision began to spin.

"Our forgiveness won't give you what you need," replied Bran as the boys turned to walk away.

They stopped to look back one final time, knowing they shouldn't. The old man remained rested on his knees, whimpering weakly alongside his most regrettable error.

Movement lingered behind him, slow and sinister. From nowhere known, shadow arms crept around Gregory. He shrieked, letting out a terrified scream as the black mass held him in a deathly grip. The shadow emerged from the misty swamp. It was gigantic. Its glowing eyes towered over the old man, looking down on him like he was nothing but a bug caught in a spider's web.

"Take them!" Gregory's voice venerably cracked. "I offered you them!"

The mass looked to the boys, its eyes glowing like the strongest torchlight. It did not sway, but tightened its grip on Gregory and began to edge away. The old man cried in desperation, knowing exactly where he was headed. He reached out, his nails digging into the soil.

"Please!" Gregory screamed as he heard the wave of water part behind him. The shadow descended. The old man clawed wildly and scratched the leg of his granddaughter, dragging her unceremoniously across the ground. Her long blonde hair was the last to be seen; fog concealed them all. And the final sound of tortured echoes drifted through the woodland. The screams were sickening before they came to an eerie halt.

*

The land was deathly. So silent that they heard only the faint intermittent drops of rain which fell from the trees and into the swamp. Marcus and Bran watched on, expecting the beast to return to claim the old man's offering. But there was nothing, only the flapping of the black book's open pages as it rested innocently in the mud.

An orange morning light filtered through the treetops, shining in patches on their bodies. The mist lifted, shying away like a monster slinking back to its lair. They sat, overwhelmed, conserving what little strength remained.

"You did good, Marcus." Bran smiled and nudged his mate with his elbow.

Marcus returned a polite smirk, playfully returning the gesture. "You, too."

They paused, sighing loudly.

"I guess we should get out of here?" asked Bran.

A nod was all Marcus could muster.

"Hey," reassured Bran. "What's done is done. We tried, didn't we? I mean… we really tried."

Again, Marcus nodded. "We did."

"It won't be for nothing. We'll tell the whole world what happened here. Jack's loss will not be for nothing, neither will all the others."

Marcus agreed, patting Bran, thankful.

"Let's go then," sighed Marcus, strapping one pack over his shoulders.

In single file they walked along the pool's edge, envisioning Gregory's final thoughts before he sank beneath the surface. Bran shuddered at the idea, still cautiously inspecting the muddy bank. He slipped once, twice, three times. The third sent him down the slope and closer to the water's edge. His heart pounded like a hammer, bringing back events he hoped in time to forget.

"You alright?" Marcus called, looking down from the ledge.

"Uh huh, just help me up, will you?"

As Bran waited, he looked at the water. He couldn't tear his gaze away from the eerie stillness.

"Grab hold," shouted Marcus, throwing down a branch for his friend to grasp. "Gotcha!"

"Pull me up!"

The climb was not that easy. The mud was slippery and felt like icy sludge under his feet.

"Almost there," groaned Bran, his hand clasping onto Marcus's as they exchanged a friendly wink.

Out of the corner of his eye, Bran sensed something moving. The earth itself seemed to churn and toss, rolling over in an attempt to grasp him. Bran thought about several things at once. He tried to shout at the top of his lungs, but only a feeble sound got past his lips. He stopped suddenly when he noticed the clump of earth.

"Special?" Bran couldn't believe his eyes.

Jack lay face down on the slope, his entire body camouflaged in the thick mossy muck.

"Jack!" Marcus cried ecstatically, clenching his collar and pulling him over the drop.

The once missing boy was awake but obviously exhausted. His expression of relief was enough to put the boys in a tight embrace.

"It's great to see you, buddy."

"Yeah, we thought we'd lost you."

Jack sat up, astonished by everything around him.

"It's OK, buddy, it's OK," said Bran calmly, removing his torn shirt and wiping the dirt from Jack's face. "We have so much to tell you."

Jack didn't respond, didn't hear the words being spoken. He was too content in a world of his own. A world where the sun rose to the call of a brand-new day. A world where the air was fresh and calm and where a soft breeze played gently as it brushed past his ears. A world where he was not alone. He had almost forgotten all of it.

Chapter Forty-Nine

Birds call from the safety of their nests, their song flowing over the forest floor. Olivia's tired eyes slowly open and squint at the light of the sun. Its rays beam through the fullness of trees that appear brimming with fire. Drops of water trail from her pale wet skin. Her dripping hair swings from side to side. She feels her body travel weightlessly through the air, though her legs remain loose and idle. She lifts her weakened head, gazing up at the chest of a man who carries her. His arms are strong, but they are comforting as he walks. Although she cannot see his face, she can see the shadow of his mouth. It's familiar, like she has seen it somewhere before. Olivia rests her head back, still watching him. The sun forms a halo around his head.

"Where am I?" she is whispering softly, her voice shaking.

The man glances down with a kind smile. His stride never slows as his feet tread carefully across the moss.

"You're exactly where you belong," the stranger replies. A reassuring grin is cast down at her, his dimpled chin stretching as his eyes return to the path.

Olivia begins to sob uncontrollably.

"You alright, my dear?"

"Oh, it's nothing," she says, smearing the tears from her face. "It's just the sun. I had forgotten just how beautiful it really is."

They both look upward. The heat of the day warms their skin as geese glide gracefully overhead in an ocean of endless blue.

"Aye, it is just that," said the stranger.

The sound of a flowing stream catches their attention. The water glistens with the reflection of that beautiful blue sky. The stream's soft splashes bounce in the light like twinkling crystals.

Olivia tries to rest, but she dares not shut her eyes. She cannot face the dark. Not again.

"I can't go back there," she cries, her arms wrapping tightly around the stranger's torso. "I'm not strong enough."

The man stops, pressing his forehead gently to hers. "You are the strongest I have ever known. You are so brave, little one."

Olivia weeps and buries her face flat into his chest, thinking of her loving mother.

"The horrors I've seen…" Olivia whimpers.

A shadow flickers across the stranger's eyes as he looks down at the girl's distressed face. It is as though they have connected, sharing memories past without the use of a single word.

"You know, don't you?" asks Olivia. "You've seen it?"

"It was a long time ago."

Amongst the Mists

Chapter Fifty

A giant boulder stuck out from a hillside, its grey surface flat and smooth. A narrow stream tumbled alongside. The water churned to each sudden drop, falling rapidly until it reached the bottom and smoothed to a calm and steady flow.

Bran, Marcus, and Jack rested lazily on top of the rock. It was warm to the skin as they lay on their backs and allowed the sun to wash over them while they listened to the tranquil sound of the flowing water.

The day was dry and hot. The call of hidden crickets cried out from around them, catching their attention as they pounced unexpectedly from the tall and sheltered grass. Jack sat up, surveying the vibrant colours of greens and blues. Removing his shoes, both feet dangled from the rock's edge feeling the cooling spray of moisture from the river that travelled swiftly below. Flexing his toes, the sensation consoled him, and for a moment he forgot his trouble and pain.

Something twinkled from the fields. Its dance flickered to the reflection of the shining sun as the heat haze waved in a dreamy motion.

Jack slid from the boulder, carefully following the stream and descending the hillside. The ground soon flattened, displaying large patches of wildflowers growing across the plain. He crept on through, the pleasing display of blue bells tickling his unprotected feet.

The reflection he sought glistened, mirroring back at him, like the glint of a watch's face under a beam of sunlight. Dangling in mid-air, the light spun like magic, twirling in the tender push of the breeze.

Jack walked closer, while looking back to see Bran and Marcus hot on his trail.

Jack reached out, grabbing the small object hooked to the claw of a branch. A piece of flat metal rested lightly in his palm. It appeared old at first glance, rusted around its curved edges. A thin chain looped its end, feeding through a punched hole to keep the plate from falling.

"What you got there?" asked Marcus.

Jack turned around, holding out his find and delicately handed it over. "Some kind of jewellery perhaps?"

Bran stood quietly beside the stream, happily watching bits of foliage float by.

"It's military, you plank!" said Bran.

"Uh?" Marcus hung the chain from his thumb before throwing it back to Jack.

"Yeah," continued Bran. "Haven't you watched any war movies? It's one of those… what's the word?" He thought for a second before snapping his fingers. "Dog tags!"

"Take a look at the plate, they stamp them. It tells you who exactly it belongs to."

Attempting to wipe away the rust, Jack turned the plate, examining the surface of both sides.

"Well, anything?" asked Bran, moving away from the stream.

Jack threw it. The *clink* of the metal chimed through the air before Bran caught it one handed.

He twirled the chain playfully until there was no chain left, mummifying his finger. Holding the plate to the light, the aged letters were hardly readable as he tilted it to decipher the grooves.

"Well?" asked Marcus.

Bran lowered his hands and turned to reply. They could see he was serious. The drumming inside his chest matched the rhythm of a vein twitching within his neck. The chain was flat in his hand as it began to slowly slide away, dropping to the ground like rotten garbage. He hesitated, whispering the words quietly at first, as though saying them aloud might risk bringing him back.

"Pvt G. Degg."

Epilogue – July 2025

Bad dreams again. It never fails. Every night like clockwork. There is no escape.

The sounds of childhood fears slither into his defenceless mind, poisoning his subconscious with memories he has spent a lifetime longing to forget. The result is always the same. Lying there paralysed, his brain yearns to speak, to scream, but his body won't respond. All he can do is wait. Wait and silently wail as he continues to fall through an endless black abyss. The pressure is immense. Spinning through darkness he notices gradually it is harder and harder to breathe. He extends his chest, drawing back... nothing. The air, too, has gone, leaving the pressure in his head to build until both ears viciously pop. The journey is ending, he remembers this part. Toppling deeper and deeper, faster and faster, the voices echo from a distant realm. There is no way to understand them. He has tried many times. Each voice blends into the next, finally combining into a distorted cacophony that bleeds into his eardrums.

Branches slap across his body while he hears twigs snapping. Leaves strike him like whips on naked flesh. His body stops, lying still. Like a dream within a dream, he cannot move nor speak, only he must watch like all those times before.

Flat on his back, the ground is absent beneath him. And above, not even the sky exists. Shadows of wide tree trunks stand tall nearby and far, their height never ending as they reach into the unknown. The voices stop and finally, yes finally, his facial muscles relax.

There is nothing else to see. The space where he rests is cold and quiet. A beam of light begins to descend towards him. It is small at first but grows rapidly as it nears. Its colour is white, the strongest white he has ever seen. It wants him. No, it needs him as he wills his mind to awake. It falls like a meteor, destined to destroy everything in its wake. Willing himself to break the bonds, his body remains limp and numb. A roaring tremble approaches that shakes the space above and below, and now the white light is almost too bright to bear. He feels his pupils burn. Yet now he cannot blink. And just before his vision deteriorates, the single light separates into two. Glowing wildly, like eyes he recalls so well.

Jack awakes with the noises still lingering in his head. He breathes in greedily, slinging the quilt from his bed. Sitting up, he goes through his morning ritual of endless grunts and groans. A mobile phone *pings* an irritating tone from his bedside table. Swiping the screen, he can't help but notice the date. 21 July 2025.

Thirty-nine years. He counts again to be sure, throwing his phone carelessly on the pillow. Two aging hands rub at sleep filled eyes, compressing the bridge of his nose. Playing children can be heard from beyond the crack of an open window. Childish banter whizzes down the street accompanied by the sound of squealing brakes. Their summer break is just barely beginning.

Downstairs, Jack sits silently at the kitchen table and slurps whatever remains in his coffee mug, left over from the night before. The house is quiet, *restful*. The wall clock ticks therapeutically as the neighbour's cat prowls along the windowsill, pointing its ginger arsehole at the glass.

Bloody charming!

Jack taps on the window with the rim of his mug, causing the cat to have some kind of fit before it vanishes into the nearest bush.

The letterbox rattles with an irritating *flap,* as several envelopes and an attempted delivery card fall freely onto the doormat. Jack looks at the printed card. *A parcel has been left in your safe place.* After much searching, it is apparently now under a miniature garden gnome.

Pissin' Amazon drivers!

Inside, the television powers up and he skips through channels while grumbling about how the BBC are a bunch of robbing tossers. There is rarely anything worth watching these days. Not unless you're willing to suffer yet another holiday special of *Mrs Brown's Boys* without being tempted to claw out your eyeballs.

The date on the channel guide displays *21/07/2025*. And now a hot flush of sweat waves over him.

Must I be reminded!

From the kitchen, the scent of burning toast drifts its way through the house. The radio's on, playing its regular morning slot of guess the year. While the kettle comes to boil, the toast springs up in violent protest. Genesis belts out from the speaker, playing a hit where the lyrics draw a blank, but the tune is catchy. He chomps down on his incinerated breakfast as music fades gradually to the presenter's overly joyful voice.

"That was *Invisible Touch* by the one and only Genesis right there. If you managed to guess it right, well done to you, hitting the top of the charts on the 21st of July 1986. Doesn't it make you feel old? Stay tuned for the –

The cord is snagged from the socket. The half eaten toast now lies spread across the floor tiles. Jack stumbles through the house, losing his slippers in the process. A buzz is heard from the living room that draws his attention to the television screen that is intermittently starting to scramble, the date jittering as he reaches for the remote.

21/07/1986.

Jack blinks hard as the numbers jiggle left to right like jelly, sporadically returning to the present date. He rushes to the door, unlatches the chain, and steps out into the open air. The day is humid. As Jack wanders to the light, his hardened skin scrapes across the cracked council slabs. He feels dizzy and sick as his unkempt garden begins to shift under him.

Ring, ring.

A bell chimes on a bicycle zooming down the street. He doesn't see the bike but he hears the noise all the same. A child calls out to another, reminding Jack of thirty-nine years prior. Tracing his memory back to that year, that day, he hears the voices of the friends he once had. The friends he'd lost.

It was never the same after what happened, not when they returned. The isolated landmark of Sleathton was pasted over every station in the United Kingdom. Bodies, many of them, had been found buried, scattered across the forest. In some cases, families managed to identify them as their own. The boys themselves spent the rest of their summer cooped up in a stuffy police interview room, having to explain their story time and time again. But the authorities didn't buy it. There was always one problem. What does a series of murders need?

"A killer," Jack says to himself.

The name Gregory Degg was meaningless, no matter how many times it was mentioned. He was a shadow. A name on nothing more than a few pieces of paper. They told the authorities about the swamp, the standing stones circling a dark bottomless pool. They spoke of the creature. The Sprit. The monster which haunted the lands. Yet, no sighting was ever proven by acceptable evidence. Not even the landmark of the standing stones could be located. By the time summer was over the case went cold, and the boys were left to their devices. Funny, it was never the same to be around each other after that. Jack just guessed it reminded them too much of that time they ventured to Sleathton. Of the time they witnessed… It. The Sprit.

Jack's head mellows and he slouches against the warm red bricks of his home.

His neighbour, Mrs Prowes, or Helen if you wanted to be friendly, marches round her garden with hose in hand, speaking to her flower beds as she waters them.

Sad old loon! thinks Jack, sidestepping back to the door.

"Morning, Jackie," she sings off key, followed by a posh upper-class wave. "Good morning." Jack's hand is almost on the door handle.

"How do you think the garden's coming along?"

"Very nice, Helen."

"And the roses? Don't they look lovely?"

"They do, yes, Helen."

"And the fuchsias?"

"Yes, Helen."

"And the bedding plants?

"Yes."

"Oh, I just love this time of year, don't you?

"Well –

"There is something special about it."

It would be more special if you wound your neck in!

Jack clenches his fists and imagines all the things he could do with her garden hose.

"Yes, Helen… its perfection."

Mrs Prowes leans over the fern that separates the property. Raising her eyebrows, she snobbishly ganders at the ground.

"Why don't you ever let me help you with your garden?" she asked.

"Why? What's wrong with it?" replies Jack, joining her nosey observation.

"Oh, nothing. Just plenty of weeds to pull, that's all. They certainly sprout up everywhere don't they?"

"They're my wild flowers."

"Oh."

"I'm going for the wild look... can't you tell? Rather happy with it, too, as a matter of fact."

Helen drops the hose and places her hands to her mouth in embarrassment.

"Oh, Jackie, I'm truly sorry," she said, presenting a sympathetic smile.

"Forget it, Helen," replies Jack, looking at the skin of his wrist. "My, is that the time? I must dash."

His back is already turned by the time he's finished speaking.

"No problem," calls Mrs Prowes. "Have a splendid day, despite all the upset, that is."

Jack stops in the doorway, rolls his eyes and steps back to the path.

"Upset, Helen?"

She quickly peers up from her flowerbed.

"Yes, you know, all that nastiness."

"Nastiness?"

"Yes, such unpleasant business."

Is she taking the piss!

376

"Unpleasant business, Helen? You might have to help me out a little."

She pierces her trowel into the soil and removes a single gardening glove.

"You haven't heard, Jackie?"

"It's Jack, Helen. And no, clearly I haven't."

"That young child vanishing in the woods."

Jack's face scrunches.

"Woods? What woods? Around here?"

"No, up north. It's that big wilderness estate," Helen replies, trying to think of the name while snapping her fingers.

"Sleathton?" asks Jack.

"Yes! That's the place," continues Helen. "They've just built that new village up there. Typical a child should wander off. I can't believe you haven't heard. It's been on the news for days. Do you not watch the news?"

Jack delays his response. "Uh… not really, Helen."

The woman tiptoes over to her door step and walks back quickly.

"Here," she says, passing Jack a folded newspaper. "It's all in there. Apparently, there was a spot of bother around the same area some years back."

Jack looks at the folded paper then at Mrs Prowes.

"A spot of bother?"

"Why, yes," said Helen, moving in closer for the whisper. "Bodies… and a few so I've read."

Jack grips the folded paper and begins to roll it in his hands.

"I've gotta go, Helen."

*

On the coffee table in front of him, the newspaper remains folded. Jack sits nervously on the edge of his seat, both hands clamped harshly around the back of his neck. He reaches out but hesitates, as though the printed ink may bite.

Just read it, he thinks, trying to steady his pounding heart.

Jack straightens the paper with the flick of his wrist, licking his thumb and skipping immediately to the headlines. He stops when he catches sight of the title and anxiously begins to read.

Child Missing.
Last seen in New Thyme village.

Deep within the ever-growing wilderness estate of Sleathton, the small resettlement of New Thyme has been struck by horror this past week, due to the disappearance of a local minor. Eight-year-old Olivia Maud Bradwell was last seen wandering the outskirts of the small village community six days prior. We have been given reason to believe that no sightings have been reported since. For the past several days the local authorities have conducted around the clock sweeps of the estate, many men, women, and even children volunteering in an effort to find the missing girl and safely bring her home. The child's mother attended a brief press conference at Divisional Police Headquarters when she appealed for anyone with information to come forward.

Spokesman: Sergeant F. Hall.

"It is in desperate times such as these that the power and faith of the community is tested. Should anyone believe they can help and who are willing to aid us in this investigation, please do so. Your supportive efforts will go towards finding young Olivia and putting an end to the family's suffering.

"I would like to express that at this particular time, the disappearance of Miss Bradwell is still currently being processed as a missing person's case. We have no supporting evidence to suspect any kind of foul play. Nor do we believe that Miss Bradwell is a runaway. I will ask, if anyone has any information, regardless of how small, to please come forward and contact your local authorities. It just might save a life. Thank you."

All villages hold their secrets, and the nestled hamlet of New Thyme is no exception. During the course of the early 1950's, the village itself was abandoned after a number of questionable disappearances that were never solved. It wasn't until the summer of 1986, that a widespread investigation struck our television sets, shocking the world after a number of unidentified bodies were recovered with the assistance of three young boys. The three young adults, who happened to be completing a full circuit course of the estate claimed to have witnessed the cause of the horrific events, lending new light to the investigation. After a period of several months the case unfortunately turned cold. And by the autumn of 1987, a press release followed stating that there was no choice but to close all investigations for lack of evidence.

Now, thirty-nine years later, the vast estate of Sleathton finds its new victim hidden somewhere below the treetops. Let us hope that with the combined efforts of Police and public coming together as one, the young Olivia Bradwell will soon be found safe. And in doing so, it will put to bed the trend of regular occurrences that has haunted the village of New Thyme throughout the decades.

Jack folds the paper, placing it gently on the table. He feels sick, his mind swimming in memories of the nightmare he endured, the memories he was warned never to speak of. He sits back in deep thought, both hands tingling as though they have fallen asleep.

They'll never find her.

No matter how he tries to calm himself, or how many times his mind attempts to stray, the thought spinning round his head remains the same.

They'll never find her.

He thinks of that place. The gruelling darkness that entraps him every night as soon as he closes his eyes to sleep. He senses the fear as though he's back there right now, forcing him to feel just like a child. On the table, the front cover of the paper shows a colour image of a girl grinning at him. He has seen her before, in a dream perhaps?

Jack holds up the image. The picture itself shows the youngster at what could only be guessed as a children's birthday party. She wears a pointy hat, held on her head by a single string of elastic. In her hand, she poses with one of those party blowers at the ready to bring it to her lips.

She certainly is beautiful, he thinks, his arm veins visibly twitching.

Standing, Jack walks up the stairs, returning with his coat buttoned and a rucksack tightly in his grip. The front door opens, letting in a ray of sunlight that reflects pleasantly across the wooden floor. He pauses in the doorway, allowing the morning air to sweep calmly past him. Holding his breath, he counts to five before letting the door slam firmly behind him. A peacefulness occupies the village. The sunlight illuminates the walls of sandstone houses, while birds chirp cheerfully in song as they venture from garden to garden. All is tranquil, the only disturbance is a plane flying low overhead, accompanied by the clear echo of Jack's hurried footsteps fading, as he walks down the street and vanishes from sight.

About the Book

The idea of a childhood adventure always seemed to appeal to me growing up – the anticipation, the excitement, but most of all, the freedom and responsibility to take on the world alone. Of course, coming from the overpopulated city of Stoke on Trent, vast open spaces were few and far between. The story of *Amongst the Mists* is one of complete fiction, including all characters and locations, although many of the story's ideas were greatly influenced.

Tales of folklore and mythical locations are such a powerful part of history. They are the legends that our ancestors recited as lessons to their children. They are handed down from generation to generation. Without them, these once iconic creatures and landmarks would become lost to time. The creation of Sleathton and the myth that lurks within came to me from the telling of such stories. One in particular is the legend of the mysterious Doxy Pool; a proclaimed bottomless body of water that can be found on the path that runs across the top of the Roaches in Staffordshire.

Doxey Pool, The Roaches, Staffordshire.

1

Since 1949 locals claimed to have witnessed a strange creature emerging from the dark water on early mornings that would entice you to the pool's edge before dragging you by the neck to a watery grave. The creature's form has adapted over time from a blue nymph to a sinister green skinned mermaid known as Jenny Greenteeth, who waits below the surface to drown both the young and elderly.

Another myth that influenced me is a creature that was briefly mentioned in my previous novel located in the highlands of Scotland. This mythical creature is called the Shellycoat: a curious fae creature rarely spoken of and even more rarely sighted. This spirit resides in the shallow waters and has given his name to many rivers and streams across Scotland. Although considered to be quite harmless, this bogeyman is prone to misleading wanderers who trespass on his watery territory, crying out loud as if drowning to distract their victims.

Of course, with any mythical creature a setting like no other is required. Somewhere to make your skin crawl and the hairs on the back of your neck stand on end; a wilderness to make you feel isolated, lost and alone with a sense that no help will find you. The vision for Sleathton came to me while researching a number of past disappearances in my local area. During the late 1960s, several children were reported going missing in the Cannock Chase area of Staffordshire, a vast forest reserve that, over the years, has gathered many mysterious stories. These disappearances sparked a number of intense searches throughout the forest and are known today as the Cannock Chase murders.

To this very day sightings are reported from time to time of children (noticeably a young girl) wandering the forest's ground alone, dressed in white, her eyes missing, and displaying only sunken dark sockets.

Acknowledgements

Thank you to my wonderful wife Emma, the most encouraging person I know. My children, Brandon and Meredith, for providing me with the time, love and support to write my second book.

To Sue Scott, thank you for the thorough editing of my work to date. Your patience with me is beyond words. Not forgetting your well received advice during each project and friendship made along the way.

To Jim Ody, thank you for your continuous guidance and support. Your advice is always well received. I look forward to sharing many ideas.

To Shelagh Corker, thank you for editing this book and for all your suggestions.

Thank you to Question Mark Press Publisher, and all the authors that show great support for one another. Your determination to see every book grow and succeed is truly inspiring.

To Emmy Ellis, thank you for your help & marvellous cover talent.

To Zoe-Lee O'Farrell & Elli Toney, thank you for all the committed hours spent on promotions and tours. Words cannot express my appreciation.

A big thank you to Andrea Neal for BETA reading and to all ARC readers, who dedicated their time to work through this book.

About the Author

QMP Author.

Born and bred in the county of Staffordshire, Matt is a keen reader of classical, horror and fantasy literature and enjoys writing in the style of traditional ghost stories. During his working life, Matt joined the ambulance service in 2009, transporting critically ill patients all over the UK. After writing his first novel, Matt was welcomed into the family of Question Mark Press publisher and now dedicates his time on future releases. His hobbies include genealogy and hiking, and he enjoys spending time with his wife, Emma, his children, Brandon and Meredith, and his family.

Connect with M. L. Rayner

Facebook: www.facebook.com/MLRayner

Amazon Author: www.amazon.co.uk/M.-L.-Rayner/e/B08LTXNSH4/

Goodreads:
www.goodreads.com/author/show/20902655.M_L_Rayner

Question Mark Press:
www.facebook.com/QuestionMarkPress
www.Questionmarkpress.com

Instagram: https://www.instagram.com/m.l.rayner/

Email:
Matt_rayner43@hotmail.com
Questionmarkpress@gmail.com

?

Question Mark Press

Where Strange Things Happen

Question Mark Press has a wonderful motley crew of authors, all brought together through the mutual admiration of the written word. Their tales will leave you open-mouthed. Laughing or hidden behind the sofa, but guaranteed to entertain.

2021 Releases so far...

Printed in Great Britain
by Amazon

77878177R00226